Black Pansy
by
Suellen Ocean

Black Pansy
by
Suellen Ocean

Published by
Ocean-Hose
P.O. Box 115
Grass Valley, CA 95945
www.oceanhose.com

Also by Suellen Ocean:
The Celtic Prince
The Lies of the Lion
The Guild
Gold River
Gone North
Secret Genealogy
Secret Genealogy II
Secret Genealogy III
Secret Genealogy IV
Acorns and Eat'em
Poor Jonny's Cookbook
Chimney Fire
Hot Snow
Blue Violet

Table of Contents

Pansy - a flower, the wild pansy of Europe
Pansy - "thought," "to think"(pense),"ponder."
"Pansophy" Universal wisdom.

Spring 1861

Black Pansy is Mabaline McCrutchon. Her friends call her
Mabel. Flawlessly beautiful, her Negro hair she wears pulled tight
against her head while she writes, let down long and flowing when
she saunters across the floor in a long white cotton nightdress,
plaited into thick girlish braids when she goes about town to
complete errands. The descendant of mostly white progenitors, the
usual Colonial mix who populated America's newly-gained
territories they took from the Natives, Mabel had been the odd one
in the family and had come to the world, blessed or cursed, she
was not sure, with the skin coloring of the slave class. Aghast that
Mabel would reveal the true origins of the McCrutchon clan,
Mabel was kept secluded from most of her family's social
occasions. Free to read all the latest literary works and newspapers,
Mabel's seclusion provided a wonderful opportunity for spending
long afternoons in a hammock, under the boughs of two ancient
trees. She had become brilliant. Beautiful and brilliant, but
unaware of this until she was offered a ghostwriting position with
the *Pittsburgh News Herald.* As each of the ghostwritten stories
gained popularity, it became evident the *News Herald* editor was
not the author. Eventually the editor fessed up and gave the stories
the pen name, "Black Pansy." Speculation was rampant and rumors
began to circulate that Mabel McCrutchon was the author. The

Pittsburgh News Herald denied it fiercely, saying only that the author was a dashing Frenchman from Baton Rouge.

Through his Aunt Lena, Charles Churchill went to Pittsburgh on a philanthropic journey arranged by highly respected Quakers. While he was traveling, Charles was a frequent guest in Quaker communities. Auntie Lena set her hopes in Charles, he'd been the more thoughtful of her brother's ten children and certainly of her brood of seven who worked hard and were respectable, but when presented with an opportunity of generosity or compassion toward others, outside their immediate blood line, their faces went blank. Charles on the other hand, had proven repeatedly to care for those less fortunate.

After the schooner ride, a black horse-driven carriage carried Charles through dusty roads to Pittsburgh, and would carry him to the *Pittsburgh News Herald* where he would meet the editor who was doing a story on Charles and the Churchill family's philanthropic endeavors.

Mabel McCrutchon was in the back of the building when Charles Churchill walked in. A large wooden post and coat rack allowed her, as usual, to peer and watch the day's business unfold. Every day the *News Herald* received the usual neighbor's complaint, unruly dogs and occasional murder and mayhem and always a drunken disturbance that citizens felt it was their duty to report. Mabel thought of these *citizen informers* as "tattle tales" so usually ignored them, going about her work but kept one ear open in the slight chance something important would spew from the mouths of these "good citizens." But today when the bell tinkled and the door shut and the morning's sunshine warmed the room, there was something different about the air of the gentleman who stopped and looked down at the wooden floor when his feet brought a squeak to the boards. The squeak made him smile and look around. His glasses were as far down the end of his nose as his bone structure would allow and he looked over the top of them. Mabel smiled. She'd known men who wore spectacles in order to look bookish. Mabel knew immediately that the man who'd just walked in was not only well read but well read about.

"Good day," Charles said hoping someone would come forward.

Mabel stood hiding behind the pole, she'd been politely told to refrain from meeting directly with the public and to stay out of sight as much as possible. It was not due to Mabel's obvious dash of colored blood but more out of fear that Pittsburgh's citizens would figure out who Black Pansy was.

"Good day," Charles repeated and looked straight at the pole Mabel hid behind. He leaned in to get a better look but she held her position firmly. Eventually, impatience and curiosity got the best of her and she peeked to get a better look at him.

"Can I 'hep you sir?" Victor, who compiled the weekly news asked. He was in his middle thirties, unmarried, living with a woman whom he insisted was his "sister," and all but Mabel

3

believed him. Victor wore his thin, straggly hair pulled back in a ponytail. His face was long and gaunt but his intelligence and quick wit made up for his homeliness. As Victor repeatedly wiped his hands on an oily black rag, he listened carefully to the stranger's words.

"Good day," Charles said again, clearing his throat and looking back at Mabel's spot behind the post, this time with an apparent irritation which prompted her to reveal herself a bit more but only by tossing her head of thick black curls and returning to her business making a show of importance.

"I'm here to see the Editor, Mr. Whitethorn."

"Mr. Whitethorn is predisposed," Victor told Charles. "If you'll relay your business to me, I'll make sure he hears it."

"May I leave a note?"

"Sure can," Victor said, wiping again, his black inky hands on a rag and ripping newsprint for Charles to leave his note.

"Will he be in tomorrow?" Charles asked, peeking at Mabel.

Victor took the note Charles had written and glanced at the signature, "Charles Churchill from Connecticut, referred by Benjamin Norfolk of the *New Jersey Society of Friends*. Ah, the New Jersey Quakers," Victor said, a tone of trust and pleasure in his voice.

Charles cleared his throat and seemed pleased.

Mabel sat down at her desk, her wooden chair making a loud sound as she pushed into it. She began tapping her pen on her desk, rap, tap, rap tap... both Victor and Charles turned to her and stared.

Mabel's large dark eyes returned their stare, she smiled faintly, pleased with herself for drawing their attention. "Mr. Whitethorn is in discussion with our author."

"Author?" Charles said inquisitively.

"We have an ongoing story in the newspaper, great story. Mr. Whitethorn meets with him regularly. Black Pansy, perhaps you've heard of him?"

Charles thought deeply, "Sounds a tad familiar but no," he shook his head, "I don't recollect. What's the story about?"

"It's about men who bet on horse racing and cock fighting," Victor said enthusiastically.

"Oh, that does sound a fine story," Charles said, smiling at Victor, neither taking any pains to disguise their pride.

"And the wives who find their secret notes and start betting and winning because the men have been fixing the horse races and cock fights..." Mabel blurted out, to which Victor turned his face shocked that she knew the next story installment and he did not.

Embarrassed, Mabel did her best to convince both men she'd only heard bits and pieces of story ideas.

Charles walked over to her desk. His black suit coat was wrinkled but of the finest Irish linen. His white cotton shirt had so much fine stitching in it; Mabel could not believe that anyone would spend that much time on one man's shirt. *He must be extremely wealthy.* Charles' age appeared to Mabel to be about five years older than she, which would make him around twenty-four. His beautiful thick, dark-brown hair had several waves in it, which he wore down to his ears. She thought he was in need of a haircut but he seemed to enjoy running his hand through it to keep it swept away from his face. If Mabel could guess she would say Mr. Charles Churchill, though he had a very English name, was the product of northern Britain, Scottish to be precise but one could never tell these days. Why, look at her. Why did she appear to have Negro ancestry when no others in the family did?

"Are you Mr. Whitethorn's secretary?" Charles said, breaking her daydream.

Mabel bit her lip and let out a deep sigh, nodded and said in a rather resigned tone, "Yes, I am Mr. Whitethorn's secretary. I'll see that he gets your note Mr. Churchill."

Charles was not ready to leave. The way her thick black curls flopped about her head and her full bosom fit tightly into a dress that was buttoned from the floor to her neck and the way the fullness of her hips swung when she rose from her chair intrigued and stimulated him. Not missing that, she stared at him as if to inform him she is looked at that way regularly and no man has yet to convince her of his sincerity.

I'll take that as a challenge, he thought. *What a brilliant and beautiful girl.* "Well," he said diplomatically, "Miss?"

"McCrutchon," she said softly, letting down her guard.

"Scottish name?"

Mabel was so stunned that he didn't see her as a colored woman she was without a response and only stuttered, "uh, uh, uh, Scottish? Uh, yes, actually my McCrutchon clan is very Scottish. You too?" she asked looking into his Scottish face.

"No," he said seriously as if no one had ever mentioned it, "English. My branch of the Churchill's is very British. Perhaps you've heard of the Duke of Marlborough..."

Mabel looked at him stone faced. She was in no mood to hear his pedigree. If there was anything that irked her more, it was pulling blood rank on her or anyone else. As far as Mabel was concerned all men were created equal and it was nigh time the world realized it.

Charles put his head down, embarrassed at his pompousness. "Good day Miss McCrutchon," he said gentlemanly, then turned and headed for the door.

As the afternoon sunlight shot through a small window high above the front door, casting a shadow upon Charles, Mabel stood and silently watched him leave but right before he did he turned and startled her.

"Erskine," he said to her with a wry smile.

"What?" she said, embarrassed that he caught her dreamily watching him leave.

"Erskine... Clan Erskine."

"Erskine?"

"My grandmother was an Erskine... from the Scottish Highlands," he said genuinely and with a delicate smile.

"I thought so," Mabel said, "there's something in the cheeks and the smile of a Scot, I get it right every time."

"I'll bet you do," he said, making Mabel's heart jump. He turned and walked into the unseasonably warm spring afternoon.

As a child, Charles Churchill had seen men work hard in his father's Connecticut Shipyards. Two of their ships had figured prominently in the war of 1812. As his hired carriage rambled by farms outside the city limits of Pittsburgh, he watched men labor in their hay fields, delighting in the peaceful, pastoral scene. He wore a smile upon his face but his thoughts were upon the troubles of the world. Charles knew exactly where the country was headed and that was into war. The Southern states were not about to give to the demands of the North and free their slaves. There was too much cotton to pick, tobacco, and rice to plant. Without the slaves, the Southerners believed their economy would collapse and the plantation owners had grown accustomed to extravagant life styles, built upon the backs of slaves. It would necessitate force to get them to abandon what the North and plenty of Southerners would agree was an "evil institution."

It occurred to Charles what the repercussions might be if he were to begin courting one so lovely as Mabel. He shrugged and looked at the scenery but could not shake her. Mabel did not comprehend the effect she had on men, especially when she lopped about her thick mane of long chocolate brown hair. Charles admired that about her. *She was sexy but didn't know it.* The more he thought of her as he rustled about the wooden seat of the carriage and the more it jostled and vibrated his groin, he grew so stimulated he was grateful the ride was a long one. He knew at once he would have to dismiss her from his mind if he was to arrive at his lodgings in respectable shape. Strength of mind Charles Churchill certainly possessed and his ability to control it was good enough to keep the shapely silhouette of Mabel McCrutchon in the back of his mind.

Mabel left the *News Herald* and walked slowly along the boardwalk that led from the back street housing the newspaper office. The *News Herald* was not a large establishment. They had few reporters and the bulk of their paper was used for the fictional story that Mabel was ghost writing. But with the prospect of a war on everyone's mind, nominally educated citizens and colleagues of the Editor had become field reporters and life in the office was becoming emotionally charged. Mabel longed for the quiet atmosphere of the past. Weeks before, she and Victor were the only ones in the office, enabling her to meander along on her story. But now the atmosphere was so fearful and emotionally charged it made it difficult to write and interruptions of people coming in and out, the big wooden door slamming constantly, disturbed her creativity. She wasn't getting much writing done, necessitating her spending her evenings writing, sometimes until late into the night. Tonight would be one of those nights.

Mabel said good-bye to Victor then sauntered absentmindedly along the boardwalk, in the warm afternoon sun. Her thoughts turned to her Auntie. Mabel's mother Vivian, was rather cool to her and her Auntie Louisa had made up for it, doting on Mabel, teaching her good manners, sewing her pretty clothes, crocheting delicate shawls and guiding Mabel about her thick mane of hair, teaching her various ways of pinning it up. Mabel adhered to much of her Auntie's teachings but was immensely fond of kicking off her shoes, lifting her petticoats and walking barefoot in the beauty of the family back yard that was gorgeous all year long. In January, the twigs on the dormant trees held a beautiful rose color while underneath fluffy snow covered the flowerbeds. In the spring, large flowering shrubs bloomed in delightful succession. Flowerbeds under the windows bloomed at night, sending their aroma only in the evenings. It came wafting into the home's open windows. And in the summer, one big hammock between two ancient oaks and vines that climbed any which way they desired, cloaked Mabel in a peaceful scene of greens and golds. The lawn was always moist and birds seemed to enjoy keeping her company while she lay in the hammock with her tablet writing throughout the long hot evenings and days when Mr. Whitethorn encouraged her to stay home and work on the story.

"Mabel?" Mr. Whitethorn said behind a filthy pair of rimless spectacles.

When her Editor spoke, Mabel answered. "Yes," she said, walking to his enormous oak desk waiting to lend a hand. Citizens had begun flocking into the *News Herald* with information about the growing armies of the North and South. Whitethorn hired extra reporters to go into the community and gather news. He was working on a story about Kentuckians who were leaving in groups heading south to join the Rebel Army. Mabel gathered information from reporters and citizens with reports of Kentuckians going to Ohio and Indiana to join the Union Army. It seemed to all of Pittsburgh that war was eminent. All the talk and heated arguments about slavery and freeing colored slaves made Mabel nervous since her Great-Grandmother had been a freed slave and Mabel had taken after her. Most did not notice but those who did and let her know sent a chill throughout her body. It was well known that free people who had even the slightest trace of African ancestry were kidnapped and taken to the auction block. Whitethorn and Victor were protective of Mabel and encouraged her to stay somewhat in the background, often escorting her home. Both Whitethorn and Victor despised Mabel's mother Vivian, wondering how she could be so inconsiderate of her daughter's social needs by keeping her from the McCrutchon family gatherings. What better way for a beautiful young woman to meet an equal suitor matching her intelligence and wit than to attend parties and socials full of diplomats and military heroes?

Every time Mabel heard the bells on the door jingle, she hoped it would be Charles Churchill. What had he come to Pittsburgh for and why had not Mr. Whitethorn mentioned him? She gave him Charles' message but the only conversations he would engage in were those about the story she was writing. He prodded her daily, firing questions at her, which she good-naturedly answered. The story was always to the reading public's approval, funny and witty, the readers could not wait to meet the handsome author from Baton Rouge. There were rumors and speculation that Black Pansy would be coming to Pittsburgh and heated literary discussions as to whether Black Pansy was pro slavery or not. Mabel laughed at it all, giving her incentive to toy with them, coming close to the topic then backing off entirely. She had her own feelings about slavery; of course she was adamantly against it, as was most of her family.

The spring days grew longer and one day the bells jingled on the door. It was Charles Churchill. He did not look the same cheerful fellow and his clothes were worn. He appeared to be lacking sleep and though still a handsome man, was in need of nurturing. Mabel did not hide behind the posts, using the best manners Auntie

Louisa had drilled into her she came out and greeted him. Both Victor and Mr. Whitethorn raised eyebrows as neither had ever seen Mabel put on the charm as she did for Charles Churchill who smiled gratefully at her attention.

Charles seemed eager to talk, as did Mabel. Such a vigorous discussion sprang forth from their greetings of "How are you?" that Charles insisted Mabel accept his invitation to join him for lunch at the hotel across the street. She quickly grabbed her hat and shawl and the two were headed out the door. She accepted Charles placing his hand at her waist, as they glided across the street. Neither Victor nor Mr. Whitethorn had ever seen Mabel take to anyone like that, except for children which she not only had a fondness for but a natural way with. Victor and Mr. Whitethorn shook their heads in disbelief, smiled at one another then quickly returned to their duties, both thinking how strongly the *News Herald* depended on Mabel's diligent work. Especially Whitethorn, Victor noticed he grew visibly shaken, giving Victor something to ponder all day and into the night.

The hotel staff had known Mabel for several years, since arriving at the *News Herald,* she'd enjoyed lunches there often.

"Sarsaparilla, please," Mabel said when asked what she'd like to drink, making Charles realize how young she was. Charles would have preferred stronger drink but refrained and joined Mabel with a sarsaparilla. Mabel began firing questions at him, much the same

13

way Whitethorn had just been firing them at her. Charles face was a bit grave.

"I don't know how to respond," he said trying to sound cheerful. "There is no doubt you have already surmised what my business is here in Pittsburgh..."

"No," she said, shaking her head, her long, thick, dark brown braid hanging over her shoulder as she turned her head and gazed out the window onto the increased activity in the street.

"Well surely you realize what the nature of my business is..." he paused, trying to form his sentence carefully, "I was sent by the *New Jersey Society of Friends...*"

She looked at him squarely, "Yes, Quakers... friends of those in bondage."

"Yes," he sighed, slowly unfolding a white linen napkin and placing it on his lap in anticipation of the food he saw coming toward him on sizzling hot platters. He was hungry, having not eaten all day, nor much at all lately and was relieved to know he could speak with her about his business.

"Where are you staying?" she pried.

"My understanding is that you are a secretary, not a reporter."

Mabel blushed. Her mother often told her she was too aggressive and that it was not ladylike. "Forgive me."

He laughed, "There is nothing to forgive. I'm staying at Nathan Rutherford's farm, about three miles out of town," he said looking into a delicious beefsteak, not noticing the shock on her face.

Mabel leaned forward and whispered, *"Nathan Rutherford's?"*

Charles realized he'd said too much and that Mabel knew more than he'd expected of a young secretary. He put his head down, put down his sharp knife, pushed his plate out of the way and folded his hands on the table. "Am I going to be chastised by a young woman I barely know, or am I going to enjoy this delicious meal?" he said then gave her a stern look.

"Forgive me," she said again, and then returned to her aggressive questioning. "Do you know Nathan? For how long? Do you know the man's reputation?"

"Mabel, I know Nathan well. I've known him all my life. He's my cousin."

The horrified look upon Mabel's face gave a slight tremble to Charles's arms but he hid it well and stared longingly at his food. "Let's have a nice meal and then we'll talk... politics is it?"

"Politics?" she shouted, drawing the attention of the waitress. "Politics? Hatred and bigotry... why Nathan Rutherford belongs to the gang of the most vile..."

"Spy," he said, sliding his plate back in front of himself, grabbing the knife and digging into his steak. He took a bite then took a deep pleasant breath, "Delicious," he said then wiped his face with his napkin and took a sip of cold sarsaparilla. "Lovely lunch, lovely."

Mabel continued to brood. She leaned forward and whispered, *"Spy? What are you talking about?"*

15

"Nathan Rutherford is a friend of the slave. He's a spy. He joins up with bands of ruffians and finds out what their intentions are. He attends Abolitionists' meetings and reports back. His barn is part of the Underground Railroad."

Now it was Mabel who was sighing. She sat back in her chair and said nothing.

"I'm pleased you didn't know. It means the group is doing a good job of keeping it secret. There are no leaks."

Mabel nodded.

"Interesting way of getting to know one another," he laughed. "My God, this is our first conversation," he stared at her wondering if she realized how unusual their familiarity was.

"We both work for the same side," she said, looking again outside, this time frowning.

"What is it?" he asked, looking out the window.

"Since we've been here I've seen three sets of young boys. Obviously, they're gathering in groups to head to either Rebel or Union Army outposts. It shan't be long now," she said looking into his deep-set, dark, brown eyes.

"No," he said, looking into hers, "it shan't be long."

"Auntie, why must I soil my thoughts with talk of war? I see it every day, I hear it every day. It's imminent but must I forego my thoughts because it happens that I've fallen in love during a time of impending war?"

"No darling. I don't believe you should. You've waited... we've all waited for you to find someone you're fond of," she put her wrinkled, hand upon Mabel's head and stroked her long braid. "Go get your hairbrush darling, let me take this braid out and..."

"Oh Auntie, do you think it's real? Do you think he'll really love me? And what about his family... will they accept me?"

Auntie shook her head. She would have loved to lie to Mabel and tell her yes, yes, yes, but she knew that the pain would be too great if her niece's life did not turn out as planned. Whose life did? "Mabel dear, all I can tell you is to have faith, remember your manners and... much as I hate to say it... always be aware that you're different than the white people of Pittsburgh or anywhere else."

"Yes, I know Auntie," Mabel said, then cuddled up next to her on the love seat.

"Did I hear you say Mabel is different?" they both heard Mabel's mother shout from her bedroom. "Yes, my Mabel is different, but she is beautiful. She is the most beautiful of all the McCrutchon women... such a shame she turned out... well... she turned out..."

"Vivian will you stop with the pity? It's Mabel who suffers because she has colored blood that shows. Lord knows I have more than she does, and quietly we're proud of it but outwardly we go on about our lives as if we were as white as any other, at least Mabel is doing something to help end it. And at least Mabel knows who she is!"

Mabel cuddled up closer to her Auntie Louisa. These arguments came often, between her mother and her aunt, especially when her mother had more than two glasses of sherry. They didn't happen every night, nor even once a week, but when they did, it was the reason Mabel's father retreated to his workshop in the evenings and stayed there long after Mabel's mother had gone to bed.

Charles began coming to the *News Herald* three times a week. Once he and Mabel became comfortable with knowing each other's political stance and agreed on most issues, they left it aside and during their lunches, spoke with one another about their lives as children, their hopes for the future and especially of his family. Like Mabel, Charles had a fondness for his Aunt. There were ten children in his family, six of them boys and Charles was neither the oldest nor the youngest but his Auntie Lena had singled him out when she began noticing he was the most considerate as she too had a compassionate, caring heart.

Neither Auntie Lena nor Charles were Quakers, both were dutiful Methodists but behind closed doors enjoyed laughing and talking about the silliness of their church doctrine. It was through a friend of Auntie Lena's that Charles had found his way to Pittsburgh. The friend was a prominent Quaker, without a wife, and Charles had often wondered if this gentleman was carrying on an affair with his Auntie Lena who *was* a widow. But Charles resigned himself to believe that their giggling and constant smiling at one another was innocent.

One day Charles showed up at the *News Herald* filthy and bedraggled. Mabel quickly grabbed him, took him behind the counter and escorted him out the back door to a supply shed that housed a water pump and towels.

"Charles, you look frightfully awful," she told him. "What ever have you been doing?" she said while cleaning him up as if he were a little boy. He smiled, enjoying her touch even if the scrubbing was rough. When she ran a damp towel too far past his navel and down to his groin, he grabbed her hand tightly, forcing her to stop. Mostly innocent to the carnal needs of men, his reaction caught Mabel by surprise.

Charles breathing was quick and heavy. How he longed to lock the door and take her into his arms, especially the way her long, thick braid kept fanning across her bodice and he could see several buttons had loosened. *Had she done that on her own?* He had not noticed earlier because as soon as he'd arrived at the *News Herald* she'd hustled him out. *Did she long to taste his lips as he did hers?*

"Mabel," he said not letting go of her arm. She pretended to be perturbed at his strong grip but she barely tried to pull away. He pulled her close, close enough that he could feel her ample bosom pressing against his chest. He kissed her lightly on the lips and let go of her hand. Mabel was dizzy with love. Her head spun round and she closed her eyes to steady herself. He stood up and leaned her against the wooden counter, pushing his body into hers, just enough to feel her close and breathe in her scent, the essence that was Mabel McCrutchon. There is no way that Charles Churchill would violate the innocence of the young girl he held vulnerably but oh, how he longed to. He took a peek at her full bosom, kissed her neck and took her braid. Like an artist's paintbrush, he ran it across the beauty that was her face and danced it about her breasts. Mabel held still, savoring every moment. Charles pulled back, his breathing still heavy. The considerate young man that his Auntie Lena had recognized was in play here today as he reluctantly pulled away. He felt ashamed. Darkness came over him. Mabel's eyes showed confusion but relief. As if nothing had transpired between the two of them, she returned to cleaning the mud off his face and clothing, being very careful to stay clear of his groin.

Charles was careful to clean himself up before he went down to the *News Herald*, not wanting a repeat of the awkward situation he and Mabel had found themselves in previously. He'd been entrusted with an honorable position and had been presented as a respectable gentleman to be entirely trusted. If news got back to the New Jersey and Connecticut philanthropical social circles that he was taking advantage of a young colored woman in Pittsburgh, he would be ostracized. However, Charles didn't see Mabel as some of the Eastern Socialites would, many of who were hypocrites. They talked night and day about freeing the slaves and ending the institution of slavery. The women had sewing circles and made quilts and clothing for the Underground Railroad but Charles knew without a doubt that many would frown on him if he returned home with a Negro bride, no matter how intelligent, beautiful and well-bred she was.

Charles grew deeper in love with Mabel each time he saw her. And each time he knew his future was but a dark cloud of doubt and could be very painful for Mabel if he did not form a concise plan. His nights were spent worrying about his family accepting her but he left his days free to think only of her great beauty and intelligent wit.

"Have you read the latest chapter of Black Pansy's novel?" Charles overheard a woman ask her friend one day at the drug and sundry store. It wasn't the last time he overheard Pittsburgh's citizens speak of it. The story was a big hit and with the war looming the author, Black Pansy, had begun to weigh in on the morals of slavery. Black Pansy had yet to take a stand but chose instead to present both sides and let the reader decide. Talk was about how well informed and knowledgeable the author was. All the women could not wait to meet "him" and young eligible women longed to get a date with him after a picture was "leaked" to one of the other newspapers in the city. Mabel and Mr. Whitethorn laughed at the photo, neither had any idea from where the photo had come but the scoundrel who leaked it would not be chastised as Whitethorn and Mabel were the only ones who knew who the real Black Pansy was. One day when Mabel and Whitethorn were alone in the news office, they both had a good laugh.

"Looks just like you," Whitethorn said.

Mabel pulled her braid up to her lip as if it were a mustache and danced around acting like a man. "I'm Black Pansy," she said in a deep voice, "I am the commentator for the war between the North and South." They were both laughing so hard neither heard that Charles had come in through the back door. He was not hurt but was covered in blood, which was secondary to what he had just heard.

"Mabel is Black Pansy?" he said softly.

She and Whitethorn turned around quickly, their laughter ceasing, alarm spread across both their faces.

"It's OK, I understand, I won't divulge, I'm proud of you Mabel he walked up to hug her but the look of horror on her face at the sight of him covered in fresh blood brought him to stop short.

"What's happened?!" Mabel shouted, terrified at what his answer might be.

Charles looked down then back up again. His look verified their worst fears. "The ruffians figured out that Nathan Rutherford was a spy. They beat him pretty badly. I found him bloodied up real bad. If I hadn't come home when I did..."

"Will he live?" Mabel asked.

"Yes, he's going to be alright. The doc stopped the bleeding. He'll be alright in a few days. At six feet four, Nathan is a strapping fellow; they didn't take him down easily. He had fifteen runaway slaves who scattered every which way when those fellas came. I don't suspect the ruffians knew Nathan had any runaways staying at his place. It was a discreet operation. But we need to scour the woods around the farm and find the folks... two women have babies and there are four small children and two elder folks. I was hoping..." he looked at Mabel who froze on the spot. She felt she did her part through her writing and work at the newspaper; she was terrified at becoming involved in the Underground Railroad. She had told her mother and aunt that she wanted nothing to do with it. Her life was safe and comfortable, no one molested her and it had been months since anyone spoke ill to her. She was silent to Charles request.

People came in droves to the office of the *News Herald.* Spring rains brought wet and mud on everyone's shoes but no one seemed to care. Tension was high. Mothers fretted about their husbands and sons leaving to join up with Northern or Southern Armies. Carriage horses reacted to fear and stress by kicking and injuring their nervous drivers. The sound of babies crying permeated the streets and stores were trying to keep up with demands of citizens who believed in stocking up on supplies. Children who wanted nothing more than to play were whisked away by nervous mothers who found no end of menial chores to accomplish. The hysteria was filling the local hospital with patients, church pews were full and edgy nerves brought arguments and more drinking at the bars.

"Mabel, you don't look well," Whitethorn told her. He walked toward her desk where Mabel had laid her head into her folded arms. He put his hand upon her soft cheek to see if she was feverish. She looked up at him with swollen red eyes.

"I've not slept well... but I finished another chapter."

Whitethorn took her journal quickly and walked to his desk, unlocked the drawer and slid it in before another patron came through the door. He walked back to Mabel and whispered into her ear, "Go home. Take a week to rest. Work on the story at home. It's too hectic here."

She shook her head no and looked helplessly into his eyes. Except for the fact that he had taken credit for her literary masterpiece; he was an angel to her. Mabel spoke with Whitethorn about topics she would never discuss with anyone, not even her Auntie. They shared similar views on politics and society and both were apprehensive and fearful about the beginning of the war.

The door slammed and Victor came through, breathless and waving a telegram, "It's from the Secretary of War. It's a notice to the railroads not to transport Confederate troops of any sort. We'd better get this story out. All the Jones boys hopped on the train yesterday to join up with the Confederate Army. This telegram says railroads who carry boys south will be guilty of treason."

Mabel threw her head down on her desk again. Whitethorn looked at Victor and shook his head. Victor nodded.

"I think we'll be better off without you Mabel. We could use your desk, in about an hour I've got three reporters coming..." Victor lied.

Mabel smiled. "Thanks Victor. Thanks Mr. Whitethorn. I'll go home. But..."

Whitethorn smiled, "If Charles comes in, I'll explain it all to him."

As Mabel grabbed her cape, the sound of gunshots right outside the office brought a quick panic. Victor stopped Mabel and Whitethorn froze.

"Those damn niggers, they're comin' up here to our free state... god damn Abolitionists are shelterin' 'em... even given 'em jobs..."

Victor could see it was one of the local teenaged boys who'd gotten into the Kentucky whiskey that had been flowing readily around the city.

"Go on home Milton," they heard a voice of reason shout, "go on home."

"I'm goin' down to Harper's Ferry... I am... I'm goin' down to Virginia... I'm join'n up with the Confederate Army I is... goin' be a soldier and fight for the right for a man to own a slave... damn niggers..."

Before Victor or Whitethorn could stop her, Mabel had grabbed her cape and headed out the door. She walked past the drunken lad and held her head high.

"There's one now," the drunken Milton said rudely.

Victor came out of the office, swung a fist right into the lad's drunken face.

"Alright... alright..." Milton said, so drunk he felt little pain, "I's jus' kiddin'... we all know pretty Mabel McCrutchon's no nigger... why she's a right fine little lady..."

Victor punched him again and this time Milton fell backwards and was knocked out. Victor looked up to see if any more trouble was waiting. A large crowd had gathered and he could see the grave face of Charles Churchill staring. He nodded to Victor.

Charles pushed through the crowd and caught up with Mabel who was delighted to see him. She unabashedly fell into his arms.

"Oh Charles," she said leaning into him as they kept walking. "Isn't it dreadful?"

"Yes it is," he said turning back at the crowd. He wasn't sure the feelings of the thirty or so people who somberly looked on but knew that Mabel must be kept safe.

As Charles carriage made its way downhill to Mabel's neighborhood, the clomp, clomp of horse hooves on the cobblestones brought her comfort. She sunk into Charles strong body, breathed in his scent and kissed him lightly on the neck. She looked behind and could hear another round of gunshots from the same area. She knew that the controversy had only just begun.

"I've brought your daughter home," Charles told Mabel's Auntie Louisa as she greeted them at the door. "There was a scuffle in town and rude words were exchanged toward Mabel..." he said staring at her. "I beg your pardon, I've forgotten my manners, I'm Charles Churchill.

"I'm Mabel's Aunt Louisa," she said looking Charles up and down with more than approval.

"Forgive me, I assumed..." he said embarrassed.

"Please come into our home, no one else is here. Mabel, you look dreadfully tired, I told you not to stay up so late writing..." her Auntie Louisa said to her, and then shot Charles a look. Mabel's novel writing was meant to be a secret known only to she and Whitethorn.

"He knows Auntie," Mabel said, hanging her shawl on a coat rack and escorting Charles to the sofa where they sat comfortably. Auntie Louisa noticed Mabel admiring Charles, as only a young girl in love would do but was dismayed that a stranger would know the biggest secret in Pittsburgh. She was quiet and downcast.

"Charles, you must be surprised to find that I'm Black Pansy," Mabel said with a hint of pride in her voice.

"Yes, surprised but not surprised," he smiled, pleased that maybe they were putting the afternoon's events behind them but when Mabel sighed and leaned into him he knew she had not forgotten the fear and social embarrassment the young lad had brought upon her. Auntie Louisa smiled and sat down in a large stuffed chair with a hanging stained glass lamp perched above her. He envisioned Mabel sitting there at night reading.

"Does Mr. Whitethorn compensate you for the success you've brought him?"

Mabel shrugged, "We haven't discussed that yet."

"She gets the same stipend she always did," Auntie Louisa said disapprovingly.

"He's good to me," Mabel said while Charles and Auntie Louisa stared incredulously. "Mr. Whitethorn has been running the *News Herald* in the red for quite some time. I'm happy he's able to finally make a profit."

"Mabel, you should be compensated. I'll speak with him," Charles said protectively.

Mabel glared at him. "No you won't. I can take care of myself regarding the matter of my pay."

He smiled. Mabel was feisty. He would need that in a woman when the time came to meet his family and make her introduction into Connecticut society.

On Wednesday, Charles suggested he and Mabel meet socially with Victor and his "sister." Mabel had been home for a week and Charles could tell it was wearing on her. Being secluded at home was fine for writing but her emotions were stung by not knowing what was going on outside her back yard. Charles had suggested Victor and "his sister" come to Mabel's. Charles would provide a nice meal and they could sit on the patio outside and converse. Mabel would have none of it. She insisted on meeting Victor and Annie at the finest restaurant in downtown Pittsburgh. Charles bowed to her request and on a beautiful evening in early May the four found themselves sitting in a quiet restaurant.

Annie and Victor had never met socially with Mabel before. Victor had kept his personal life separate from his work. They were so uncomfortable, wondering how they would carry on a charade of being brother and sister, they spoke up right away.

"Mabel," Victor said apprehensively. "I've something to tell you."

Mabel smiled and winked at Charles. "Yes, go ahead, Victor, what is it?"

Victor looked at Annie who was also uneasy and averted their eyes. Like many of Pittsburgh's citizens, they attended church and knew it was considered a sin to live together as man and wife without going through the legalities of it.

"Annie's not my sister," he said softly and quickly.

"What?" Mabel said, "Could you repeat that? I didn't hear it."

Charles gave her a look but she avoided his rebuke. She and Victor were great friends and on many occasions had made fun at the other's expense.

Victor looked at Annie. The thought of having to say it the first time was hard enough but now he had to repeat it? Annie nodded at him. "Go ahead Victor, say it again."

Mabel laughed loudly and put her hand on Victor's. She drew close to his face and looked directly into his eyes, "I'm teasing you. I *know* Annie's not your sister. I never believed it for an instant. Besides, she doesn't look a bit like you." Mabel leaned back pretending to size them up. Using her hands, she waved them about to show that she didn't believe they could have been from the same family. "Look at you Victor. You're tall and have big bones. Annie is blond, tiny and small framed."

Charles glanced back and forth between Mabel, Victor and Annie. Mabel was acting strangely, as if she'd been drinking, which he knew she hadn't. Victor shot Charles a look, confirming Charles' suspicions Mabel was acting out of character. The stress seemed to be taking a toll.

"What's the latest coming from the *News Herald?*" Charles asked, hoping to change the topic and the mood.

Victor jumped in. "The War Department sent 5,000 muskets and ammunition to Cincinnati."

Mabel and Charles were interested and leaned forward. The waitress came to their table to pour water and leave a basket of bread, no one acknowledged her except Mabel who politely whispered, "Thank you."

Charles scowled, "That's a hefty delivery. Why Cincinnati?"

"It's for Kentucky, right?" Mabel asked, Victor nodded and Charles was impressed that Mabel understood U.S. War Department strategy.

Victor nodded. "Yep, it's meant for the faithful and reliable Union men of Kentucky."

Charles was thoughtful. "Arming Kentucky?"

"Only to be used for defense of Kentucky."

Mabel nodded, then looked up when she heard someone call her name. It was three local women she'd seen several times at the *News Herald*; personality types she considered tattle tales. They waved at her, Mabel smiled and waved. She noticed they were looking at Charles and once she realized, was saddened that they had been phony, had she not been sitting with handsome Charles, she doubted the women would have acknowledged her. She caught Charles looking at her. *Is he reading my thoughts?* She smiled. He smiled.

"The Confederate States of America..." Annie murmured, "Will they succeed?"

"No, they will not. From north to south the rivers will run with blood but the North will become the victor and slavery shall be no more," Mabel answered.

"Gee, sounds like something Black Pansy would say," Victor said taunting her.

Mabel was stunned and sat back in her seat but Victor was not about to lose his opportunity to return the jostling. Annie was uncomfortable. She and Victor had been discussing the identity of Black Pansy before Charles and Mabel arrived at the restaurant. They pondered over Mabel being the author of the popular story. "Don't worry," Victor told her with a half grin, "I won't tell if you won't."

The uncomfortable tension was broken when the waitress brought their food. They were all hungry and ate readily.

After Charles delivered Mabel safely home, his carriage driver, a free Negro named Burford, spurred the horse forward and spoke to Charles. "Mr. Churchill, Mabel McCrutchon is a fine lady. The folks in the community would be dismayed if any ill came of her."

Charles was surprised at his driver's words, he had tried to engage him in conversation for a week and had not succeeded in much more than "Yes Sir, No Sir" and cordial greetings.

"I didn't know you were acquainted with Mabel," Charles said, wondering what rumors he may have to indulge. *Don't all young girls have secrets?*

"Everyone knows Miss McCrutchon," Burford said with a smile and a look that told Charles he knew more.

Charles sighed.

"Oh no, Mr. Churchill," he said quickly, "No bad to report. Mabel is one of the pearls of Pittsburgh. Many a man, white or colored would enjoy her company... smart, pretty, from a nice family." Burford frowned and looked back at Charles who was very attentive, "Shame they keep her locked up the way they do. Someone should steal away with the poor girl."

"Yes, I have thought the same myself... Burford?"

"Yes Mr. Churchill."

"Call me Charles... Are you free to journey?"

"Journey? Five miles is a journey Mr. Churchill, what distance do you have in mind?"

"I'd like to go south and I'd like to bring Miss McCrutchon along, are you free to travel?"

Burford became agitated. Charles could see he was perspiring and his face was drawn, a dark cloud descended upon him on the warm spring afternoon. "No Sir, I would not be comfortable traveling south. Hooligans are everywhere on their way to join up with the Confederates, I'd be in great danger Sir. I have a wife and four children. No Sir, I could not journey south."

"Oh come now Burford, you seem a man capable, and one who knows to stay out of trouble."

"Mr. Churchill, I'm free here in Pittsburgh but I'm a wanted man in Georgia. I escaped but four years ago and my wife and children only known freedom little more 'n two years, whole family has a price on our heads outside a free state."

"I see," Charles said as if he hadn't already known. "I will pay you one-hundred and twenty dollars for you to transport Mabel and myself through Kentucky and down into Mississippi and back. The whole trip will take about five weeks."

Burford laughed, "Mississippi? Mississippi?" he laughed again and shook his head. You must think I am a silly fool. Mississippi? Mr. Churchill..."

"Charles."

"Mr. Charles, you seem to be forgettin' men are preparing for war. Any day now... any day."

Charles leaned back and took in the sights around him. Pittsburgh was alive with the anticipation of war yet the spring flowers continued their yearly profuse blooms of purple and various shades of reds and pinks. Vines trellised throughout picket fences and vigorously wound around trees. Fruit trees were in bloom and bulbs shot up through the soil forcefully, each day thousands of new bright yellow daffodils, red tulips and purple crocus spread across the city.

"You'll pose as my slave and I your firm master. I plan to ask Mabel to marry me, so she will pose, legitimately, as my fiancé."

Burford's heart plunged. "Mr. Charles, it is a serious crime for a white man to marry a Negro..."

"But Miss McCrutchon is not a Negro."

"Not to you Mr. Charles but to pro-slavery folks she's a colored woman and they'll throw you in jail, wrench Mabel from your arms and take her down to New Orleans where she'll fetch two-thousand dollars for some greedy, puffy, red faced slave trader with two much whiskey on his breath. No Sir, Mr. Charles. Not for two-hundred dollars."

"Three-hundred dollars, Burford. I will pay you three-hundred dollars, that's a fine offer."

Burford was silent for about five minutes. Charles was behind him so could not see the warm smile spread across Burford's face.

"Black Pansy has got the whole city stirred up," Victor told Mr. Whitethorn who raised an eyebrow but kept sorting through the pile of papers on his cluttered desk.

"I overheard men talking at the hotel dining room and women discussing it over calico fabric shopping at the dry goods. Why I even..."

Whitethorn stopped him, "What were they saying?"

The men were angry, they were pro-slavery but the women were somewhat sympathetic. The story's taken a horrible twist."

Whitethorn frowned but nodded. "You read the last chapters?"

"Sure have! I like the part where the men who dragged the slave woman were sentenced to twenty years hard labor."

"You liked that," Whitethorn nodded thoughtfully.

"I loved it but the men in the hotel were angry. They were talking 'bout how they should go down to Baton Rouge and tar and feather Black Pansy, if they just knew who he was."

"They did huh?" Whitethorn was visibly shaken but Victor didn't let up. He was worried for Mabel's safety.

"Black Pansy has remained neutral through all four chapters, but now, just as war is breakin' out..." Victor paused, trying to drop a hint he knew the true identity of the author stirring heated discussions across the city and into the countryside.

Whitethorn's wrinkled hands trembled, He'd already sent Mabel home but he would not stop the flow of excellent literature coming from the bright, beautiful girl. Too much was at stake.

"Black Pansy has taken a stance that's dividing our community," Victor warned.

"Slavery has divided the country Victor, we've just seen the south secede. We're going to war. Let the people be consumed with a good story. I'd wager even the Rebel soldiers 'ell be reading *American Heroes* in their tents."

"Imagine that..." Victor said, "our own author changin' minds and changin' the course of history."

"Well..." Whitethorn cleared his throat," I must send word to Baton Rouge that Black Pansy must continue *his* anonymity, for *his* own safety.

Victor looked at him dubiously and shrugged. "Yes, make sure *he* understands the danger."

Whitethorn gave him an icy stare.

Sequestered in the safety of her home and surrounded by the beauty of the spring Mabel spent long hours in her hammock writing. Every peculiar noise she heard reminded her that war was near. She wrote what she heard and saw in her vivid imagination. She'd hear the footsteps of little boys playing soldiers in the street and the worried voices of their mothers calling after them, so wrote of dying soldiers and their sorrowed widows. Through the tangled vines that wove through the fence of her secluded garden, she peered onto a new world of insecurity. Knowing that thousands of people were reading her words, she voiced what was in her heart and poured forth the anger she held against a world her mother insisted hated her. Mabel remembered the spiteful words that occasionally fell from people's mouths and penned them into the mouths of her characters, making real each soldier, Wagoner or everyday citizen whom she felt needed a tongue-lashing.

"There's a fire in the street! Fire!" Victor shouted to Whitethorn. "And a mob! Look, they're burning *American Heroes!*"

Whitethorn walked to the front window and looked out. "Lock the door Victor, run back, and lock up We're in for a world of change. Book burning..." Whitethorn shook his head, "how original."

"You're keepin' your head 'bout you. I guess the Editor should appear calm but that mob's out after us Sir."

"The law will be here soon. We've got our rights guaranteed by the first amendment."

"Laws or no laws, that mob's growing larger. We should prepare to stay the night here in the office."

"No we won't either," Whitethorn shouted. "Go on and leave if you will, I'm telling you Pittsburgh's legal system will not fail to protect the *News Herald.*"

Victor was sullen. "You're prob'ly right," he said sadly, "Jus' hope they protect Black Pansy."

Whitethorn nodded and patted him on the back and quickly escorted him out.

Charles visited Mabel daily while making plans to steal away with her, never once mentioning his intentions. He enjoyed watching her write. Thinking intently, pen propped deliciously into the side of her mouth, her lips she would sometimes allow him to steal a kiss from, just out of view, they thought, of her parents and siblings. Safe from the woes of life beyond her garden, she flourished with the roses that bore forth young buds eager to open wide their petals to the warmth of the filtered sun and dew of a spring morning. She unwound her thick, long braid and let the scent of her hair reach Charles' nostrils, electrifying his senses. She let him touch it and twine it round his fingers. Mabel was in love and she was in love with being in love. Using Charles as the ideal, she wove a gallant war hero into her story, using his description, making him a lady's man whom all women adored and wanted for themselves. The more she wove Charles Churchill into her story the more women readers she attracted. Racked with guilt, Whitethorn gave her small bonuses, which she shared generously with her younger siblings.

Day after day Charles arrived in his carriage while Burford waited patiently in the shade of a large oak. He'd agreed to accompany Charles down south but on the condition he pay him four-hundred dollars, two-hundred to his wife and children before he left and two-hundred upon their return.

"Mabel..." Charles said.

"Yes," she said attentively, eyeing the structure of his face and the depth in his eyes. In her story, she used his likeness to create a valiant Scots-Irish lieutenant of the Union Army, a single man whom all the women adored who had yet to meet his equal in wit or beauty.

"You do know I care deeply for you," Charles asked knowing full well how she thrived on his love and attention.

She nodded. The thought of it delighted her as much as the scent of violets or fresh cinnamon in an apple pie or the pleasant sound of a frog chorus after the rain.

"I need to go away," he said, putting his head down melodramatically, averting her eyes.

"Oh no!"

"Yes, parting from you is the last thing I want to do, but I have business that needs my attention. There is no other way but for me to leave."

His words hit Mabel like the sting of a slender willow branch slapped upon her cheek, a painful reminder of life's disappointments. *How had I not seen this coming? I was a strong confident woman, no man had yet to stir me though many had tried. I was content and now I am devastated - oh love, how could you be so cruel?*

Mabel's flushed, angry face was not what Charles had expected. "Mabel? Mabel!" he shouted.

She glared at him.

He looked away and gulped, thinking twice about his proposal - did he not know her? He looked back again. Her dark eyes penetrated deeply into his psyche, her angry heart brought scarlet to her full bosom that rose and fell with a passion he longed to devour. Marriage would allow him to devour it, to devour her.

"Please marry me," he said softly as he buried his head into her bosom.

Stunned, Mabel stared at the top of his head. She looked around, understanding how inappropriate the scene would be to those who had not heard their conversation. She stroked her hand through his soft, brown hair. She ran her hand up his cheek and felt no stubble; Charles was meticulous unless pro-slavery ruffians had mugged him in a barn. Mabel held him close and kissed the top of his head.

Charles' breath fluttered and he struggled to catch it. Outside their garden world could be heard the sound of clanking metal, carriage and wagons being serviced, barrels of grain sliding off of wagons and into storehouses and the firing of guns by gunsmiths preparing for war. All of Pittsburgh had quickened its pace. Horses cantered up and down the street, tempers flared.

As Mabel held Charles close, she held her head up and looked over the trellis into the world beyond. She had lived in this garden for nineteen years. She had always been safe. Yes, her family had been ashamed of their keeping her secluded but still they had loved her, they had all loved her in their own ways. Now, against her heart lay the head of a man who loved her more than any of them had. He cared not what skin color she bore, he loved her, he adored her, and she knew he would fight to protect her. She looked around at the garden, her hammock, her favorite blanket draped across to keep her warm on cool evenings where she lay and not only wrote her now famous story, but dreamed of someday having a man just like Charles. There was only one answer.

"Yes, Charles. Yes."

He looked into her face that resumed as the soft, kind girl he had loved since the day he walked into the *News Herald*. He nodded and held her tight and let out one last sigh. Their world was at war.

Burford was apprehensive but joyous at the prospect of making four-hundred dollars for no more than five-week's time. What fun he and his family could have with that money, they would never be poor again with a four-hundred-dollar financial boost.

Charles face was pensive as he walked back to the carriage.

"How does Mabel's mother feel about you taking her away?" Burford asked him.

Charles thoughtfully looked out at the expanse of green as they sauntered away from the city and into the countryside toward his cousin, Nathan's home. "Burford, you seem awfully concerned about Mabel and her family."

"Yes Mr. Charles, always lookin' out for the young ladies."

"Mabel's mother doesn't know."

"Mr. Charles, I don't like to give advice but I know something about women and you had better not wait too long to ask her mother."

"Yes, I'm well aware of the traditions that accompany marriage. I told Mabel I would return tomorrow to ask her father for her hand. I'll tell them then."

They were both silent as the streets of Pittsburgh turned from cobblestone then dirt as they headed into the countryside. Although Nathan Rutherford was recuperating nicely from the beating he'd taken at the hands of ruffians, he was on the porch waiting for Charles who could see from a distance that his cousin was troubled about something. Charles let Burford head on home, taking the carriage with him for the evening. Nathan had transportation if an emergency was to arise. Burford was to return in the morning and accompany Charles back to Mabel's home to break the news to her parents and to Mabel who had no idea of Charles' plans.

"Nathan, is the situation under control?"

Nathan nodded but scoured his yard before turning his back and escorting Charles into his modest home. Nathan was a bachelor who stood six feet four. His intimidating presence and peaceful disposition usually kept him out of trouble, but now that the word was out he'd been deceitful, the pro-slavery hooligans were undoubtedly planning something. Nathan's large tanned face and wide round blue eyes and light freckling on his face gave the man a boyish look but the look he now wore was one of wisdom mixed with fear.

"What is it?" Charles said, he too looking behind them.

"They came back again last night, drunk and carrying torches. This time there were at least a dozen men and they wore white robes. They were ready to burn my barn."

Charles sighed and sat down. "I see your barn is still there. You look fine."

Nathan continued looking out the window. "It will be a long time before I regain a sense of peace. Some of them are temporary residents or hired from down south to retrieve runaways. Luckily, one of the men had loose lips at the alehouse and one of my neighbors heard what they were up to, all the neighbors came to my defense and the men left. Later the neighbors came inside and said that there had been rumors that I was harboring runaway slaves. They insisted I stop, for their safety as well as mine. Most were kind, a few were quite angry but several others, neighbors I trusted, gave transportation to the families to a safer site. I guess I'm done harboring fugitives. My only hope now is to protect my house, barn and crop."

Charles curled his bottom lip in disgust.

"It was terrifying," Nathan said waving his arms around in imitation of the robed men with their torches. "Can you imagine facing a dozen hateful men who'd been drinking at the alehouse all day? They were so pickled, I could see them stumble, one man fell. Luckily nothing was burned."

"We should find out who picked up the tab at the alehouse."

Nathan chuckled, "Good idea, I think that can be done. Are you still going south?"

The thought of it awakened Charles' emotions. "Yes, I've asked Mabel to marry me."

Nathan did not smile; he turned toward the mantle at the fireplace. With his back to his cousin he spoke, "Are you sure that's wise?"

Charles laughed. "Wise? I'm sure it's *not* wise. Mabel is a young woman with emotions like the waves of the sea. Up, down, up down, breaking against the rocks and turbulent... calm and beautiful. Wise, no, but I'd be a fool not to."

"I see," Nathan turned and faced him. "You're taking her with you?"

Charles nodded. He knew the seriousness of taking a mulatto woman into a slave state but his instincts were usually correct and they told him under this situation that all would be well... in the end. "Yes, Nathan. I'm going to break it to her parent's tomorrow. We'll be leaving in three days. Burford has agreed to drive but at an outlandish price."

"Three days? That soon?"

"Yes, it's a good idea to get Mabel out of Pittsburgh."

Nathan laughed. "You mean out of the flames and into the fire don't you?"

"I suppose I do," Charles said as he stared into the kind face of his father's sister's son. "I suppose I do."

"Did you hear about the trouble down at the newspaper office?" Nathan asked anxiously.

"Of course! Sounds like some of the same bunch you're dealing with. Whitethorn is terrified. He's hired his own ruffians to protect the building. He and Victor have been working shorter hours; Whitethorn has curtailed a lot of the reporting." Charles would have preferred they talk about something else.

"You haven't told me what your mission is... Mississippi is it?"

"I haven't told anyone. Louisiana."

Nathan let out a deep sigh. "You are courageous. Jesus Christ Charles. You're driving into Rebel territory with two Negroes right as war is breaking out. It's insanity!"

"Mabel is not a Negro."

"No she's not, she's probably just about as white as any Pittsburgh citizen but to pro-slavers she's Negro and if they take her from you she'll be sold. Beautiful girl like that would fetch over two-thousand dollars."

"Nathan stop! I will protect her."

"What has possessed you to take her?"

"I need her."

"For what?"

"I can't answer that. I'm not sure why, I just know I need her."

Nathan shook his head and gave Charles a very disapproving look. "Do you honestly believe Mabel's parents will consent to it?"

Charles laughed heartily. "They'll have no choice. I'm sure I can convince Mabel to go with me. Once she's made up her mind there will be no stopping her."

"I've a pretty good idea what you're up to. Can't say for sure what you're doing but I was told before you came that you would be taking instructions from the Connecticut Quakers and that I was to trust that you were well guided."

"This is true," Charles said, somewhat relieved. "Any advice on how I should approach Mabel's father to ask for his daughter's hand in marriage?"

Nathan laughed more heartily than he had for days. "Do you think I'd be living here by myself if I knew that? I've passed over a few lovely ladies for fear of their fathers."

Charles smiled. Family rumors had been that Nathan was a big loveable farmer with a meager income who had a taste for beautiful women who were bred to wed wealthy men. "Yes, they can be intimidating but Mabel's father is a gentle man, it's her mother that concerns me and her protective Aunt."

"I'm not acquainted with the McCrutchon clan but I believe Burford knows them. He may know them well, that's why I recommended him as your driver."

Charles looked incredulously at Nathan. "Why didn't you mention that before?"

Nathan pondered, frowned and shook his head innocently, "So much going on, Christ, I had runaway slaves living on my premises. I was preoccupied."

"Please elaborate on Burford's relationship with the McCrutchons."

"One of those, his wife's cousin's sister's..."

"You mean they're related?"

Nathan leaned forward, "I told you. Mabel *really* is a Negro."

"Will you stop saying that! It means nothing to me!"

"No but it means everything to a slaver. Two-thousand-dollars is a lot of money and she's worth every penny of it."

"Whose side are you on?" Charles said angrily at Nathan and then stood up to retire for the night.

"I'm on your side. I'm on the side of the enslaved race held in bondage by men who want to own beautiful women like Mabel."

Charles glared at him. The events of present had worn his nerves as thin as the fabric on his cousin's abused overalls. "Are you saying that my love for Mabel is purely physical?"

"She is beautiful."

Charles shook his head. His glasses perched on the tip of his bony nose, squinting his eyes tightly as if that would help his mind comprehend his cousin's accusation. He looked up at the man towering over him. "Good God, you really believe that don't you? You don't understand. In New England, the Irish girls have been marrying free Negroes and raising beautiful families. The French

Canadians have been intermarrying with the Natives for quite some time. I've a taste for exquisite beauty. Mabel suits my taste. Yes, she's beautiful. I'm not ashamed of desiring her. You of all people should understand that. How many women have you had? Furthermore, Mabel is intelligent... well beyond average. I'm through discussing it. Good evening Nathan."

Nathan pouted. "Forgive me cousin... perhaps... I'm a bit jealous." He finally sat down. The emotions of the past week had made him tense. He feared for his life and had begun to question his decisions. He was well into his thirties and had neither wife nor children. "Charles, you just whisk in here and take the prettiest, smartest girl in all of Pittsburgh. There isn't a man in Pennsylvania who wouldn't love to have Mabel McCrutchon as a bride. Forgive me. I wish you only the best."

"Thank you Nathan. I'll do my best to keep her safe. You're not the first man to tell me she is the jewel of Pittsburgh."

Nathan laughed. "Burford has been hot on her since they were children."

"I see. Should I be concerned? He is traveling with us. He'll have occasion to be alone with her."

"Burford? Nah, he's married now, has four cute kids. He married a nice woman. Burford's a good man. Don't let anything happen to him either. Jesus Christ Charles, are you sure you want to do this? Are you crazy? Traveling with two Negroes to New Orleans during a war over whether the white man should enslave Negroes or not?"

"I suppose it takes a little bit of crazy to have become involved in the Underground Railroad. It must run in the family."

Burford arrived early the next morning to take Charles to meet with Mabel's parents.

"Dear God," Charles told Nathan, "Burford is outside already. Look Nathan, he's sitting out there waiting for me. The sun has only been up for an hour."

Nathan looked outside and saw Burford sitting in the carriage in the warm sun, smiling, a book propped between his legs. "Looks like he's in no hurry. Maybe Burford likes to get away from the wife and kids."

Charles grunted.

"A bit grouchy this morning Cousin?"

Charles was silent.

"You'll do fine. I thought about your situation while I lay in bed last night. Mabel's father... you're not worried about right?"

"That's right," Charles said trying desperately to flip his own hotcakes on a cast iron grill.

"You ever cook before?" Nathan asked him.

"When I was a boy, a few times."

"Well let me know if you need help... anyway, you're worried about Mabel's mother and Auntie."

"That's correct," Charles said as Nathan got a glimpse of his charred hotcakes.

"And you're not going to marry her yet but you want to travel with her?"

"That also is correct. Cousin you're brilliant," Charles said sarcastically.

"The mother has always wanted to keep Mabel hidden because she loves status but the Aunt wants what's best for Mabel."

"What are you getting at?"

"Tell them that you are going south to get an award for man of the year," Nathan said then laughed heartily at Charles' gullibleness.

Charles threw the spatula down making a racket. "I'm going into town for breakfast." "I'll be back this evening... after dinner... in town."

"Burford, why didn't you tell me you were related to Mabel?" Charles said in a grouchy tone.

"Good morning Mr. Charles."

"Quit calling me Mister."

"I'd rather not omit the Mister, it reminds me that I'm on the job."

Charles sighed. "So why didn't you tell me you're related to Mabel?"

"I'm not."

"Nathan said you are."

"That's incorrect sir, *my wife* is related to Mabel."

Charles sighed again. "Well, why didn't you tell me your wife was related to Mabel?"

"Didn't know you cared Mr. Charles. It wasn't any of my business. I like to keep my mouth shut about those things."

Charles was impressed. "You're a wise man Burford. Your wisdom will come in handy on our journey."

"Thank you Mr. Charles."

Pittsburgh was quieter than usual and both Charles and Burford appreciated it. They lingered around until after lunch, then made their way down to Mabel's house. Thankfully, the quiet pervaded her neighborhood as well.

"Perhaps everyone has accepted that there's war to the south of us," Charles told Burford.

"Oh, I don't know that sir. Just 'cause it's quiet, that doesn't mean anything. Maybe folks are restin' up for some big shenanigan. Maybe folks are just tired of all the talk of war. Maybe Pittsburgh wants to stay out of it."

Charles let out with a sinister laugh then exited the carriage and walked the stoned pathway to the large home of the McCrutchons. He was no longer afraid of two old women. It was Mabel he wanted. He was in no mood to play silly parlor games with anyone, including Mabel. The big door had a large oval beveled glass window. Through it, he could see Millie, the youngest of the

McCrutchon clan running down the stairs to answer the door. Millie had white porcelain skin and hazel eyes. Her cheeks were rosy from running quickly down the stairs. At eight years old, Millie had known Charles was coming and Mabel had confided in her that it was an important day.

"I've come to see your father and mother."

"Not Mabel?" Millie asked.

"Yes Mabel too."

"Mother... Father... Mabel."

Mabel had anticipated Charles' visit and dressed appropriately. The tall collar and sleeves of her cotton, floor-length, calico dress were laced. A gray color fabric with tiny pink and purple flowers Charles found quite appropriate for spring. *She is fashionable,* he thought, *my mother would like that.*

Mabel greeted him with her usual smile, "We'll go into the parlor," she said, perfumed hanky in one hand, her hair done up with ribbons.

"Why, so we can play games?" he said quietly to release tension. "Nothing, just talking to myself," he said after she gave him a wary look.

"Mother... Father... Charles is here."

"Good morning, Mr. Churchill," Mabel's father, Lionel, said as he rose from the table and shook Charles' hand.

"Good morning Charles," Mabel's mother, Vivian, said knowing exactly why Charles had come.

"Vivian... Mr. McCrutchon," Charles said politely.

"Please, please... call me Lionel."

"I will... Lionel... and please... call me Charles."

"I'll get right to the point. I wish to marry your daughter. I would like to marry her in Connecticut, that is my mother's wish. I'd also like to take Mabel with me to New Orleans."

Everyone gasped. Vivian had a dreadful look on her face and all the color ran from Lionel's' leaving him an ashen gray. Mabel was stunned. Millie giggled.

"Why, Charles you never mentioned this to me," Mabel said, angry that she hadn't been warned. She had a responsibility to Whitethorn to keep up her writing. "Mother has never allowed me to venture past the boundaries..."

Charles cut her short. "Well Mabel if you're to be my wife, I'll be making decisions for you."

"What?"

"Well... some of the decisions for you," Charles said quickly losing confidence.

Seeing his daughter take command of the situation brought color back to Lionel's cheeks.

Vivian smiled, "What's in New Orleans that would inspire a gentleman to travel when a war has just broken out?" She raised an eyebrow and looked toward Mabel as if to say, *and with a colored girl?*

Charles was in no mood to go through this again. The argument with Nathan had been enough. "Mrs. McCrutchon, I'll take superb care of your daughter. No harm shall come to her. No harm shall come to me. I've some business regarding my father's shipyards that none other than myself can attend to," he lied. "I would like Mabel to come. I've all the necessary paperwork, Mabel will be my fiancé and Burford will travel with us."

"Burford Jones?" Vivian said, and then looked at Lionel. It was through Mabel's father that Burford's wife was related to the McCrutchon clan.

"Yes. Burford Jones."

Lionel stood up again and shook Charles hand, "Charles, you'll make my daughter a fine husband. I respect your strength," he said over the top of his glasses into Charles' eyes as if to say... *you're going to need it.*

Vivian consented by embracing Charles, warm and reassuringly. She gave him a kiss on the cheek, and then with a smile and a whisper so soft no one heard, said *"Keep her away from Crocker."*

"Did you find out who paid the tab at the Alehouse for the white robed scoundrels who terrorized you the other night?" Charles asked Nathan as they sat together in his small home and discussed the events of the day.

"I did." Nathan pulled a dirty, wrinkled paper out of his overalls and read it to Charles. "Bartholomew Miller. He owns a large lumber mill east of Piedmont, Maryland and he wants his slaves back."

"Have you heard word of them?"

"Those with families went to New York, the singles are on their way to Ontario," Nathan said with pleasure in his voice.

"Very good. Makes a man feel good to help another man gain his freedom."

"Or woman," Nathan said to Charles who nodded.

Heading South

Mabel gripped the sides of her seat in the coach that Burford resolutely held at the helm. Off duty, Burford was a joker, a glib remark always on the wait. But once Burford reported for duty, he was all business, especially this time. If Burford had any fear, which Mabel knew he must, he did not show it, only a determination to accomplish the mission safely and return home to his family a lot more prosperous.

Charles, on the other hand was the nervous of all three and through the expression on her face, Charles could read Mabel's confusion as to why he withheld the itinerary and purpose of their trip. He grabbed and squeezed her hand. His apologetic look gave Mabel no confidence the trip would be without consequence.

Once leaving Pittsburgh, Burford had been instructed to travel at a moderate pace along the Ohio River. Soldiers from the North would be traveling in great numbers on the steamers down the Mississippi River to New Orleans so Charles chose to stay away from the great river until they reached Natchez. During the early miles, their mood was somber and few words were spoken. Mabel surrendered to reality and leaned snugly against Charles' shoulder. She'd not been this far south nor this many miles from home.

In the evenings, they stayed at inns and alehouses where she had her own room and wrote with wild abandon. The beauty of the surrounding nature inspired her. The next installments of *American Heroes* would sport vivid scenes of America's backwoods beauty.

Charles was grateful she could occupy herself as he had maps to study and correspondence to compose, particularly one to his mother for whom he'd not written for far too long.

Mabel never once gave it a thought that her writing would give hints to the identity of the author, Black Pansy, but back in Pittsburgh, Victor was the first to point it out. "Mr. Whitethorn... Black Pansy..." he said biting his lower lip, "Mabel..." he said aggressively, to which Whitethorn nodded, finally acknowledging his beautiful and brilliant ghostwriter.

"Mabel's writing has changed," Victor told him, "she's writing about soldiers... brother against brother..."

"Her writing is brilliant!" Whitethorn chortled.

"Yes, true, but she's incorporating the road and natural history into the story... there are many who know Mabel has left with Charles."

Whitethorn had lain awake worrying the same after receiving Mabel's latest package. A whole chapter for which he was grateful but cringed at how much the writing resembled a young woman out into the world for the first time, the dusty road with all its trappings. "It will be harder to deny but we must do so vehemently."

Victor rolled his eyes and began biting the inside of his mouth. He too had laid awake most of the night, the excitement and turmoil over the rumblings of southern rebellion had been overwhelming. They'd kept the front door secured and worked in the back rooms out of view of the public who on occasion wanted to storm the *News Herald* and string up Editor Whitethorn and occasionally Victor because of something they'd read in *American Heroes*. To make things worse, Victor's mother, a staunch Baptist, had heard he had his "sister" living with him. As his mother, no one was more familiar with the sex of her own children and she had no recollection of bearing a daughter. Victor was in deep with explanations to her.

Burford kept up the moderate pace but Charles realized they were not making enough miles so they began traveling during the night. With fewer travelers or military on the road, they made better time but their backsides were blistered and their emotions gray.

"We're in the heart of Rebel country now Mr. Charles," Burford said, looking back at Mabel who sat close to her fiancé.

"Yes Burford, Rebel land."

"I know you read maps and question military when we stop, but sir, I pray your traveling calculations are correct. I've four kids at home..."

"Burford, I'm known for my attention to detail and though I can't reveal my sources I have the current status of the Rebel and Union Armies.

"Mmm...hmm," Burford said looking at Charles dubiously, believing him to be bluffing.

As the miles rolled on, Mabel began to let go and enjoy the scenery. She watched wild waters tumble down slick boulders along the banks of rivers and streams. The thought that Natives peered at them at night through gnarled forests brought Mabel more alive than any moment in her young life. All was peaceful most days, though sometimes the sound of distant cannons broke the serenity. Mabel believed in the cause that young men were dying for and thought it ironic that she whose great-grandmother had been a slave now rode freely through the green rolling hills of Kentucky, side by side with a fine man from a prominent New England family.

Prominence was not what mattered most to Mabel. It was character that she needed in a man, not some silly farm boy who'd not read Harriet Beecher Stowe nor the writings of Frederick Douglass. Charles had read them all and knew the injustices of the world. Every stop they made was calculated. In advance, he'd known of President Lincoln's call for 75,000 volunteers to put down the Rebel insurrection. When the news hit the streets that Robert E. Lee had rejected the president's request to lead the Union army, it was not news to Charles. He seemed to know in advance, what both sides were planning. Was it sheer genius? Was he a spy? *Who was this man she was now betrothed to?*

Foremost on Charles' mind was that they must make it to New Orleans and back to Pittsburgh safely. The President had set up blockades at all Confederate ports. The deeper south they traveled, the more Charles coddled her. She would catch him staring at her then ask that she wear her hat, a big floppy thing he'd bought her with peacock feathers so profuse you could barely see her face, which was entirely the point. And gloves. The gloves were fine on days when it was cool, rainy and overcast but on warm days, she refused to wear the gloves or hat and it became a tenuous situation between them.

"I'll sit on my hands if I must," Mabel said angrily.

The look he gave her was one of sadness. Above all people, he knew and believed deeply that Mabel McCrutchon was a fine, decent human. How petty it was that folks cared what shade her skin was. And now a war had broken out over it?

It was evening when they drove into Tennessee. The trip had worn them down but they'd been good company to one another, telling things about themselves they'd not otherwise have known. Burford told them he could play piano and violin and the Pittsburgh Presbyterians appreciated his skill. Charles said he could ride a unicycle and Mabel could sing like a songbird and had never revealed that to anyone outside those who'd heard her sing in her garden.

The day had been warm but the evening was growing cool. Mabel was more than happy to don her gloves and bundle up, including the frivolous hat that Charles warned her, "Could save your life... or at the very least... your freedom."

Burford usually waited for Charles' cue but both he and the horses were exhausted, so took the liberty to pull into the next alehouse that presented itself.

"What are you doing?" Charles protested.

"Mr. Charles, we're all fatigued, 'specially these poor horses."

"No Burford. We must push on. We'll stop when we get to Nashville."

"Nashville? Why it'll be midnight 'fore we get to Nashville. What's wrong with this place?" Burford asked as the carriage sat outside an alehouse with a sign that read, "Blue Grass Inn - Come on in."

"I'm dreadfully hungry," Mabel complained.

"We've food in the basket... crackers, jerky and fresh apples," Charles begged, but Mabel was quick to jump out of the carriage and Burford climbed down, both unaware that two men and three uncouth women were staring at them through the open door.

Slowly and sarcastically one of the men asked, "Is that a N-e-g-r-o-w?"

"It is and a right pretty one," said the other man who looked like he'd been eating up more than his share of hog corn.

Jealously, one of the women complained, "What 'er you lookin' at? Think N-e-g-r-o-w women are better 'en whites? Ya'all on the wrong side if'n you do. I reckon you two boys aughta go join up with them Northern boys ifn' you love N-e-g-r-o-w women so much.

"Ah Sally, you know I think you're the prettiest thing since Daniel Boone sold land to all them white settlers but I aint's never seen no hoity toity colored girl before. Why she's downright purdy," he whistled, beer foam stuck onto his yellow, tobacco-stained mustache.

"I seen 'em before," the other woman said, her face hidden between long strands of unwashed hair. All three of the women looked in desperate need of bathing while the two men looked as if that day they'd had a swim.

"I seen 'em in Louisville and Lexington, they sew 'an make pretty things for rich white women."

"Yea, the white women teach 'em manners, educate 'em 'an all that," the other said.

"Please get back in the carriage," Charles pleaded. "Please, I have a list of stopping places and this place is not on it."

Mabel turned and looked at Charles. Suddenly she realized what he was saying and the way a lamp flickered inside the inn was just enough for her to view five menacing faces all staring at her. "Burford, Charles is right. Folks like us are not welcome here..."

she looked back into the inn, ready for a fight but now was not the time, she could see she would not win this one.

It was midnight when they rode into the bustling city of Nashville. They could hear loud and lively music as minstrels of both sexes and every economic stratum displayed their talent. Up and down Nashville's main boulevard, beautiful women sang to the lively tunes, their nights made when a gold piece was dropped into visibly placed cans. Saloons were still open for business and wild women were still collecting coins from willing patrons. The sky was a deep dark blue and the moon white and full. Mabel inhaled the cool fresh air.

"I believe in the Constitution and the Union," came a loud voice from a saloon.

"Death to all Yankees and Abolitionists!" followed another. The war was ready to break out and it seemed young men were eager for one last hurrah before marching off to the beat of the fife and drum.

Mabel studied the fashions and watched the manners of women as they lifted large dresses and billowing petticoats when crossing the street. She caught the eyes of several of the women who smiled politely but turned quickly away. Then Mabel noticed that they had women, like her, with color in their skin, their servants who trailed behind them. *For what? To keep an eye on them? Fix their hair when it fell? Mend their dresses when their tight corsets ripped from laughter after overindulging on corn whiskey?* The servants barely looked at Mabel and she wondered why. What harm would become of them for giving her eye contact? *Were even their eyes enslaved?*

Charles took Mabel's arm and they walked together but only after he made sure her hat and gloves were on. He seemed to be the most at ease since the week before they left. A lot had happened. Her verbal accosting in the street in front of the *News Herald*, Nathan's beating by pro-slavery thugs, Charles facing her parents. He had a lot to let down from and they both knew much more was to be placed before them. She looked at Burford. He too was enjoying the evening; a sense of amusement spread across his face and it was nice to see him smiling.

"Stay close," Charles warned him.

"Mr. Charles, we'll all stay close. I plan to stay right by your side. In Pittsburgh, I'm a free man but in these slave states, I'm your servant. Beat me if you have to, make it look real."

"Let's hope we don't have to resort to that but thanks for the permission," Charles said dryly.

Mabel winced. Was she supposed to say the same thing? She would not. *Oh, how could the tint of my skin separate me from my own world? Make a slave of me when I was born of a free mother, free grandmother, and a straight white line forever down her mother's tree?* Her father's grandfather had married a colored servant, a mulatto. What did that matter? Had she not proven a good mother and wife and bore him more than a half-dozen healthy children? Hadn't she brought beauty and strength into the McCrutchon clan? And now a war of it? What hypocrisy she lived with.

Charles grabbed her arm and tilted her hat to cover better her beautiful tinted skin. She smiled at him and felt the warmth of his love. Letting go, she put punch into her step and the three of them entered the fray of Nashville. The last party.

It was in Nashville that Mabel felt strong carnal urges toward Charles and he toward her. She longed to hold him the way a married woman was able and he relished the day that he could consummate his love for her. She'd been watching Charles day after day and felt her presence had affected him as well. When they stopped in the beautiful green forests of Western Virginia and Kentucky to tend to their personal needs they had caught each other peeking. He when she removed her dress one day, behind a tree, to remove ants that had come crawling onto her skin, and she, once when he removed his pants to shake loose the leaves and twigs that had invaded. She wondered if Burford had not been there would she have forsaken Christian and social morals and indulged in a little kissing and touching? She was quite sure she would have and she looked at Charles when they passed under the swinging sign of the Nashville Hotel. He smiled and squeezed her hand.

They left early the next morning and began traveling down the Chickasaw Trace.

"Mr. Charles, we need a full day's rest for these horses. Need a Blacksmith too and the carriage needs repairs. Any suggestions?"

Charles was thoughtful. Every one of his stops was coordinated with a list, knowing that each proprietor was a friend of the slave, either an Abolitionist associate or a Quaker family, sometimes both. But a livery stable and Blacksmith could pose problems especially if they asked questions that he may not have answers for. Charles studied his list.

"We'll try to make it to Abraham Camp's stand. I'm sorry but his is the closest stop that I know is safe to stop for that long. We'll stop at Salerno's stand for food."

"If we make it there alive," Mabel joked bitterly.

Charles looked around; he'd done that constantly since leaving Pittsburgh, always watching over his shoulder. Since leaving Nashville, those they'd encountered along the road had been aggressive. Many travelers were ragged wayfarers or farmers on foot. Northern farmers walked home along the trace after floating their goods by barge down the Mississippi, selling their goods in New Orleans, then selling their barge.

"There are a lot of robberies on this road," Burford told Mabel, he as nervous as she but refusing to show it.

"We've our guns," Charles said confidently.

The trees were thick and beautiful but the shade made for wet spots that did not dry. There were times when the carriage became stuck and Charles and Mabel had to push it.

When they neared Salerno's there were fifteen wagons belonging to Chickasaw Natives who ignored their arrival. Charles knew that these men and their families were keen to the impending war but were avoiding confrontation. Hidden between the Chickasaw wagons was a carriage, similar to theirs. Mabel caught Charles eyeing it suspiciously. Though Charles' itinerary had not listed Salerno's as a friend of the slave, he felt safe stopping because it was listed as a presumably safe place to stop briefly. Mabel walked ahead and without thinking removed her hat and walked into the stand. There were more Natives inside who were not rude but ignored her. At a table having lunch and obviously heading south to join the Rebels, were six men. Charles walked in just in time, before they had a chance to accost Mabel.

"How dare you disobey me!" Charles shouted rudely to Mabel who looked bewildered and appalled at his manner. "Return to the carriage at once!" Charles demanded.

Mabel's wide eyes darted about the room. Every single man, woman and child was now staring at her. Immediately she realized she must not act the free woman that she was but a woman in bondage whom Charles "owned."

"Yes Sir," she said, "so sorry sir," she repeated hanging her head and retreating to the carriage. She passed Burford who had just entered. She glared at him and he knew to walk out with her, both stayed put in the carriage, Burford unlocked the gun case and removed the revolver.

With all eyes on him, Charles ordered a glass of rum and a slice of cake he saw on the counter. Another young man dressed as finely as he approached him.

"Is she for sale?" he asked.

"No... pretty isn't she?" Charles said crudely.

"Yes, she is," the man said, turning around again glaring back at the carriage outside. "She could almost pass for white."

Charles was lost on how to respond.

"I'll give you two-thousand for her."

"No, no," Charles said, a lump in his throat. *Dear God Burford get the guns out.*

"Twenty-five hundred?"

Charles shook his head no. The man looked down and saw Charles' hand that held the short, stout glass of rum was shaking uncontrollably. Again, the man looked outside toward the carriage. He kept looking at Charles' shaking hand and back to the carriage. Sizing him up he said, "Your wife?"

Charles stared at him. He did not know how to answer that. She would soon be his wife but she was not now and laws were strict about marriage between Negroes and Whites. He began to sweat uncontrollably.

"What have you got there, you devil you? Belong to someone else does she?"

Charles tossed coins onto the big timber slab that served as a bar. "Good day," he said to the stranger. Charles was out the door and quickly instructed Burford to make more than moderate progress down the Chickasaw Trace. Mabel said nothing for a long time and for the first time she did not lean into him even though he leaned into her. He desperately needed to feel her close.

They made their way down to Abraham Camp's stand but found it shuttered.

"Burford, can't you fix the wagon and tend to the horses yourself?"

Burford balked and mumbled, "I could Mr. Charles, 'spose I could but it's not my specialty. I'm not experienced with horses, just good at drivin' em, always have someone else caring for them."

"We need to get off the road. Next side road you see... if it's wooded and we can take cover, turn down it. We'll rest the horses and sleep outside for once."

Burford followed Charles' instructions and before the carriage had come to a full stop Charles said to Mabel, "Come with me. Burford... Mabel and I are going to stroll, shake our legs, do you mind?"

"No, Mr. Charles, you can stroll all you want. Do you both some good," he said then looked at Mabel with a look that said, *you go with him, get over this, we are in dangerous times.*

Mabel did not want to budge but sat frozen on the carriage seat. Charles could see she had been crying. Her eyes were very red and her face was swollen.

"Why did you bring me? You don't need me. Where are we going and for what?"

Charles spoke softly and extended his hand. "Please Mabel get out of the carriage, let's walk... please?" He tugged on her hand but she would not budge. He pulled and pulled but could not get Mabel to budge. "If you come I will tell you where we're going."

Covering her swollen, tearful face, she lifted herself off the carriage seat and Charles picked her limp body up and lifted her down. He'd never held her like that before and it stimulated him immensely. He glanced at Burford, resenting his presence. *If only we could be alone.*

Charles and Mabel walked hand in hand through a meadow. Wildflowers in all colors had just begun to bloom. A light wind blew fresh air into their faces; their nostrils gulped it in. He turned and faced her and drew her close, brushing her thick hair from her face. Her dark, kind eyes showed forgiveness. He kissed her lips. Afterwards she put her head into the hollow of his shoulder and sobbed.

"Mabel, there are five children, little more than babies that I promised I would escort to Pittsburgh. Their mother was a slave, beaten so badly she died."

Mabel gasped. She shook her head no. But Charles had to shake his head yes. She looked up at the carriage, then back to Charles. "We're bringing them back in that?"

"Yes! You are to pose as their mother and I their father, a slave dealer. It will be extremely dangerous. What we've seen this month, the turmoil, it could get much worse and probably will. I know I should have asked you but I knew your heart was good. Five colored children Mabel, three little girls and two boys ages two to seven. I don't know how we'll do it, but with the war breaking out, we had to act quickly. A Quaker representative in the countryside outside New Orleans is caring for them. The legal owner of the children is looking all over the south for the children; he had plans for all five of them. Mean son-of-a-bitch is what he is, bastard. Doesn't feed his slaves well, doesn't decently clothe them. We've got to save them. Don't you see?"

"I do Charles. I do." Mabel looked at the beauty of the evergreen and oak woodland forest that surrounded them. A small pond was in the distance. There was nothing but untarnished nature. She wondered if this meadow would be a battlefield, for the northern free states against the southern states fighting for their right to sell children by the pound.

Oh, how Charles wanted to engage Mabel's body under the stars and the crescent moon. But he was a gentleman and she was a fine lady, the jewel of Pittsburgh, she deserved his respect. So Charles, Mabel and Burford set up their bedrolls and lay out under the stars. Had they not been exhausted they could have stayed up all night lying flat on their backs talking like little children but by about 8:30 they were sound asleep.

Around midnight, Mabel turned over and felt a man's hand covering her mouth. She could not scream nor cry out. She could not move. It was the man from Salerno's Station who had tried to "purchase" her from Charles earlier in the day. He bent down and dragged her about a foot when he heard the loading of a cylinder into a revolver. It was Charles.

"Let go of the lady and don't turn around."

"Mr. Charles? Mabel?" Burford's terrified voice rang out.

"Burford," Charles shouted, his revolver still pointed at the intruder, "there's some rope in the back of the carriage, retrieve it please and tie this man's hands with it. Take him to a tree and tie him there till the wolves get 'em or if he has any luck left someone will eventually hear his cries. Mabel, go ahead, gather your things. Of course we're leaving. Burford... I'm going to stand here with my revolver pointed right at this gentleman. I'm sorry if I can't be of assistance, for you with the horses."

"That's alright Mr. Charles. We'll be ready to go shortly."

"Mabel, are you OK?"

"Yes," she said, not wishing to say any more as if her voice might someday give her away.

The three were soon back on the road again.

"Charles?" Burford asked, "Why were you up at that hour?"

"Burford, that man wanted Mabel. He told me he wanted Mabel and I could see it in his eyes. I knew he'd follow us and wait. I never went to sleep. I promised Mabel, her parents, her aunt, Victor, Whitethorn and even you Burford that I would let no harm come to Miss McCrutchon. I intend to keep that promise."

Mabel leaned in tight next to Charles. He wrapped his coat around her to keep the chill off as they headed toward the Mississippi border.

The incident the night before gave Mabel renewed vigor. Although she spoke less, she thought more about the story she was writing and at every stop grabbed her pen and wrote it down. She took advantage of every station that offered the opportunity to post her manuscript back to Pittsburgh. The incident had her penning away the description of the evil man who tried to steal her away. He became a new villain. Pittsburgh loved it. Black Pansy as an author was growing famous but Mabel had no idea her story had reached such heights. *Harper's Weekly* and *Herald of Freedom* had done editorials, both suggesting that Black Pansy was turning the tide of thought against slavery. Jokes were made about Black Pansy helping in no small way to win the verbal war for the Union.

But *Harper's Weekly, Herald of Freedom* nor Mabel McCrutchon knew to what depths of despair the country would soon fall during this "War of Rebellion."

It was very early morning when Victor and Whitethorn arrived at the office. They'd decided to come in early and leave early before the crowds started rat-tat-tatting on the door. Every day, all day, a parade of citizens with varying inquiries had worn Victor and Whitethorn down. But Victor received a pay increase and Whitethorn had begun using a competitor's presses to print his paper, leaving the *News Herald* office less hectic. Prosperity from Black Pansy's stories was flowing rapidly into Whitethorn's hands. Telegrams of praise were frequent. Pennsylvania and neighboring states clamored for more of the story. American households constantly inquired of one another if there were new chapters of *American Heroes*. "The writing is fresh and poignant, as if Black Pansy himself was commanding the war and dictating the next social era," the *Harper's Weekly* proclaimed. Word reached Whitethorn that the president's wife; Mrs. Lincoln had begun reading it to her husband who is said to have enjoyed it immensely. Whether it was true or not Whitethorn did not know. There were numerous photos, sketches and portraits of the author, all fake of course, and there were several phony interviews.

Mabel's Auntie Louisa had no small part in her niece's success as an author. A former school teacher, she'd been dotting Mabel's i's and crossing her t's and making occasional edits for quite some time. To prevent exposing Mabel as the true author, Mabel had been mailing the manuscript pages to Auntie who would discretely deliver them into the hands of Editor Whitethorn but not before a few changes were made. Whitethorn gave her Mabel's stipend, which she diligently secured away. Auntie Louisa's changes and additions improved the story greatly as she kept abreast of the country's politics while Mabel was away and as a young girl, Auntie Louisa had traveled through Baton Rouge so knew the lay of the land and the feel of the area.

The secret that Mabel McCrutchon was Black Pansy was tightly kept. Besides Charles, those who knew were: Whitethorn, Victor, Victor's "sister" Annie, Mabel's mother and father and Auntie Louisa. Of course, there had been rumors early on but they had been successfully squelched. It seemed no one suspected Mabel any longer.

Once they arrived in Natchez, Charles was forever pulling Mabel closer and propping up her feathered hat, while she dazed and gazed at handsome men from exotic places and they at her. The men from Paris or Madrid, with their thick accents, showed no modesty when flirting with her nor did the tall, Dutch, northern farm boys who smiled sweetly. Mabel basked in the excitement. Schooners from upriver transported people and products into New Orleans. Kentucks sold corn and whiskey. Northerners made cattle deals. Spanish and French influence was everywhere and Mabel loved it.

"Why must I hide?" she protested. "Mulattos are everywhere! Everywhere!" She twirled around, spinning this way and that, her adrenaline spiking, her personality following suit.

Charles reminded himself that Mabel was only nineteen years old and that it was not unusual for beautiful young girls to be enamored by handsome young men who aggressively pursue with the skill of a spider jumping to devour a moth. But she was his butterfly; the jewel of Pittsburgh and now it appeared also of Natchez.

"The Mulattos you speak of may appear to own their freedom but probably do not," Charles told her. "Look carefully, they're trusted plantation representatives. See that woman on the platform negotiating cloth purchases?"

Mabel turned and looked but stopped short to admire an olive-skinned, black haired, Spaniard with a goatee and a smile.

"Not there," Charles griped, taking his hand and twisting her head toward a very fair Negro woman in the depths of investigating bolts of cotton and wool. "She's probably the head seamstress for a large plantation. She's shopping for fabric to make the under garments for slaves."

Mabel frowned.

"See that young fair-skinned colored woman with the little boy?"

Mabel turned to look.

"She's carrying a basket and is keenly aware of her surroundings. See how intense she is? She probably works in the kitchen of a large plantation. Her little boy?" Charles shook his head at Mabel, "does not stand a chance, that's why the pensive face on the mother. One of these days her master will tell her the boy is going on an errand to town but he will never return. He'll be sold. She may never see him again."

Mabel frowned at Charles. "You're disgusting. You don't know these things. I'll bet I would be just fine walking around without my hat. I'm well aware of the conditions of the enslaved," she protested but kept all his thoughts in mind to use in the next chapter of her story.

Charles was not done. "You see that man there?

Mabel turned to look but did not know whom he was speaking of.

"The man at the root beer stand... silk vest, gold pocket watch, pencil thin mustache, black shiny boots... he's a slave dealer."

"No? How can you tell?"

"I just can, he's got that look. I've seen them in Maryland and North Carolina. They are the most uncompassionate humans. They would have to be. He's the kind of man who takes little boys and fattens them up so he can sell them by the pound. No heart, absolutely no scruples."

Just as Charles relayed this the mother with the little boy walked past them. She shot Mabel a look, eyeing her, wondering what her life must be like. She eyed Charles. Mabel grew uncomfortable. *She must think I'm his mistress*. Mabel tucked her face under her floppy hat and grabbed Charles' arm. She held him close and eyed the scene around her with an altered view. She knew he was correct. This was Natchez - these Colored People were not free - someone owned them, someone owned that mother's son, *she doesn't even own her own son*.

Mabel's mind got to working on her story. Every so many chapters she created a new hero. It surprised her how many of her heroes had Charles' attributes. They were close to their destination. They would retrieve the children from the sequestered hiding place and return them to Pittsburgh where they would, she assumed, be sent on to the Underground Railroad Committee who would find homes for them in Canada.

It was dusk when they arrived in New Orleans, she Charles and Burford all wore foreboding countenances. It had rained for two days straight. There was talk of a hurricane but Charles spoke with men in taverns, Oystermen, who knew how to read nature's cues and they said they didn't suspect any hurricanes, just the usual tropical storm.

"You're on the Gulf," one of the oystermen told Charles. "You can expect tropical storms. How're you traveling? Come down by schooner?"

"No, no," Charles said, "Came down the Choctaw trace then on down the trace to Natchez."

The Oysterman looked askance at him, incredulously shook his head and pointed a finger in Charles' face. Charles could see the years of sunshine and sea had weathered the man's round face. He was not much older than him but the hard work outside had aged him and brought cataracts to his eyes. "I don't know what your business is... in New Orleans... but if I were you... I would finish it up and get my tail feathers back north. The North is trying to blockade the ports and the cannons have begun to fire. There's to be some fightn'. Just know it. I'm 'bout ready to join up myself," he said, making Charles question his wisdom in discussing his business with him. "Don't get me wrong Mister, I'm one of them who think a man's got no right own'n another man. But this aggression coming from the North... it's got to stop. We'll handle our affairs down here our own way. Can't go stoppin' decades and decades of enterprise all at once now can we? What will happen to our cotton and rice production? What will happen to Southerners if we let 'ol Abe and the Mrs. tell us how to conduct business? The way I hear it, slaves are headin' to Lincoln's doorstep thinkin' that he and his wife... Mrs. President," he said, laughed, then took another swig off his clay beer mug, "are gonna' take care of 'em.

Now them darkies all wanna come home, they miss their old masters. The plantation life ain't all bad it just ain't."

"If you'll excuse me, I've important business to attend to. Good day," Charles said, tipped his hat, his heart a little fainter, his energy spent.

Mabel couldn't get enough of the Southern charm presented to her at the hotels they stayed in. Charles made sure she was served breakfast in bed, crepes with fresh fruit from the Caribbean, tea and eggs. He tried to make up for the discomfort she'd endured and strengthen her for the return trip.

"It's not known what misfortunes we may encounter," Charles said to Burford at the hotel, sitting in a high backed red velvet chair under a rose pink chandelier looking through the window out into the streets of New Orleans.

Burford nodded. He was long past worrying about what *may* happen, they'd arrived and now needed to complete their task. He sat in a similar chair, except his was royal blue. He sat in front of the same window and was content to savor the moment. It was a beautiful spring day and the sun lay warm and brightly upon their laps. A shadow of a large bird passed their window and the smell of sweet blossoms wafted into the slightly jarred window. Everywhere he looked, he saw French and Spanish wrought iron works of art, trellises, gates and balcony rails. Red brick contrasted against purple and white flowers spilling from hanging pots.

Beautiful people of various ethnicities brought a parade of entertainment. Small colored boys tap danced in tattered clothes. Teenaged boys sold bananas they'd salvaged from the water when they fell off the banana boats. The bananas sold quickly due to the recent blockade of the Port of New Orleans, fruit was growing scarce. There were boys selling newspapers and shining shoes. Half of New Orleans streets were filled with people and products that were just off a boat. A culture that brought African women with colorful turbans wrapped round their heads and baskets overflowing with melons and oranges. The other half of New Orleans looked as if they'd come from the north or the east. Farmers, lawyers and immigrants looking for work or to sign up with the Rebel army. Burford saw several intoxicated men lying on benches and more well-to-do people than he'd ever seen in his travels.

Charles watched Burford relaxing and enjoying himself. Because he'd fled from Georgia, Burford felt the likelihood of any one recognizing him was slim but New Orleans was a hub for slave traders and there was always a chance a traveling overseer could recognize him. *How kind of him to chance it*, Charles thought.

Charles insisted Mabel purchase fresh clothes, which she did, then entered the hallway wearing a blue dress. She pulled on her petticoats and lifted her hem, revealing new shoes. But sadly, she had the same floppy, feathery hat. Charles had insisted.

"You look beautiful," Charles told her while admiring her freshness after a bath.

"As do you, Mr. Charles."

She was well rested and enjoying her stay.

Both Mabel and Charles watched Burford stare out the window. He looked peaceful but had not had the privilege of purchasing new clothes or delighting in a bath. His time had been spent finding a Blacksmith and carriage repair then dropping into bed for a sound sleep.

"Burford," Charles said pulling cash from his pocket, "Get some new clothes and take a long hot bath. Mabel and I will be meeting with someone. We'll meet you back here for dinner. We'll have one more night of New Orleans southern hospitality then be on our way. How are the horses faring?"

"Mr. Charles, I believe it's wise to trade those two horses for two fresh ones.

Charles was embarrassed that he'd not thought of that himself. "Of course! They were fine horses, your intuition was spot on. I trust you'll choose wisely. Tomorrow we leave bright and early. And Burford, if for some reason Mabel and I don't return by dinnertime, dine alone, put it on my tab, the horses too of course, and stay put until we return. Don't be alarmed if we don't return until long after dark. But please..." Charles lowered his voice and glasses that as usual had slid down the bridge of his nose and he looked over the top of, "stay out of sight as much as possible, for your own sake. Don't let anyone interrogate you. Tell them you've been told not to share your master's business or reveal private information."

"I appreciate that Mr. Charles, your caring and all..."

"I'm sorry to have to place you in that role but you do understand."

"I sure do, I can't wait to get home to my wife and children."

Charles patted Burford on the shoulder as someone might do to a child. Mabel and Burford shot each other a look.

"Come, come, Mabel," Charles dictated, and another look was darted between she and Burford. Burford looked away.

Mabel eyed Charles cautiously. Something had come over him. Yes, he had a lot on his mind but was she seeing another side to the man she'd agreed to spend the rest of her life with?

"Come along Mabel, quickly. We're to meet with a party of two men and one woman. I've met the woman," he paused, gave a warning glance to Mabel, "but I've not yet met the men."

Mabel raised her eyebrows, rolled her eyes, plopped the floppy hat onto her beautiful head of floppy hair, lifted her full petticoats and was his obedient but sarcastic *servant*. "Whatever you say Charles."

Charles had reserved a buggy and driver (or had asked Burford to do it which was why he hadn't had time to bathe) and he and Mabel were soon riding across the city. In the area where the hotel was, she hadn't noticed much military activity but as they rode into other neighborhoods, that the South was going to war became apparent. She was shocked to see more than one family saying tearful good-byes to Papa as he headed off to stop 'Northern aggression'. Would he return again? And if so, would he be the same husband and Papa? Mabel thought not and tried focusing her thoughts on more pleasantries like the smell of fresh bouquets blowing in every breeze.

Charles instructed the carriage driver to follow the river. Because the inland route proved quicker for them to reach New Orleans, Natchez had been the only spot where they'd reached the Mississippi River, but now Mabel was seeing the beauty of the river and the large Plantation homes built along its shores. If she hadn't known the magnificence was built by the sun up, sun down labor of slaves, she would have enjoyed it more, she would have liked to, they were the biggest most stately homes she'd ever seen. Enormous spreading oaks with park-like meadows between each plantation. Gigantic porch overhangs, supported by large white columns. Squirrels darted between the trees and birds of prey like the hawk and falcon glided above. Songbirds nesting in the trees sang wonderful melodies. Such grandeur, such splendor, *such greed,* she thought and cocked her chin, grit her teeth and held onto her hat as the driver reached a straight portion of road and spurred the horses.

"Slow here please," Charles told the driver.

"Saint Francis?" he asked.

"Yes."

The carriage pulled slowly up the long road until it reached a peaceful setting, set back from the big river, just a short walk to swim and picnic or watch the schooners. Mabel saw a dilapidated plantation. Apparently, a flood had swept through causing extensive damage. It was in desperate need of a paint job, landscaping, and carpentry work. Mabel forgot her distaste. There was something about *this* grand home in need of love and tender care. Her imagination ran way with her and for a moment, she imagined it was she and Charles' new home to renovate at a slow easy pace.

"Mabel," Charles startled her, "we're here." He turned to the driver, " If you wouldn't mind leaving then returning at 2:00?"

The driver appeared anxious to take leave of them, nodded and skillfully turned his horses around to canter down the road.

Charles had no doubt this was the place, he smiled at Mabel then took her hand.

"The grounds are beautiful," she said gulping in the fresh air that was Louisiana spring. Her eyes sparkled like the sun hitting the river, a light breeze caught her hat, she held it firm and smiled at him.

"You can remove it while we're here," he said admiring her as if for the first time. Mabel removed the hat and pulled the combs out that held up her hair. She shook it loose and let the wind catch it. Hand in hand, the gentle wind blew them to the door, a swift one caught the fullness of her dress and she struggled to hold it down while Charles pulled the doorknocker, a sculpted brass relic of the plantation's early magnificence. When the door opened there was no butler, no well-mannered servants, no chubby cooks nor exotic aromas in which to anticipate a dinner served at a long table among distinguished guests. Just a Colored boy of about fourteen. Having been told of their arrival he was quite emotionless, very polite but anxious to return to a pleasant pastime, like reading a book or whittling, or day dreaming the way Mabel had always enjoyed in her hammock. The lad politely led them down a large tall hallway, the glory of its past still permeating with the soft sounds of a string quartet and disciplined laughter of days gone by.

"Hello Charles," they heard a woman say. Mabel could barely make out the silhouette of a woman in a light pastel dress against a pastel colored wall.

"Hello Jenny," Charles said softly, then Mabel heard him swallow. Jenny took several slow seductive steps toward Charles, looking past Mabel as if she were absent from the room. Her hair was long and blond, several ringlets placed strategically as if she'd spent all day on their erotic effect. Charles shuffled backwards a few feet, his body tense as if he'd run into his executioner. Jenny stepped closer. Mabel could smell expensive French perfume, civet cat gland extraction, used to play aphrodisiac on a man's senses. She heard Charles inhale it. *Look at me Charles*, Mabel wanted to shout but the words lay stranded in her mind. She was sure she could hear the loud beating of Charles' heart. There was no questioning whether Jenny and Charles had been intimate, they were intimate now. *How long will I stand here forgotten?* Mabel asked silently, her mind daring to give Charles the rope he needed to hang himself.

Jenny, stood between Mabel and Charles, but turned and faced Mabel. Her eyes were big and a hazel blue, lifting uncommonly from their sockets, seductive but not atrocious. She wore a half smile and Mabel read so much into her expression there was no need for words. Someone needed to stab the ice so Mabel began.

"Jenny, is it?" I'm Mabel McCrutchon. It appears you and Charles have met."

Jenny laughed and her half smile became full. She put her arm around Charles' waist and like a little boy, he allowed her to escort him into the main room where more of the home's superior status remained in degraded decline.

"Where are the others?" Charles asked, pulling out of his stupor. "I'm surprised that you're here, I thought..."

She laughed again, went, and sat close to Charles balancing her slender legs and leaning on the armrest of the sofa. Charles looked bewilderedly and irritated at Jenny then to Mabel, the way he should have the moment they first stepped into the home. *But he hadn't.*

Mabel snubbed him and Jenny noticed then leaned deeper into Charles and let her long hair tickle his face. He stood up, "Mabel is my fiancé," he said and bowed slightly.

"Well, isn't thay'at good news," Jenny said in a thick southern accent, leaning all the more into Charles.

"Where are the others?" He asked impatiently.

"There are no oth'es," she said angrily. I'm here a'lone and have been with those dreadful po' babies. The oth'es left a week ago on the count 'a tha' war." Jenny began to sob. Mabel could see they were the tears and frustration of a woman not on the verge of breaking but breaking, now, in front of them both.

Mabel pushed aside jealousy and took Jenny to sit down and she could see that Charles was grateful. "We'll come for the children tomorrow," he told her.

"Oh take them now Charles," she pleaded and continued sobbing. "They're hungry Charles. I can't let anyone see them, there's been no one to cook for them or clean them up. They'a filthay' Charles, five ragged little Negro babies Charles, five!"

"What about you Jenny? Couldn't you cook for them?" He asked.

"I'd hard'ly call myself a cook!" She exclaimed then looked at Mabel who was wondering if Jenny was drunk. "Only thang' I'm good for is my daddy's money," then winked at Charles. "Take them tonight Charles, so I can go back to New Yawk. Just make shure' the Crockers don't see them, they live two plantations down.

There the smat' ones, built on higher ground, still doin' well afta' all these yeas."

"Crockers?" Mabel asked.

Jenny jerked her head attentively, "You know tha' Crockers?"

Charles stood up. He remembered the words of Mabel's mother, 'Keep her away from the Crockers'. *Good God, those were her last words.*

"We'll go and come back tonight," he said curtly, "have them ready as best you can." She laughed again, "I'll do ma' best but ah' don't know how."

Charles and Mabel walked back toward the foyer of the mansion. They both looked upward as bright light worked its way into the darkest corners as if some dead spirit still inhabited the house and was calling out to them from inside the walls. Outside the wind whistled eerily, and when the door opened, Mabel screamed.

"What is it?" Charles shouted.

Mabel backed into the mansion and slid slowly, faintly, into a squat position, her back against the wall, her hand on her heart.

"Oh Charles, there must have been ten of them, spirits, apparitions, whatever you call them. They were black-skinned, workers... they must have been slaves. They were all dressed in light muslin clothing, ragged Charles, very ragged, ripped."

Jenny walked slowly toward the door keeping several feet back, her face was pale, her eyes glassy, and in a trancelike voice, "I see it all 'tha time." She looked at Mabel and laughed. When Charles and Mabel were out the door, he held her close while she wrapped her shawl tightly around her body. Half way down the drive, they could hear Jenny laughing.

"Charles, we've at least another hour before our driver returns. Let's walk down and see the Crocker mansion."

"Whatever for?" He asked feigning ignorance.

She got excited and for a moment forgot the eerie sight she'd just seen.

"Charles, they're my ancestors! My father's grandmother was a Crocker. Her mother was a slave who was abused by her master, Phinius Crocker. The child who came of the abuse was my father's grandmother, Mary. Old Slave master's wife was so jealous she took the child Mary and gave her to a woman in her Presbyterian congregation. Mary's mother pulled plows. She was so distraught she couldn't work so they sold her, she was never heard from since."

"That was a long time ago Mabel, those people are all dead."

"But I must at least see it, oh please Charles, let's walk by there, we have an hour."

He sighed, deeply, "Are you alright, after all that?"

She shivered and wrapped herself tighter into her shawl. "No, and I'm dreading tonight. I feel terrible we didn't tend to those children now."

"We'll be back shortly. Come on, let's go see your heritage."

They walked briskly down the road that followed the great Mississippi River. The grass that surrounded them was green and the trees were leafed out. They passed a wagon full of hay driven by a black man with a younger boy at his side. Several well-dressed white children played peacefully in front of one of the homes while slaves tended the grounds.

"Probably all the white folk live leisurely while all the colored ones do all the work," she said not expecting an answer. She didn't get one.

"I suppose I should be cautious about ridiculing white folks," she said self-pityingly.

"I suppose," he said stooping to pick up a nice stick to walk with.

"Since I'm mostly white."

"Mostly," he looked at her teasingly, "mostly beautiful."

She grabbed his hand and with the other hand held onto her hat but the wind caught it and began tumbling it quickly down the road.

"Look at that! It just won't stop!" She said chasing after it and he after her until breathless they found themselves staring at the freshly painted driveway entrance of *Crocker Plantation, home of the finest Arabian horses in Louisiana.*

"This is it."

"How does it make you feel?"

"It makes me feel... free!" She said tossing her hat up for the wind to catch, which it did while she scurried up the lane and up the hill to the beautiful Crocker Plantation overlooking the Mississippi. Out of breath and panting, she was confronted with a black man who frowned at her. "Miss... Master does not take kindly to strangers using his home as a park."

Mabel picked up her hat, placed it back on her head and held it down with one hand, holding her dress from the wind with the other.

"Oh, I'm no stranger..."

"Mabel!" Charles shouted running after her. "Our driver will be here..."

"I'm a Crocker!" Mabel shouted, drunk with enthusiasm.

"What is it Paul?" Came a voice from a well-dressed, handsome man who walked up from the side of the mansion.

Mabel turned to the handsome man. He wore black silk trousers and a thin white shirt that the wind pushed against his muscular chest. His hair was brown, thick and wavy like hers and his skin tone the same as hers. He obviously bore a bit of Negro blood just like she.

"This young woman insists she is a Crocker sir."

The man smiled at her, and extended a hand to her, "Good afternoon... Miss?"

"McCrutchon," she said.

Charles could tell by the inflection in her voice that she was smitten by the handsome man.

"Mabel, it is time to meet our driver..."

The man ignored Charles and asked Mabel, "Would you like to see the grounds?"

Mabel regained her senses. Having a story to tell her family was one thing but falling in love with a distant cousin was quite another. "I mus'nt, I've very important business to attend to... but what is your name?"

"I'm Benjamin Crocker... the third," he said playfully, flashing a beautiful pearly white smile. "How is it that you're a Crocker?"

She hesitated, looked to Charles whose face said, *no don't say it*, then she looked at Benjamin and politely answered, "My great-grandmother was Mary Crocker."

Benjamin searched his brain, found nothing, so shook his head, "I've not heard the name."

Mabel looked again at Charles whose face was pleading for her to leave.

"Race horses? How extravagant," she taunted him, which he took as praise and laughed modestly.

Mabel put her hand on her hat. It felt comfortable. It brought warmth. For the first time she grabbed the ribbons that dangled from the bottom and secured the hat tightly around her chin.

"Good day Benjamin."

"And you as well Miss McCrutchon. If you ever need anything, let me know."

She took a sweeping look around and grabbed Charles' arm. The two headed back down the hill, toward the river.

"Did you hear that Charles? Benjamin wants to help."
He laughed." Look! Our driver is here!"

Once back at the hotel both Mabel and Charles were impressed with Buford's choice of new clothes. Though he chose practical and durable fabrics, he drew from men's styles he'd seen in Natchez, styles with a Latin influence, recognized by the ruffles and tucks in his linen shirt and the bright blue dye of the woolen fabric. His hair was clean and oiled back.

"How handsome," Mabel said, looking him up and down. "Happier too," she sighed then thought of the five children and the road ahead. When Charles went to settle his tabs with the hotel, livery stable and clothier, Mabel had a chance to speak privately with Burford whose wisdom she respected. Who but a former slave would understand?

"Do you believe in apparitions?"

The look that swept across his face told her that he did.

"I saw the ghosts of about ten former slaves today Burford. I wish I knew what to make of it."

"Miss Mabel, apparitions are not to be foolin' around with. Best if you let dead spirits lie."

"What could the ghosts of fifty years past be trying to convey? And why me?"

"I don't know Miss Mabel, I didn't see any ghosts myself. I don't know what a girl like you could do to help them... they're dead.

Guess you could look at their accomplishments, all the architecture they built, and the fortunes they helped amass for this country and just appreciate it. Seems that's all you can do."

"Appreciate it? Yes, I suppose they are some of America's heroes, aren't they?"

"Yes, I suppose they are," he agreed.

The next morning, as the carriage made its way to Saint Francis Plantation, Mabel noticed farms and pastures she'd missed the day before and ramshackle slaves' quarters she'd overlooked. *Had she not wanted to see it?* As they neared Saint Francis, she thought of her great-great-grandmother who'd traveled this road many times, many years before. How sad it must have been for her when the road took her daughter away, for the last time. Mabel could feel the numbness she must have felt afterwards, the indifference to her master, his will and her tasks there. An indifference that led to her sale at the slave auction.

"Ho..." Burford said to the two sable brown mares that diligently pulled the cart. Burford guided them into the road to Plantation Saint Francis. Mabel did not see any more apparitions, no more daunting dead unappreciated "heroes," nor did she want to, understanding that the living might be more grotesque than any dead spirits who haunted an insignificant estate of yesteryears.

Burford pulled the carriage into the trees and stayed behind to keep an eye out.

Jenny was waiting for them when they arrived. "The chil'en 'aw downstey'rs" she said still eyeing Charles. She gave a wide-eyed glance to Mabel, "Lucky girl," she said, then placed her jeweled wrist inappropriately low, below his waist on his backside. Charles gave Mabel a helpless pleading glance to which she smiled reassuringly.

Jenny guided them to a door that led down a steep staircase. Jenny stepped behind Charles and the three of them descended down the stairs. It was pitch dark in the basement storehouse that in the home's heyday was a cold storage for perishables, butter, root crops and it was where the master had kept his extensive alcoholic beverages.

"My great-grandfaatha' had a lot goin' on down here, Jenny said remorsefully, "He was always bringin' the neighbor's slave girls down here, my great-grandmotha' hated it. Almost shot he'm ta' da'yath one night when she caught him with one of old man Crocker's servants. She was a ver'gin I 'spose, Crocker wa'nt no molester but my great-grandaddy sho' was. That po' girl had my great-granddaddy's baby, they sold that baby right out from under that po' girl..."

Mabel gasped.

"That's enough Jenny," Charles said going to Mabel's side.

Mabel regained her composure, *I'll sort this all out later*, she thought. "Where are the children? Haven't we kept them waiting long enough?"

97

"They're down tha', that room on tha' ley'eft" Jenny said then began climbing back up the stairs. At the second step she turned around, "I did tha' bey'est I could."

Charles knocked softly then turned the handle. On the floor were piles of blankets, pillows and comforters and the young teenaged boy who had answered the door yesterday was curled up with five small children. In his hand was a book. On the floor were stacks of books. The children were thin but appeared healthy. The boy smiled but the younger children looked fearful.

"Don't be afraid, we're not here to hurt you. We're taking you to where you can be free," Mabel said while her thoughts spun rapidly. The story of the slave assaulted by Jenny's great-grandfather sounded like her great-great-grandmother whose baby they gave to a woman from their church, but how could she be sure?

The winds of the afternoon returned. Doors rattled and the wind blew as swiftly as horses could run, she wanted to run, she wanted to breathe. The wind tugged and pulled on all that was outside, it whistled loudly like a train's last call for passengers. Images of horses running in panic stampeded Mabel's brain as the wind whistled louder and more ferociously. She could faintly hear Charles' kind voice, administering wisdom to the children, lecturing them of the seriousness of their journey and their reward if all went well.

Mabel put her hand to her heart and leaned against the wall. *Was this strange vulgar woman, Jenny, a distant cousin of hers? And Charles' former lover? No wonder the apparitions were here! No wonder she felt safe at the Crockers! She wasn't a Crocker at all! She was a Saint Francis! Had her great-great-grandmother led her there... led Charles to her? Had she been led straight into the dungeon where her great-grandmother had been conceived?* Mabel felt the horrible stain of that knowledge. A monster had forced his seed upon her ancestor. *Who am I?* her mind screamed.

"Mabel? Mabel! Mabel!!" Charles shouted, frowning at her, forgetting what Jenny had divulged.

"Yes Charles, I'm here, I truly am."

"Go get Burford."

Mabel ran to the stairs. She stopped, imagined the room with the sights and sounds of yesteryear, the sound of voices, a gathering of neighbors, a party, a harvest festival, all the neighbors gathered to share in the bounty of what the slaves had grown and the slaves themselves. She shook it off, she was not her great-great-grandmother, she was Mabel McCrutchon and she was engaged to wed Charles Churchill, philanthropist, Abolitionist, they had come on a mission; she would not let him nor the children down. She passed Jenny who stood at the window staring at the wind as it blew leaves and debris all about the lawn where Mabel had seen the apparitions. *Was Jenny seeing them now?* Is that why no people were about and the house abandoned? Jenny turned to Mabel. Her face was vacant, her large bulging hazel-blue, bloodshot eyes stared out. Mabel felt compassion for her. Jenny was the only one who stayed behind, the last one to care for these children and it had broken her. Mabel flew open the door and held tightly to her hat. She saw the apparitions again but their countenances had changed, they had told their story. Mabel looked deeply into the group, looking for her ancestors. Could she see them? Were they among these transient visions? Hiding among them, she saw, faintly, a mother smiling over a cradle. As Mabel stared at her, she came to life. The cradle disappeared and a young colored girl emerged, enveloped in a cloudy haze. Mabel smiled and the apparitions of mother and daughter smiled back. They could rest now.

Mabel ran to where Burford waited. When she looked back, the apparitions were gone and a tropical storm brought rain and a flash of lightning that lit up the window where Jenny stood. Mabel could see she was smiling and a great burden had been lifted from her soul.

"I'll wait here," Mabel shouted over the wind to Burford, "Charles needs your help!"

He nodded and ran to the house. Soon Charles and Burford were hurrying out of the house with the children, all five of them.

"What about the older boy?" Mabel shouted.

Charles shook his head and raised his shoulders, he neither knew nor had heard anything about the boy.

Mabel ran back to the mansion as the wind whipped louder than before, the boy stood at the door tearfully waving good-bye.

"Who are you? Where do you belong?"

"My name is James, I belong to Master Johnson down the road, he hired me out to Miss Jenny. Now I must go back, Miss Jenny's leaving."

"James, do you want to be free?"

"Yes ma'am, sure do. Everyone wants to be free, no man should own another."

"Come with me!" She grabbed his hand and the two of them ran across the lawn, the rain beating upon them both, soaking their clothes. James did not care, his face lit up like a lantern, his cheeks were full of pride, his smile wide as the river that lay before them. Mabel hefted James into the crowded carriage and then a mean gust blew her hat off. She chased after it. To Charles dismay, she kept chasing after it as it rolled toward the Crocker Plantation. Burford turned the carriage around and started after her. It was dark and they could barely see her. As Mabel ran closer to the Crocker's, the wind subsided and her hat stopped tumbling.

"Burford, stop, go no further!" Charles demanded. "I see Mabel has stopped running. Good Lord, we don't want to venture to the Crocker's."

In the middle of the Crocker's massive stand of ancient oaks, Mabel bent down and picked up her hat. She took a long look at the architecture of the Crocker estate and the lives that must have been lost during the making of it. But the beauty touched her deeply. She tossed her hat high into the air, "I'm free! I'm free!" She sang out.

"What's she doing Mr. Charles?" Burford asked.

Charles slid down in his seat and groaned, "Just bein' Mabel, Burford, just bein' Mabel."

Hat in hand, Mabel went running back to the carriage, her new clothes drenched with the tropical rain. She squeezed in tightly, very tightly with Charles, the boy James and five little ones.

"How far are we going?" James asked.

"Up through Mississippi and Kentucky, on up to Pittsburgh, Pennsylvania," Mabel said, drunk with adrenaline.

James looked at them as if they were crazy, "Don't y'all know there's a war goin' on?"

Heading North

The situation had grown so out of hand at the *News Herald* Whitethorn had to shut the office down completely. It was on the same windy, rainy day that Charles and Mabel secured the children, that Whitethorn shut it down.

"I'm closing shop," he said to Victor who nodded absent-mindedly while going over a report on suspected Rebel hideouts in West Virginia. He looked well-rested, well-fed and his head of hair he wore in a long ponytail looked freshly washed.

"I don't think you understand. I'm closing shop."

Whitethorn caught Victor's attention but knew he didn't understand the depth of his words. His faithful employee said nothing.

"For good Victor, I'm shutting it all down."

"Why?"

"It's become so hectic, I am sick and tired of hiding back here."

"But we're in a state of war, the people need to know..."

"There are two other newspapers in Pittsburgh," Whitethorn said resolutely.

"But we're the only true Abolitionist paper, the friend of the enslaved."

Whitethorn shook his head and averted Victor's incredulous eyes. "Shuttin' her down. I've made up my mind."

"What about *American Heroes*?"

Whitethorn looked guilty and sheepishly tried to avoid the subject, muttering only that it was being printed somewhere else, and the office was no longer relevant.

Victor sat down. He looked at his big oak desk with compartments. One for incoming mail, one for out, a spot for stories people had brought in, places for pens and ink. Then he glared at Whitethorn. "What about Black Pansy?" He said maliciously.

Again, Whitethorn looked guilty. "That's no business of yours Victor, I've decided. I thought you'd take it better than this, I'm sorry. Now gather your things, swing by the bank they have a check all made out for you. I added a little extra to hold you over until you find another position."

Victor said no more and angrily gathered his things into a crate and exited out the front door slamming it loudly. He headed down the sidewalk and towards his room in an alley behind busy restaurants and pubs. He must have passed six different people who greeted him but he did not hear. By the time he got home to Annie who was waiting for him, word had spread to his small corner of Pittsburgh that Victor was angry about something and would no longer represent the *News Herald* because he carried his work supplies in his arms in a crate.

"Well, what's got into you," Annie said seeing the sour look on his face.

"What's all this? Your supplies from the newspaper?" She gasped as it sunk in, "You lost your job?"

He nodded and sat down at their small table where she had homemade bread, fresh milk and oxtail soup waiting for him.

"Whitethorn thinks he's made it big now cause'a that story Mabel's been writing."

"He has made it big. He must be mak'n a fortune! I heard *American Heroes* is popular all across the country. I hear they're readin' it in Europe. Imagine that. Mabel must be makin' herself a fortune."

"Mabel doesn't know about the success. He was coverin' expenses before so didn't pay her but a paltry stipend. He's makin' a big fat profit now."

"He gave you a raise."

Victor smirked.

"Guess there's nothing you can do about it, he is the boss. You'll get another job. Mabel sure will be disappointed when she gets back, she likes you. Why I was just talkin' to her Auntie Louisa the other day..."

"What did she say?"

"Just how much Mabel likes you, what good friend's ya are an all. That's all," Annie said in a high voice that caught his attention.

"Did you tell her you know?"

"What? About Mabel bein' Black Pansy an' all? Yeah, she knows I know."

Victor dropped his head dramatically onto the table.

"Have some fresh bread and butter, 'll make you feel better. I made some collard greens too..."

He shook his head at her.

"I knew her Auntie knew. Didn't think it would hurt none."

"Mabel's life could be in danger if word got out. Tempers are high now Annie, there's a war goin' on and Mabel's story's makin' a lot of folks mad, real mad."

Burford pulled down a side road as Charles instructed. A huge empty barn lay at the end of the road. Charles hopped out and opened the barn door then motioned Burford to pull in. Charles looked around making sure no one saw, then swung the heavy door shut behind them.

"I wish I could say we were spending the night in this nice warm barn. Come on children, step out for a bit. This is all designed to deliver you safely to Pittsburgh. Come on Mabel, you too... everybody out."

They all climbed out and Burford climbed down, he was wet and cold from driving the horses. Mabel was soaked and had begun descending from her euphoria.

Charles' began making an awful racket banging around under the seats but soon he popped his head out with a smile, "All set," he said, "come take a look."

They all walked over and looked in. The whole bottom of the carriage was hollowed out. There were blankets and pillows inside a big wooden storage space.

"Well..." Burford grinned, "I never suspected."

"Just enough room for the little ones, the smallest of course. They're looking for five young, colored children. If we have two up front, it will look as if Burford is Daddy and Mabel is the mother. I of course will pose as Master, no offence taken I hope," he said sincerely to them all. Both Mabel and Burford looked down.

"What about me?" James asked.

"They're not looking for a fourteen-year-old runaway, not yet anyway, Jenny will cover for you James until we have the chance to get some miles behind us. Come on all, pile in. Sorry children, we'll trade off from time to time."

The little ones completely understood. They'd been coached for weeks and they understood both the rewards and the cost of freedom.

Mabel wondered where Charles went sometimes when they stopped. He must have had high-ranking spies amongst the Rebel Armies because he knew where the skirmishes and battles of this new war would take place.

"Burford, where do you think Charles gets such up to date war notices?"

"I've been wondering myself Miss Mabel. Mr. Charles must be an important man."

"I think maybe the sympathetic wives and sisters of war strategists," was Mabel's guess.

"I hate to sound disagreeable Miss Mabel," Burford told her, "but men are known to take sympathy with the anti-slavery cause as well."

"You're right Burford, sympathetic brothers."

"And fathers, uncles, cousins, grand-parents."

"Yes," Mabel said, snuggling closer to the two children whose turn it was to sit up front with the boy James and the adults as they patiently waited for Charles return. He was at another one of his "stops." Sometimes these "stops" would have them back-tracking several miles. Mabel wondered if she would ever get home.

"Hard to know those little children are cramped under the floor like that, isn't it Miss Mabel?"

She sighed and shifted her weight, the head of the child known as Bessie resting on her lap. "Yes, I begin to worry when I hear them wrestling around in there but it beats facing a life of slavery."

"Yes it does."

Bessie smiled and held Mabel tighter. James, who was riding up front with Burford turned around and flashed her a big grin. Escaping was his surprise and adventure, Mabel hoped Jenny was doing a good job covering for him. Their success depended on it. *Was Jenny stable enough to fool James's master? What about her trip to New York?* Mabel worried incessantly. Every time she heard the three little ones scratching around under her seat, she sighed and Charles would place his hand on her knee. Two children were always crowded in with she and Charles and they rarely stopped to shake a leg.

Charles was cheerful when he returned. "There's a farm just this side of the Mississippi state line, we'll stop there for the night. We'll be in good hands."

The news didn't seem to cheer Mabel. "Charles, I don't know how much more I can stand knowing those poor babies are underneath us... and we've been just plain lucky that we haven't been stopped, poor, poor children."

"We'll see if maybe we can find two of them safe passage with others."

"What others" Mabel was surprised.

"No promises. Burford, can you get a little more speed from the horses?"

"Yes sir! Been waitin' for you to say that," Burford said and professionally spurred the horses into an increasingly fast cantor, then both horses broke into a run.

Mabel tied the strings of her hat tightly up underneath her chin.

The directions Charles received were confusing and Burford drove in circles, passing the correct road several times before finally turning correctly. They reached a locked gate, greeted by a white man who swung open the gate while Burford hurried their carriage through. They parked at a series of hitching posts above a swiftly rolling stream. There were several single horses tied, another smaller carriage and a large wooden agricultural wagon. The surrounding nature was well preserved, the setting had existed for decades. Well-tended gardens surrounded about ten workshops, and weeping willows provided shade for picnic tables and to cool the foundry.

"This is nice Charles," Mabel said, removing her stiff body slowly, stretching out her back.

"It's an old French settlement. They're French Jews, the Inquisition drove them from France. They understand persecution."

"Bonjour Mademoiselle Dupont," Charles said to a beautiful young woman who greeted him in a simple, white dress with pink azaleas pinned to her bosom. Her hair was pinned up loosely, several long strands of the jet black hair fell loosely alongside the azaleas. She and Charles chatted away in French to which Mabel understood very little but apparently, Burford did and laughed along and agreed with them on the topic. Mabel felt tired, sore, disillusioned, fearful, hungry and anxious to remove the babes who lay cramped under the seat. "Charles..." she said irritably.

"Yes Mabel, oh forgive me for not introducing you..."

"The children," she interrupted.

"Oh yes, of course," he hurried and pried open the compartment. Mademoiselle Dupont graciously gathered all five of the children and James, and headed toward one of the dwellings.

"Do not worry about a thing," she said in a thick French accent and whisked the six children away for bathing, food and fresh clothing and Mabel hoped *new names*. Mabel grabbed her satchel and not knowing where she was headed began to walk ahead of Charles. This was the second time in a few days that Charles met with women who adored him and Mabel had grown quite fatigued of it.

Charles grabbed his bag and tried to catch up but was a considerable distance behind. Mabel, walking alone and unattended, was met by three handsome young Frenchmen who fought over the opportunity to carry her satchel. Clamoring over her she soon forgot her anger and looked back to see if Charles had seen. He smiled. *I deserved that*, his smile told her.

Mabel spent the remainder of the day getting friendly with the French Jewish Colonists, especially Hermann Davidad, who had taken an instant liking to her.

Charles grew tired of following Mabel around so went for a long walk. He wandered down to the bank of the stream, scurried down to crouch amongst the berry brambles, and gather his thoughts when Mabel and Hermann strolled up, arm in arm and walked onto the bridge just fifteen feet in front of him.

"May I kiss your lips?" Hermann asked in thick French, to which Mabel smiled and turned her head. Turning back around again she let Hermann give her a succulent kiss. *That's my woman!* Charles mind shouted. Mabel turned around again, her hands on the bridge railing, Charles could see she was smiling and like a little girl thoroughly enjoying herself. She turned around again and let Hermann kiss her again, each time more passionately.

Charles could see Mabel's bosom rise with each breath she took. Charles was infuriated but confused because he was terribly aroused by the episode.

"We'd better return," he heard her say, "Charles will be looking for me..."

She said my name! Charles was relieved but confused and from his crouched position in the brambles, Charles could see Hermann's eyes on Mabel's ample bosom. While Mabel chatted on about how lovely the setting was, the graceful trees bowing into the stream, the sound of the rushing water, Hermann maneuvered to get one more kiss from Mabel but she would not relent. "Charles..." she kept saying..."Charles..."

Charles was distraught over Mabel's infidelity but even more so over his arousal over the incident. He retired early and fell fast asleep, falling into deep vivid dreams. He saw the armies of the North and South, hot in the warmth of a spring day. He saw loved ones saying good-bye to soldiers, he heard cannons booming and saw pillars of smoke that caught in the lungs. He saw boys on the battlefields blowing bugles or drumming, boys who should have been in school. He saw colored soldiers in Union uniforms fighting for their freedom and Rebel soldiers fighting for the continued status of the agricultural South. He saw the faces of the six children and it jarred him awake. He dressed and went outside. All was quiet. All the settlement had gone to bed. Only the owls kept watch, hooting to one another, codes no human would ever know. He went to check on the children and found Mabel snuggled and fast asleep with them, a book in her lap. She looked so very young. He would forgive her short affair of experimentation. *Had not he had plenty of his own?* He had other things to think of. The Quakers of Connecticut were asking for an accounting of his expenditures. Little did they understand how much of his finances had gone into this trip. He would appease them, they were proud of the donations they'd collected especially from England, Scotland and Ireland. And Charles had communication with his family to think of. His letters to his mother and Aunt Lena had been short notes, letting them know he was fine but saying nothing about Mabel nor any *engagement*. That would come later when they returned to Pittsburgh and he was sure of Mabel's love. Seeing her now with the children, he believed she would be a fine wife and mother once she grew from her girlish ways. He returned to bed. All was forgiven. She had rebuked Hermann.

"Has anyone seen Charles?" Mabel went about asking everyone the next morning to which everyone shook their heads and averted their eyes. Hermann Davidad had created quite a stir by his adoration and attention upon the beautiful Abolitionist who was betrothed to Charles Churchill. Hermann's reputation had preceded him to the settlement. He was supposed to be on his best behavior, a sort of last chance for the man who'd been exiled from other settlements due to his cavorting, especially with other men's wives.

Though shy and fearful at first, the children in their care had begun to play with the others. They ran and laughed as all children should, they bathed and had fresh clothing and abundant food and two of the oldest boys and James would be lovingly transported to New York and from there to caring families awaiting them in Canada. The two children that would be returning with them to Pittsburgh, were happily boarding the carriage with Burford. Charles was in good spirits, said his good byes to all except Hermann Davidad who was nowhere to be seen. Charles jaunted toward the carriage in the noonday sun with Mabel running after him, her hat unknowingly falling from her hand. Charles retrieved the hat. Mabel's face questioned the need for the large plumy accessory but Charles nodded and she took it from him willingly.

"Someday I'll buy you a new hat, something that suits you, the new woman that you've become."

She looked quizzically at him. "I'm still the same girl Charles and you're still the handsome man looking out for me. I'll wear the hat, perhaps it shall bring us luck."

"We'll need much more than that."

"Amen," Burford said under his breath.

"We're giving you new names," she said to the children. "These are your freedom names. You'll be Daniel and you'll be Elizabeth and your last name will be Campbell. We'll call you Danny and Beth. Do you like that?" They smiled and clung tightly to the woman with whom they'd bonded. All were quiet for the remainder of the day. As the evening approached and they were miles from the destination Charles showed on his list, Burford and Mabel began firing questions at Charles. He had no easy answers.

"We'll have to find lodging along the way, or ride through the night," he said as they passed through farming country. The sun was setting and though darkness would come shortly, Slaves were still plowing and hoeing.

"Many of these farms are using slaves to do the work," Mabel said uncomfortably.

"Yes, of course," Charles answered as he tensely looked around. "This is the South and they do have slaves. Although they don't *all* have slaves, most of the southern farmers do their own work, with the help of their families."

Burford stiffened at the thought of his days of servitude. He kept his eye on the road as storm clouds gathered at their back.

"We're in Mississippi now, beautiful isn't it?" Charles said, thinking aloud.

"Umm...hmm..." Burford agreed.

"Yes. It's beautiful... different from the Choctaw trace," Mabel said trying to prevent the children from recognizing her fear as they drove through agricultural slave country.

"A bit different," Charles said, "They've cut more trees for their crops."

"Mmmm...hmm..." Burford said again.

The children clung tightly to Charles and Mabel. They understood that if discovered they'd be returned to their former master who may punish them severely so they would think twice before running off.

"I say we keep going... ride on through the night," Mabel said looking right and left at the beautiful farms and miles of oak and pine.

"This is a prosperous farming community," Charles said, "hear the plantation bells ringing?"

"What does that mean?" Mabel asked.

"It means we should keep on going," Burford warned.

"I agree," Mabel said. The children were silent.

"We'll be pushing the horses," Charles reminded Burford.

"They'll survive, we started late," Burford said softly.

The children were silent as their carriage and tired horses climbed the rolling, green hills.

"No young white men about, they've all gone to fight. The slaves, women, children and old men are probably the only ones about," Charles said as he scanned the area.

"Don't count on it," Burford said dryly, "there's plenty of young men with milk knee or some affliction, who carry the same sentiments. Me and the children, we probly' have prices on our heads."

"If any one passes or comes near just smile and wave," Charles told him, "meanwhile inhale this fresh country air and look forward to a brighter day tomorrow,"

"And a long night tonight, Mabel said then slouched down in the seat, clutching the hands of the children in her charge.

"There's the bell again." Burford said, crouching down in his seat, "it's calling the slaves in from the fields."

Mabel looked at the dark figures casting shadows, bending, hoeing, and plowing. There were tall skinny shapes, large muscular bodies, both women and men toiling in the last daylight. If she hadn't known the truth, she may have thought it picturesque. From a distance, it looked a peaceful, pastoral scene. But she knew better, Burford knew better and the children, Danny and Beth, they knew better.

"We 'don eva hav'a go back there do we?" Danny asked.

"I hope not Danny," Mabel answered, "remember everything we told you. I'm your mammy, Burford is your pappy and Charles is our master. Master Charles, you'll call him if anyone asks. Don't say anything else."

"Yes Miss Mabel," they both said.

The sturdy horses trudged on through the dark night. They had all agreed it wise to travel through the dark to gain miles. What they didn't expect at sunrise was to see that they had ridden right into the aftermath of a battle. They began encountering walking wounded Rebel soldiers who cried out for a ride.

"Don't engage in conversation with anyone," Charles warned.

They passed smoldering stumps and medics carrying dead and wounded. No one paid them any heed as the big black carriage lumbered forward.

"It isn't pretty," Charles spoke as the smell of gunpowder filled their nostrils and the morning sun and slight breeze blew death's stench into their faces.

"No sir, it's not."

They had ridden out of the area of cleared farmlands and were now riding into deep forests. The shadows of the tall trees offered them a promise of sleep and seclusion.

"Time to rest these weary horses and you Burford," Charles told him. "Keep an eye out for a lonely private road."

"Thank you Mr. Charles, I'm in dire need of sleep."

Finding a lonely stretch of road, they stopped. Mabel knew she'd get no sleep sitting crowded in the carriage. She'd dozed off frequently during the night. Now it was time for her to tend to her feminine needs. She spotted a small stream and Charles agreed that if she stayed close it should be safe. Letting out a deep breath, she loosened her hair and brushed it through with her fingers. Charles watched her carefully, thoughtfully. He was leery of her love for him but not for his love for her. He pondered what right he had to take a girl, fresh and inexperienced, as a wife. He'd had previous romantic encounters. Was it fair that women were labeled tainted if they partook of a little sexual flirtation in their youth? A discreet affair or two before they settled down to the demands of marriage and a new baby every fourteen months?

Mabel tucked her full skirt underneath her legs and sat down on the matty forest floor. The trees towered over her, the canopy was so thick, barely any light shone through. She rested her back and head against the straight trunk and closed her eyes. Images of the past thirty-two hours swarmed her thoughts. She glanced toward Charles who smiled from the distance as he kept a close protective eye on her. She rose and wandered down a trail a bit then sat down against another tree and closed her eyes and thought of Hermann Davidad, a man who understood his charisma and used it to his advantage, to take advantage. She thought back to the Crocker plantation and the image of Benjamin Crocker came to view, his smile, his air of kindness, would she ever see him again? Did she want too? Was she ready to devote herself to Charles? She looked over at him, to bask in his adoration and protective spirit. *He was gone!* She stumbled up and ran back to the carriage, it was gone! She'd taken a path, which path had she taken? She looked and saw trails the deer had made but which one led her back? Afraid to cry out and weary from lack of sleep, she stumbled her way through, her sense of direction scrambled. *I should have stayed put, why did I panic?* She heard voices, men's voices and did not know whether to hide from sight or ask for help. When two men in Rebel uniforms saw her first, she abandoned any other choice. She would stick to her story, their story, *I'm a slave*, she told herself. *Act a slave.* Before the two men had time to speak Mabel blurted out, "Oh, kind sirs, ah have ben' los' from ma masta' and ma chil'un, ah can't find mah way, please hep' me, please kind sirs." Mabel's hands were trembling but that would befit a fearful slave.

"You sure you're not a runaway?" One of the young men asked her, a tall lanky kid, younger than she, with blond hair and freckles.

"Yeah, you sure? We ain't allowed to provide aid to no runaways, much as we might like to ma'am. We ain't much for slavery but if we assist a slave, well that would put us in a heap a trouble," the other fellow said.

"Ah followed da' wrong path, honest ah did," she insisted, flashing them an innocent smile.

"We're heading toward the road, you follow us. Don't worry none, we'll get you back there," the lanky blond reassured her.

"Thank you 'eva so kindly," Mabel said and followed them up the correct trail that led back to the carriage.

"Mabel!" Charles shouted to which she glared at him.

Burford was awoken from his nap under the trees, as were the children who poked their sleepy, curious heads up.

"Oh Masta!" Mabel shouted, "I'm so sorry Masta, truly 'ah 'em."

"You should be, shame on you for running off like that!" Charles shot back.

The two fellows looked at Charles, then Burford, then back to Mabel who hurriedly entered the carriage. "Mah babies!" She said, wrapping her arms around them.

"Well, alright Miss, glad we could help," the lanky blond said, a little perplexed. "Have a safe journey, better watch out, these hills are fightin' country. Where you goin' anyway?"

"Kentucky," Charles said quickly, "headin' home to Louisville."

"Well alright, be safe. Maybe this 'ol war 'ell be over soon. Think so Mister?"

"Over... soon? Yes, I hope it will end soon. You must be tired of fighting."

"T'want much of a battle, just a 'lil skirmish. Wan'nt nuth'in ta make the history books," the other soldier said, then the two Rebels took one last look around. The last thing they saw was Burford's angry, black face from his position on the hard ground. It had been about twenty minutes, that was all the sleep he'd managed. Running on a sleep deficit, the usually kind man's nerves were frayed.

The soldiers walked off to meet their destinies in the new war era. Mabel and Charles looked fondly after them as they walked off. They were pleasant, polite fellows; their mothers and fathers had taught them well. *What would become of them and thousands like them?*

Burford glared at their backs. He stood up, shook the leaves and dried grasses from his clothes. Always careful to look as presentable as possible, not because he enjoyed looking smart but because he feared looking otherwise. "I'm ready to move on," he said curtly.

"You're in charge," Charles told him.

After days of riding and sleeping in decent lodging, they reached Jackson.

"We shan't stay here long, one night only," Charles told Mabel and Burford. "Baths for all, a good dinner and tonight..." he looked at Mabel. "I'm taking you to the theatre. That is... provided Burford will watch the children."

Burford nodded but said nothing. He'd been too long uncomfortable, too long caring for other's needs, too long in the Slave South and way too long away from the niceties his wife and children brought him. He'd long since forgotten about the second installment of two-hundred dollars he'd receive when he returned to Pittsburgh, thinking it not near enough after all he'd been through and the danger he put himself in. He was growing tired of Charles Churchill and his "do this... do that" attitude.

Charles sensed Burford's growing resentment. Privately he said to Mabel, "I hate to go back on a promise but Burford needs rest. I believe I've pushed the poor man to his breaking point. Would you mind if I let him have the room to himself tonight and I bunk with you and the children? We'll get a room with three big beds."

Mabel was shocked. Her dark eyes spread open like he'd never seen, she looked down, looked at the children, back at Charles then let them wander down Jackson's main boulevard. He could see a smile spread faintly across her lips. From behind, she shrugged, as if it did not matter one way or another.

"I'll get the rooms... Burford!"

As promised, Charles booked a separate room for Burford and a luxurious room with three double beds, for Mabel, the children and himself. Mabel thought the room overly decorated with long flowered drapes adorning the windows. An oak dressing table complete with doilies, a brush, a comb, a pitcher and washbasin made it comfy. Within easy walking distance, a bathroom down the hallway, housed a claw foot tub. Mabel washed up the children, Danny and Beth, privately in the room and then tucked them into blankets and into bed. There were issues regarding the separation of colored folks from whites in dining halls and especially hotel rooms but after the first incidence, Charles had learned to sneak Burford in quietly if he sensed a problem. As for Mabel, there was never anything offensive spoken by hotel or lodging staff. The children were quietly brought to the room, unseen.

"Whatever shall we do this evening?" Charles taunted Mabel as he watched her as she sat at the dressing table brushing her tangled locks of chocolate brown hair. She could not hide her expression for he could see her reflection in the mirror. She'd removed her dress, but remained quite fully clothed in lacey, cotton camisole and petticoats. She was very tired and he could see it in her eyes. Her arms were bare. He walked to her side and took the brush from her hands. With each stroke of the brush, he followed it with a stroke of his hand. Her eyes were closed. Sensing she was mesmerized by his gentle touch, he kissed her neck. She did not open her eyes but stretched her neck so he could kiss it again. He stood over her, looking down into her fully matured breasts spilling out over the camisole. He ran his hand down to the curves of her waist. She was still laced tightly. He knelt down and put his hand to the floor, his fingers touching her ankles. She winced. Charles could hear her breathing quicken. He slowly ran his hand up her calf but when she delicately crossed her legs, he ran his hand back down her leg and up the other leg. He could feel the fullness of her calves and longed to feel the thickness of her hips and thighs. Though her legs were still crossed, she twisted in the chair allowing him to carefully slide his hand all the way up her leg to the curve of her thigh. Her skin was soft and downy. She threw her head back and her breasts protruded further out of the camisole, her nipples barely hiding behind the stiff cotton lace. He stood and kissed her neck softly, repeatedly. He inhaled the aroma of her hair. She awakened his manliness. The protrusion in his trousers held back his desires no better than her heavy breathing hid hers. She stole a glance and longed to know what treasures hid behind the cloth. She'd not yet seen a man's aroused body, except in illustrations or risqué paintings. How she longed to be naughty, to touch it, stroke it, feel it deep inside of her. *How delightful that would feel.* But she must be strong, she was treading dangerous territory, her reputation was to be preserved. Her respect was foremost.

"Charles," she said, "it is warm in here, is it not?"

She rose from the dressing table. Her lovely brown skin still flowing from the white, cotton, camisole. Charles backed up and beheld her radiance.

She smiled softly. "I am sleepy."

"And I am a gentleman. Although I do thank you for a taste of your lovely charms."

Mabel was up early with pen in hand.

"Writing already?"

She nodded but ignored him, choosing instead to pen all the thoughts she'd gathered.

"I need to post these chapters to Auntie Louisa."

"There should be no problem, not in a big city like Jackson, Mississippi. We'll have breakfast, in here of course, with the children, then we'll walk down to the post office and..."

Mabel frowned, "Crowd back into the carriage for more grueling days."

"Mabel..."

She turned to him when she heard her name spoken so delicately. Her eyes sparkled; the whites of her eyes were free from the redness of previous days.

"When we return..." he paused, afraid of what she might say, "do you still intend to marry me?"

"Yes, of course," she said but without looking him in the eye.

"I'm relieved..." he said walking toward her, "I was afraid..."

"Shh..." she said, "we've many miles to travel, many weary miles, through a countryside that may be war torn. Neither you nor I know what tomorrow may bring. I've no remorse for last night. I admit I enjoyed it. Much more than I'd imagined." She smiled and he noticed that she brushed her body close to him while wrapping her shawl around her bodice. She inhaled and her breasts rose and fell again at thoughts of last night. She gave him a coy expression, "Shall we go?"

"Charles, have you noticed we haven't been to church?"

His amusing smile spoke volumes about his religiosity. His philanthropic life left her no doubt he was a good, kind, generous man. His success and discussions they'd had left her no doubt Charles Churchill was a spiritual man. She however, being kept from view throughout her childhood, had drawn strong social ties through her small neighborhood congregation, even if those social ties were with women much older than she and today she longed for Christian fellowship.

Charles' Methodist upbringing had been much different. The large church his family attended was formal and impersonal; showing up on Sunday was used more for displaying wealth and status then communing with God. His mother thrived on being one of the wealthier parishioners and the business connections Charles' father made through Saint John's suited his needs. Charles' Auntie Lena, bless her heart, met her spiritual needs through her associations with the Quakers, even though she made her weekly appearance at Saint Johns. Though his handsome features he inherited from his father, Charles had taken after his Auntie in philosophy. Like Lena he attended Saint Johns to remain respectable but found spiritual fulfillment through his diverse intellectual crowd and his philanthropy.

"Are you hinting at something?" Charles said as he and Mabel walked to the livery stable where they were to meet Burford.

"Jackson must have a Presbyterian church," Mabel said, then stopped and bent down to ask Beth and Danny if they would like to go to church.

"Masta's wife took us ev'a Sunday," Danny said. The people who held Danny's family in bondage had used cruel tactics to subvert their slaves but every Sunday without fail the Master and Mistress had taken their fifteen slaves to church with them. The kindness bestowed on the slaves by several of the women of the church was a welcome respite from their daily rough treatment on the farm.

Beth reacted fearfully among the large crowds on the streets of Jackson. Mabel was feeling anything but.

"Pull your hat down Mabel," Charles cautioned.

"Honestly Charles, are you forgetting I'm supposed to be the children's mother?"

He'd gotten confused. He couldn't help noticing people were staring at them and whether imagined or real he felt threatened. Surely there were bounty hunters seeking out runaway slaves.

"Look Charles, a Presbyterian church!"

Before he could stop her, Mabel had wandered to the front of the church and stood in front of the freshly painted small white church with a white picket fence surrounding it. Fresh yellow daffodils and wild purple violets bloomed beneath the fence, thriving in the warmth of the bright morning sun. Sunday morning services were attracting a large crowd, families held the hands of their children and filed reverently in, all freshly combed, bathed and in their best clothes.

Charles couldn't help but notice there were few black people in attendance. He had no intention of attending but Mabel was swept away in tradition and hypnotically walked into the church, a stolen runaway baby in each hand.

Burford grew uneasy as time slipped by and neither Mabel nor Charles appeared. The Blacksmith who ran the livery stable had asked him too many questions and Burford had a sense for a man who did not like colored people. He had no money to pay the livery bill and the Blacksmith would never consent to his leaving without settling.

"Mr. Charles will be here soon. I'm sure of it," Burford said confidently. He knew better than to show fear.

"Let's hope so," the Blacksmith said then walked to the sleek horses and stroked their necks. "I reckon a man would not want to lose these horses over a livery bill." The horses whinnied and pulled at their ropes. Burford tried to calm them, knowing they were reflecting his fear and that a livery stableman accustomed to horses, would read their mood.

The man walked to the carriage and looked it over. "Mighty fine rig you've got here. What does this Mr. Charles do for a living that he can afford such finery as this? Plantation owner? Slave trader?" He said, inspecting the impressive carriage.

"I'm not at liberty to speak sir, Masta' says I don't talk to nobody 'bout his affairs," Burford said foregoing his usually excellent grammar. Slave states like Mississippi did not allow the education of its Negro population.

Charles had no choice but to follow Mabel into the church. He pushed his way past the crowd so that he could sit next to her. She smiled and slid over. He looked around and noticed all eyes were on them. He slid down some more and did not turn around nor look at anyone while the minister began his sermon. Mabel seemed to forget their predicament, choosing to feel safe among complete strangers because they were of the same faith. The minister had crafted a fine enough speech about the Lord's gracious forgiveness of sins and man's sinful nature but his springtime allergies had flared up this morning and his dear wife had to run to his aid with a handkerchief more than once, prolonging Charles' agony. He thought of slipping out to rescue Burford but dare not leave Mabel and the children, especially while she was oblivious to the danger she'd just placed them.

When the sermon finally ended and they rose to lively organ music, to file slowly out of the church, Mabel leaned over to Charles. "Did you hear that Charles?"

He scowled. His wish was that they did not speak but just quickly remove themselves.

"The picnic! Didn't you hear? The minister invited us to a picnic." She smiled at everyone to her left and right believing she was among kindred spirits, true Christians in every respect.

An older woman heard her and tapped her hand, "Do join us, it's out behind the church, lots of wonderful dishes, we've been preparing weeks for this." The woman glanced down at the children, frowned then took a long glance at Mabel and then Charles. She quickly exited the church. Mabel did not notice. Like a child, Mabel turned away from the front door and headed out the side door with the children in tow. Charles had no other choice but to let her go, hope for the best and go rescue Burford.

"I told you, Mr. Charles will be here shortly," Burford's angry voice bellowed out of the barn.

Charles ran toward it then stopped, composed himself and entered the livery stable.

"Ah, there you are," the man said to Charles. "I thought you'd run off on your Nigger."

Before Charles had time to reply, Burford had taken his fist and slammed it into the jaw of the Blacksmith who fell backwards, hitting his head on one of the supporting wooden posts.

"Good God Burford! What have you done?"

"I've got a temper Mr. Charles, you just haven't seen it before," Burford said then calmly took the horses and led them outside.

Charles bent down over the unconscious Blacksmith. Hoping he would revive shortly, he looked for the counter where he would pay his bill and upon seeing the invoice, Charles placed more than enough to cover the bill, held it in place with a small iron tool and followed Burford outside.

"You've got to get out of here Burford." Charles looked left and right, no one was about on the side street. It appeared that the church picnic had attracted a large crowd. He'd have to convince Mabel to leave immediately.

"See that clump of trees? Take the carriage there and wait for us, talk to no one! Do you hear? No one. Get inside the carriage. Hide Burford, until we come!"

Charles hurried to the church picnic. To his dismay, all the picnickers were white and they stood in a long line waiting to be served by very young colored servants whom he could see were frustrated but dared not show it.

"I wanted lemonade!" A skinny, unattractive, white woman shouted at a flustered young black girl. There were eleven servants trying to please a hundred pushy, disrespectful Christians on what was turning into a very warm day. Charles scanned the crowd for Mabel but did not see her.

"Charles!" he heard her shout, the two children, grasping onto her skirt. Mabel, plate in hand was just about to the front of the line. "Charles!" she smiled and waved.

Charles looked at the scene in front of him. There seemed to be no one guiding the inexperienced servants. There were several open pits where meat was roasting but was unattended and close to burning. There were four varieties of drinks; lemonade, root beer, ginger ale and iced tea but none were marked and the silver pitchers all looked the same.

The crowd was hungry and lashing insults at the servants and growing more impatient and disrespectful. Children who ran free began helping themselves to bread and in their exuberance knocked over bowls of cookies, which the young black girls kept righting back up again. Charles heard one of the Christian women shout at one of the servants, "Don't touch that! Keep your cotton-picking hands off the food!"

From fifteen feet away Charles could sense Mabel's anger. Her face was aghast that anyone would say that to the poor girl who was trying her best to please the ungrateful crowd. Just when Mabel was about to direct *her* anger at the rude-mouthed woman, a small dog ran into the crowd and up to the bread. Paws up, the little dog grabbed bread in its mouth and scurried off. The rude woman ran after the dog. Amidst all the confusion, the servants kept patiently trying to do their best but the situation grew worse with each passing moment. As Charles feared, the fire on all three pits was too high and the meat was burning. Not one of the servants gave up trying to make things right for they knew that within this Christian crowd were men and women who would later

133

take great reward in punishing them. As the frenzy grew higher, Charles plunged into the crowd, grabbed the two children, smiled politely at the picnickers and though he did not run, walked very quickly away. Without looking back, he headed straight for the carriage where he hoped Burford would be waiting. Mabel was not far behind. She ran. But she looked back. She looked at the beautiful little white church with tall spires, the well-tended green grass that surrounded it and the little white picket fence with daffodils and purple violets. It wasn't until she looked again toward the slaves in the hot Mississippi sun that she let out a sob. And then it all came out. She ran but she sobbed uncontrollably. Burford hurried from the carriage cab and climbed up front to take the reins of the two fine horses that seemed as anxious as them all, to be on their way.

"Charles," Mabel said defiantly, "you can bet Jackson Mississippi, in a hundred years is not gonna clear itself of self-righteous Christians who believe themselves superior to the colored folks. It's not so today and won't be for a long, long time!"

"I'd give it two-hundred years Miss Mabel, at least," Burford said. "Hee-yah!" he shouted at the horses who jumped into a canter, then seamlessly into a flawless, rhythmic run from which they did not slow until they were well on their way up the Choctaw Trace heading toward Nashville.

The Choctaw trace wove through beautiful forests of blooming shrubs that wafted their flowery scent for miles. When they reached the Pearl River, they wanted to stop and spend time in the beauty and serenity of the area but all agreed it was too risky. They could not be sure that someone was not close behind after Burford's surprise show of anger. Neither men had dare mention it to Mabel, who sulked since leaving the church.

"We'll stop for the night at Red Bud Springs," Charles said, "there's a tavern and lodge that will be friendly to us. It's a pleasant place to wake up to, with three natural springs. It's tended by an Indian Squaw and her husband who's a fur trader."

"How do you know this Charles?" Mabel asked sarcastically.

"My sources tell me."

"Excellent sources Mr. Charles."

"Burford... when will you stop calling me mister?"

"After having to pose as your slave... more than once... Sir... with respect... I believe it's a good idea I keep it up."

"I suppose you're right," Charles said, then covered his face with his hat and let the sound of the horses lull him to sleep.

When they finally reached Red Bud Springs, they were relieved to find their visit had been expected. Their hosts, a young, vibrant Indian woman from the Quapaw tribe and her equally invigorated French-Canadian husband took Mabel and Charles to their lodging, secluded rooms in the attic above the tavern. Other than it being quite warm, they felt secure and protected.

Burford was the most relaxed he'd been the whole trip and appreciated that their hosts had plenty of hay for their horses to eat all night long. "Getting a little thin," Burford told the French-Canadian, "they were still fat down in New Orleans." To which the man did not say much, it was not his nature to chitchat but chose instead to do most of the work bedding the horses down. Burford was extremely grateful and retired early to his room.

Beth and Danny were restless and tossed and tumbled about the floor. "They feel comfortable," Mabel told Charles as she watched them play.

"I do too," he said, stretching out on her bed.

"Hey," Mabel said teasingly, "didn't they give you your own bed... AND room?"

"They did and I'll retire to it in due time. We haven't had much time Mabel..."

She averted his eyes. "I'm so sorry about today... I was such a fool," she confessed then sat next to him on the bed. He put his arm around her.

"It's been a long journey and you've done very well. Especially since it's the first time you've been out of your garden," he teased.

She laughed. "That's true Charles, I've never been out of Pittsburgh. Other than my job at the *News Herald*, church on Sunday and the few businesses I frequent, I'm a stranger to this world."

"It's not a very kind one... I'm afraid," he said apologetically.

"Oh, I've had a lovely time... all and all. The apparitions in New Orleans..." she looked at him for answers, "were unexpected. And I hadn't expected to see the Crocker Plantation, and hear the gruesome tale of Jenny's great-grandfather with the Crocker servants. Charles, I'm sure that was my great-great-grandmother, that's why I saw the spirits... and Jenny... all of it. I was led there, I know it Charles. As cruel and sad as that history was I feel drawn to it... that big mansion... the racing horses... that nice man. What was his name?"

"Benjamin," Charles moaned.

"Yes... Benjamin," Mabel said, alert and vibrant thinking of the plantations facing the mighty Mississippi. "I'd love to go back some day... someday soon," she said as if lost in a dream.

"Oh I don't know Mabel, there's a war going on. It's only just begun. I heard someone in the tavern say Lincoln is asking for volunteers, men to spend three months in the army."

"You're not thinking of going... are you Charles?"

He shook his head no. He stood up. "I'm tired Mabel."

She could see that he was discouraged. She stood up too. They both were so tired neither could feel the flames that gathered around them. She gave him a weak peck on the cheek. He retired to his room.

Mabel stayed up late into the night writing. Now that she was safe, she felt alive, inspired and a bit mischievous. After the

137

episode at the Presbyterian Church, her thoughts had changed about church. Knowing that some, if not all of her church members read *American Heroes*, she wove a thinly veiled expose' of the church. It was scandalous and racy. When she finished it, she felt proud and would have given anything to see their faces when they read it. Suddenly she realized she wanted to share her thoughts with Charles, not realizing it was two o'clock in the morning. Still dressed she snuck out of the room, quietly closing the door behind her. She went to the door adjoining hers where Charles was sleeping. She knocked. There was no answer. She tried the door and it was not locked. She went in and quietly shut the door behind her. It was dark in the room and she came to her senses. *It's late.* She was about to retreat when she caught a faint glimpse of Charles. He was lying unclothed; his sinewy body twisted in the covers, the moonlight just enough to let her eyes feast on a completely bare side of Charles Churchill. Mabel's eyes ran down his whiskered face, down his sloping shoulder, down his torso and thighs and down his strong, long legs. She giggled a little when she saw his large bare feet. Her giggle woke him. He did not move but opened his eyes to see her standing over him. She turned to leave.

"Mabel?"

She froze.

"Mabel?"

Embarrassed she turned around slowly. The moonlight lit her face. He could see she was flushed and stimulated. He dared not move for fear the blanket he was twisted in would expose his nakedness but when she started tip-toeing out he grabbed the blanket and held it to cover himself below the waist and chased after her.

"Mabel, what is it? Come sit," he walked her back to the bed and had her sit down.

Her breathing was heavy. In the thick darkness and warmth of the attic, their desires were as exposed as Charles' nakedness. Mabel said nothing but her short panting breaths told him everything he needed to know. He admired her beauty and the way her body filled the dress he'd bought her. Dainty lace along the high neckline tickled her chin. Embarrassed she turned away. He placed his hand on her back and found the strings that held back what he had desired for so long. He gave a slight tug on one string, she winced. The restraints loosened. He ran his soft hand inside the back of her dress, loosening it more. He pulled her dress down over her shoulders and kissed them. First one kiss then another. Her breathing grew louder and faster. Charles slowly brought his hand to one of her full breasts. It felt smooth and fell into his cupped hand. Her nipple, stimulated and erect slipped between his fingers. She winced again. She loved the feel of his hands cupping, his fingers going round and over her nipples, as if he could do it forever but Mabel could take it no more. She turned round to face him. In her eyes were the flames and desire of a woman untouched, a woman wanting to feel the gentle caresses of a man. Still her breathing labored as his hands moved about her breasts and sometimes to the wisps of hair that hung in front of her sultry eyes. She stood up. He stood up. The blanket that had hidden Charles fell to the floor. In the moonlight, the two stood facing one another. He entirely unclothed, she, from the waist up, was completely exposed. Her petticoats danced at her waist and taunted him. She taunted him. With her eyes she dared him, dared him to take what he wanted, what he had always longed for.

Mabel leaned into Charles arms, her back toward him. He wrapped his arms around her waist and whispered softly in her ear, "Are you sure?"

She nodded and loosened the buttons that held her skirt and petticoats aloft. They slid down her soft brown legs. They stood facing one another. Her hand in his he took her to the bed. Devoid of blankets, he gently lay her down upon it. Her eyes never left his face. He could see in them that she was ready. He placed kisses delicately about her neck and kissed her mouth passionately while directing himself into the soft folds of the entrance to their ecstasy. She felt him now inside of her. It hurt lightly but she'd known it would and he was gentle. Her hands held the stiff muscles of his back as he rode gently upon her. She could see his face in the faint moonlight. He was smiling ever so slightly. "Are you alright?" he whispered. She nodded. He quickened his pace upon her, his chest pressing against her full breasts until he'd reached his height at which point he let go, driving his moist seed deep into her wet folds. She had invited him into her intimate world. She had encouraged him. She had spread her legs so that he may enter her. It was done. There would be no turning back. She played with his hair as he lay spent upon her. He nestled in her breasts, playfully taking a nipple in his mouth and tickling it with his tongue. He lifted himself from her. She stared at his tall slender, muscular body and at his erection. She smiled and let out a deep sigh. The light would soon be streaming through the windows. They'd be in the carriage again for long days and sometimes nights but she'd have Charles by her side and she could wile away the hours by remembering his masculine gifts and anxiously awaiting their pleasurable return.

Mabel and Charles were quiet as the tired horses lumbered through the warm spring days. The road was dry and it had been hours since stopping for the horses to drink.

"Mr. Charles... uh... Charles..."

"Fantastic Burford, we've finally got past the formalities, please, please, please continue to omit the mister. What is it? What's on your mind?"

"It's the horses... Sir..."

"Call me Charles."

"Horses need a rest, they need water and hay. Any stops on your itinerary?"

Charles lifted his weight off his backside to retrieve his latest notes from his back pocket. He looked it over then pulled out a map and studied it carefully. "Not for another seventy miles I'm afraid."

"No inns, taverns or Underground railroad associations?" Mabel asked.

Charles shook his head, embarrassed of his imperfect plans. Mabel turned her head and watched the scenery go slowly by. Charles put his hand on hers and she jerked hers away. He'd known that with women sometimes the first night of passion often brought remorse, Mabel was not the first virgin he'd had the pleasure of.

"We've been passing well-traveled side roads, I 'magine there are farms..." Burford said, looking and thinking ahead.

"Well, let's give it a shot, shall we? Beth, Danny... do you remember what to say or not to say when we're amongst strangers?" Charles asked.

"Of course they do," Mabel said retreating from her pout more from responsibility than from forgiveness of herself for her unplanned sexual romp in the attic. She shot Charles a haughty look and he mentally braced himself for the coming event sure to unfold.

Burford found a road that had been used for years. He could see fresh wagon marks in the soil. "Here's hoping the farmers are friendly."

"I don't see why not. Better go back to the formalities Burford."

"Yes Sir, Mr. Charles."

For several miles, the road led through a forest of tall pines then opened to a wide meadow. A creek ran through the meadow where grass grew thickly after spring rains.

Burford looked around and could see no farms. Optimistically he stopped the horses. "This is perfect, if we can stay here for a few hours and let the horses graze and water down, I think we can continue and ride through the evening. We won't make your seventy-five mile point Charles, but Lord willing something will turn up."

"I agree. I'd love to walk; all this sitting makes a man feel anxious. Mabel, Danny, Beth, we're going for a walk."

The carriage had barely stopped before Charles had the children out. They began tugging on Mabel who glared at Charles.

"What a beautiful meadow, run around children, you've been so pent up... play, play, play," he told them.

Taking his advice, they pushed their short, slender bodies through the thick grass, pulling on seed heads and spilling them about.

"I asked you if you were sure," Charles said defensively to Mabel who again glared at him. "You came to me, remember? I was sleeping."

"Yes I know and I did enjoy myself Charles, I only wish you would have stopped me."

"Stop you?! My God, no man could have stopped you," he grabbed her wrist and pulled her close as he possibly could up against his chest. He could feel her rapid heart beat. Putting his face to hers and glaring now into her dark eyes he said adamantly, "I would never have stopped you. If it hadn't been me it would have been someone else, someone like Hermann Davidad."

Mabel gasped, *had he seen her kissing him at the creek during their stay at the French Settlement?*

"Or Benjamin Crocker," Charles accused, reminding her of her attraction to the handsome man she'd encountered at the old plantation home of her great-grandmother. A man who may be a distant relation. A man to whom she felt a strong attraction, a lure so magnetic she longed to return to New Orleans. But the scent of Charles and the serious look upon his face was what she found desirable. She would not erase the memory of their lovemaking. She could feel the desire but longed to return to the innocence and purity of before, *no one need know*. If he spoke of it to anyone, she could deny it. *Perhaps there will be no marriage.*

Their eyes defiantly met one another's. Whose anger raged highest there was none to judge. Their hearts had grown cold and their minds were angry but the heaviness of their breathing defied the truth. Neither could or would recognize the pure lust that had festered between them.

Charles looked at his pocket watch then gathered the horses and helped Burford harness them. Mabel had spent the last forty-five minutes at the creek. She and the children refreshed by splashing their faces and removing their shoes and dipping their feet into the chilly water. She felt better and she glanced apologetically at Charles but he had only a glare much like the ones she'd had for him earlier. She looked down.

"Charles..." she said, resting her hand on his knee, after they were on their way again.

He didn't give her a chance to finish. "I've known women like you," he said angrily, "they taunt men with their youth and beauty. You seduced me!" he said loudly enough for Burford to hear, who in response scurried the tired horses into a canter to drown out the argument he wanted no part of. But Mabel began arguing back and Charles responded. The faster the horses cantered the louder their voices raged. Beth and Danny had seen these quarrels many times before and though they feigned sleeping, they heard every word of the argument that made no sense to anyone, especially Mabel and Charles. Their arguing came to an abrupt stop when Burford pulled the horses to a halt.

"What's going on?!" Charles shouted.

"Soldiers... it's a roadblock Sir."

"Children, get down off the floor," Mabel shouted, "Come sit beside me, remember everything we taught you."

"Yes, Ma'am," they said in unison.

"Union or Rebel soldiers?" Charles asked.

"Can't tell, too far off."

Charles lifted his hindquarters and removed his itinerary from his back pocket. He crumpled it up tightly. He turned to Mabel, "Excuse my forwardness but..." and he stuck the crumpled page into her dress, on top of her left breast. He then crumpled his map and stuck it under her right breast. "They'll never look there," he said with wry smile. "Don't slow too much Burford, you'll draw suspicion. Everyone be calm."

"They're Rebels Sir."

"This far north?"

"Yes Sir, their Rebel flag, I can see it plainly."

As they drew closer, one of the soldiers approached them and held his hand up to halt. He was a healthy, handsome, competent, looking man about twenty-five with a thick head of sandy, blond hair and bushy eyebrows. His eyes did not linger long on Burford but lingered too long on Mabel, who amidst her fear seemed to enjoy his admiration.

"Are these your children?" he asked her.

"Yes Sir, they 'ah," she said, faking an accent.

"And you Sir," he said to Charles, "will you step out please."

Charles reluctantly climbed from the carriage. His clothes were wrinkled and Mabel saw he had dried grass stuck to his coat. He towered over the young man, just as he towered over her. His glasses perched on the end of his nose as usual. Mabel knew he was frightened but admired how calmly he spoke. He told the Rebel soldier that he was a farmer from West Virginia and that she, Burford, Beth and Danny were his slaves and that he owned them outright. When the soldier asked if he had the papers to prove it Charles pulled out official documentation but the soldier sensed something. He walked back to Mabel and asked her to please step out of the carriage. She did not know if he saw she was trembling. He asked Burford to step down. The children stepped out and clung tightly to Mabel. Their faces wore the normal expressions of slave children being interrogated because that's what they were. The soldier motioned two other soldiers to come to him and while he kept an eye on Charles and especially Burford, he had his soldiers scour the carriage. Nevertheless, Charles was thorough and they found nothing, not even the trap door to the compartment under the floor.

"Check all the bags," the soldier demanded. He knew something was amiss but without proof, he had no authority but to let them go. The soldiers went through Charles' bag and then Burford's. The commanding soldier sent one of the other soldiers back to the roadblock while the one left behind went meticulously through Mabel's luggage. She trembled violently because at the bottom of her bag was her latest writing of, *American Heroes*. She saw him pause and look at it. He looked around and could tell he debated whether to say anything. *He can't read.*

"Nothing here Sir," he said, afraid to draw attention to his illiteracy.

They all let out a deep sigh. The commanding soldier helped Mabel into the carriage. His hand held onto hers long after she was seated.

"I do hope I see you again someday," he said to her then turned to Charles. The sun hit the soldier's face. He was tanned and looked like he'd been well-fed throughout his life. "She's not for sale is she?"

"For sale?" Charles said looking at Mabel, remembering her moody temperament then to the soldier whom he realized was serious. "No, she's my slave, been with my family since she was a small child. She's nothing but trouble, we have thought of it."

"Trouble huh?" the soldier laughed and spent a long time looking at the ground then back up to Charles. "If I encounter your face ever again I'm going to relieve you of your trouble. I could build an empire with a woman like that. I don't know what you and your Colored are tryin' to pull here but I know it ain't what it appears. I can smell it... can feel it in my bones. Now go on get out'a here before my soldiers and I take your pretty servant off into the woods and show her what trouble really means. She's too high and mighty for a slave... and you're no farmer, go on... git!"

Charles held his head high and walked to join Mabel in the carriage. She could see he was angry and under different circumstances would have stood up to this man. She knew nothing of Burford's angry blow to the Blacksmith in Jackson but would have better understood the look on Charles apprehensive face as he called... begged... Burford to return to his place at the reins. It was a collective sigh of relief by them all when the horses were spurred into a trot and they were off and heading toward the border of West Virginia.

Now that Victor had been laid off his job he had time to idle about the city. He'd grown well versed in telling the story of his layoff at the *News Herald*. He applied for work elsewhere but no one had a place for him. Maybe in a few months, the Rebels would give up their fight, or Mabel would run out of ideas and Whitethorn would be back to his normal small press operation. Victor contemplated his situation every day all day. Annie was growing impatient with his obsessiveness and threatened to walk out on him if he didn't straighten up. One day he came home and told her he was going to join the Union army. Annie was aghast.

"You can't leave me here. I'm lost in Pittsburgh without you."

He shrugged as if he didn't care but the truth was he took good care of Annie and she of him. He could not though, carry on without a job and being a soldier fulfilled his new restless spirit.

"Can't you wait until Mabel returns? She'll talk sense into Whitethorn. She's so fond of you. I'll bet she'll withhold her Black Pansy stories until he makes it right."

Victor stood on their small wooden balcony, his long lanky leg propped on the railing, his boots in need of a good blacking. Victor was intelligent and had been a reliable employee but the abrupt rejection had affected him.

"I haven't told anyone, that I know who the real Black Pansy is."

"Nor should you," Annie warned him. Her delicate features contorted in frustration. Her fingers twisted nervously at her soft blond locks.

"Everybody would love... that story," he said, drawing confidence in what he knew. "I'm a fine reporter, I could write the story and distribute it myself, why I could start my own newspaper with the proceeds. I can see the headlines now," he said, running his hand through the air, "Black Pansy Revealed."

"You would endanger Mabel."

Victor became animated and started pacing around the six feet balcony. "That's why I don't say anything, never would I do anything to hurt that girl. Why, I love Mabel..." he looked at Annie and could see she was hurt.

"Why do all the men looooovveee Mabel?" she shouted jealously.

Victor abandoned all sensitivity, "Because she is so damned pretty. I got to tell you Annie, let truth be told, there ain't no man that don't have eyes for Mabel. And she's smart too, smarter 'n me and old man Whitethorn put together. She proves it by writin' that story, she's good, you know she is. Hell, everybody thinks it's some handsome fella down in Baton Rouge. Like hell it is, it's our own Mabel McCrutchon."

"Shhh, someone might hear."

"Yeah, no money in that... fool I'd be, telling the world Mabel McCrutchon was Black Pansy."

Little did he know he just did. Their rooming house had balconies that were near the windows of their neighbors. Mingus O'Brien was sitting below that open window eating his dinner. He'd heard every word and knew exactly who Mabel McCrutchon was... his cousin.

Mabel was furious with Charles... and the whole world. Her latest installment she would not send to Auntie Louisa, but would edit it herself, to make sure nothing was left out. Mabel began writing profusely and learned to write while riding in the carriage with a man she loathed and restless children crawling onto her lap. She let loose her storm. She blasted men, their superiority complex, and their lust. She blamed herself for her sexual indiscretion and wove promiscuous women in to tempt her heroes. She lampooned the Southern man to such great extent she feared a hanging surely if her journal was confiscated but she *did not care.* She did not though, forsake a few of her *moral* characters whom she had grown fond of, for in her heart knew that all men were not bad. Some had backbone and discipline. But she began writing furious escapades between imaginary men and women, modeled after real people she'd encountered in New Orleans. She did not faintly allude to these sexual encounters, but spelled them out quite clearly if one knew how to read into her stories exactly how she'd woven them. Page after page she penned. She wrote of men meeting women in hotels, women who were not their wives! She wrote of women who seduced shopkeepers, dockworkers and even Christian ministers! She wrote and wrote, day after day, night after night until she was utterly exhausted. Burford and Charles privately discussed her declining health. She would barely speak to either one. It was on a Friday evening when Charles calculated that they'd arrive in Pittsburgh on Monday, Tuesday evening at the latest. He felt responsible for Mabel's decline; it was after all, he who had enlisted her as his companion. Other than her current state, their mission had been a success. They had gone to retrieve five children and had done so with the addition of the boy, James. They were almost home and Charles was much too proud to return Mabel to Pittsburgh in such a state. He would make these next few days as pleasant as possible. He would release her from her commitment to marry him. He would apologize and bear the blame of the intimate night they shared in the attic at the lodge along the Choctaw trace. He would start by taking her to dinner once they reached Clarksburg. There he could pamper her, she could take a long bath, rest up... they would become friends again. Once in Pittsburgh he would return her safely to her parents, her Auntie Louisa, Whitethorn and her beautiful garden paradise and he would return to *his* highbrow, upper crust life in Connecticut and maybe help his father with the administrative work of the shipyards.

"Mabel?" he asked softly as they neared civilization.

Mingus O'Brien told no one, not even his status climbing, money-loving wife. The secret of Black Pansy's identity was well kept with him. Believing the secret must be worth five-hundred dollars to Editor Whitethorn, O'Brien went straight to the *News Herald* to collect his money but the office was shut down and boarded up. O'Brien looked to see if he'd been followed then wandered behind the back of the building. That was boarded up too. O'Brien was a large strapping man who delivered pianos to upstairs tenants. It wasn't that O'Brien was without brains; it's just that hadn't been cultivated. Since his big spurt in puberty, everyone in his family, everyone in the neighborhood, followed by everyone in town, rewarded him for heavy lifting.

O'Brien had been to Mabel's home on many occasions and it always irked her that he had been welcomed to all the social events, mainly because his skin did not show the traces of Negro blood that hers did. If she knew Mingus was stalking around in an attempt to bribe Whitethorn, she would turn his world inside out. She knew more dirty secrets about that man's life than he did. But Mabel was not there and wouldn't be for days. Meanwhile, Mingus

O'Brien wandered around Pittsburgh trying to flush out Whitethorn.

"Yes Charles," she said sarcastically, impatiently looking up from her writing.

"I insist you dine with me this evening... alone. Burford can keep an eye out on Beth and Danny. They'll enjoy helping him bed the horses down."

She started to decline but he didn't give her the chance.

"I absolutely insist. I will refuse to leave Clarksburg if you don't."

She rolled her eyes, let out a deep sigh, and turned her head to look out onto the road. He did not see her smile nor hear her thoughts of mischief and spitefulness.

When they reached Clarksburg, Charles spoke to the children who obeyed his every word. He told Burford that he must watch them, then slipped a twenty-dollar gold piece into Burford's hand.

"You deserve this and more. I have been a rude chap more often than I care to admit and you have been a pure gentleman..." he began walking away, then stopped, "except of course when you knocked out the Blacksmith, but no one's perfect I suppose."

Burford laughed.

Charles' statement caught Mabel by surprise. "Blacksmith? Burford knocked out a Blacksmith?"

"Yes, in Jackson..."

"Where was I?"

Now it was he who looked impatient. "At the church picnic."

"Oh...yes," her voice reflected humility.

"You see," Charles said, leaning in to her, beginning to tell the story. Mabel listened intently, sometimes frowning but had fallen into full laughter at Charles' humor. Reliving that frightening day and replacing it with laughter was good for them both.

Their choice of dining establishments was not great, there were only two. "Take your pick," Charles told her as she looked between a lonely, empty soda fountain that was about to close and a lively restaurant whose tables were full and whose patrons happily waited for the next available table.

Mabel and Charles sat quietly as they waited for a table. She with her hands folded on her lap, he tapping his foot nervously. She still wore her floppy feathered hat when in public.

"I think it's alright if you don't wear your hat in here."

"Oh, I've gotten so used to wearing it, I didn't even remember I had it on."

He smiled, "Thank you for wearing it."

She nodded.

There were families with children of all ages, the warmth of the room and the sound of silverware clinking and dishes being washed and upbeat conversations comforted her but Charles was nervous because he would be breaking their engagement off and he loved her very much. So he distracted himself by watching the people. But what he didn't realize is that he was engrossed in watching the four daughters who worked as

waitresses in the family owned restaurant, pretty in their long dresses, with their plaited hair and the older ones pinned up hair.

Charles fixated his attention on the oldest girl who smiled when she caught Charles looking at her. Mabel held her own, after all, she was angry with him, quite fed up. And he knew that and continued, unconsciously, to devote all his attention on the pretty waitress. His eyes went wherever the waitress went and when she came near Charles Mabel saw him fluster and smile at her.

"Charles?" she said breaking his spell.

"Oh! Yes... what?"

When you're with a lady it's not polite to stare."

"Was I?"

"Yes, terribly so," she said fiddling nervously with her hair hoping no one knew what commenced between the two.

"I'll try to be more considerate."

"Thank you."

The two sat silently, he a little encouraged by her jealousy, she discouraged by his wandering eye. *Hadn't she thought she was done with Charles Churchill?*

When the pretty waitress whom Charles had overly admired came to escort them to their table all the color went from Mabel's face and the color returned to Charles.

"Mabel..." Charles said, pointing to her hat she'd left sitting on a chair. She grabbed it by the string and whisked it off the chair.

They both ordered lamb and soup, vegetables and bread.

"How's your story?" he asked as his eyes wandered the room looking for threats to their safety.

"Oh it's dreadfully naughty," she said boldly.

Between the pretty waitresses and staring at Mabel, as always stunning, the mention of naughty stirred his loins.

"Naughty?"

"Oh yes, Pittsburgh will be ablaze with this next installment, it's very long, and very naughty."

He did not know how to respond. He'd been punishing himself for his *naughty* ways...

"Just exactly what do you mean naughty?"

She leaned forward so that none could hear. "Oh Charles, if one has the imagination to read between the lines, I've some terribly naughty characters."

"Do you mean between the bedcovers? That kind of naughty?"

Mabel shrunk in her chair and grimaced then nodded. "No one knows it's me, Black Pansy wrote it. I can be as naughty as I want," she whispered.

Charles looked around the room and quickly put a napkin on his lap. Their dinner was served and he spoke barely a word because he had not the chance. Mabel chatted on about her naughty stories and her sinful characters.

Thinking they would find Burford, after dinner Mabel and Charles strolled to the stable where the horses were but he was not there. Only two contented horses peacefully munching hay. Mabel sat down on a bale of hay. Still talking about her story's characters, Charles bent down and kissed her. Once, then twice, then, all the naughtiness that had possessed her for the last week came pouring from her, like a water break in the pump house, Mabel had no control. She stood up and hungrily kissed his neck and pulled at his shirt. He was taken back by her aggressiveness but did not want to discourage her; he wanted all of her flood to spill out upon him, wash over him like the mighty rush of the river. She ripped at his clothes, scratching at his back. She lay down upon a bale of hay and pulled him upon her. She moaned when his erection touched her bare leg under the full skirt and petticoats they had both lifted. His pants were down quickly. Her undergarments she removed herself and gently lay them aside. Her eyes lured him onto her, her moist opening beckoned and he responded. He delightfully slid into her again. She moaned with passion and slid deeper underneath his body. They tossed and danced about in such a frenzy neither wanting it to end but it soon did but with the ecstasy of them both. They lay panting heavily and amid laughter, they were again Mabel and Charles, betrothed. He looked down upon her sweat soaked face, how beautiful it was and to him always would be.

"Ah Mabel, I love you."

"And I you Charles. You have brought me to enjoy my body as I've never known." He opened the strings that held her breasts hidden inside stiff cotton cups. He ran his fingers across her large brown nipple and looked into the beauty of her eyes, her soul. He could not believe that she would be his to enjoy again and again. His face fell into her bosom and he let out a deep sigh.

The first chance Mabel had, she sent her latest story installment to the *News Herald*. Due to the mature nature the story had taken, she bypassed Auntie Louisa and boldly sent it on to Editor Whitethorn.

The early morning was balmy as they headed east from Clarksburg. All had agreed to make haste. Burford anticipated reuniting with his wife and children and Danny and Beth grew excited as they approached their new life.

"Can we go to school?" Danny asked.

"Yes you can," Mabel said, lovingly combing his hair with her hand.

"Will we learn to read and write?" Beth asked, while leaning her cute little head on her brother's shoulder, her dark eyes twinkling, her dimpled cheeks grinning.

"Not only will you learn to read and write but you can teach school someday, or be a minister. And Charles, I've complete faith in the people you're associated with. I've no doubt these children will be protected."

"The committee that oversees the details is caring, responsible and cautious. They're very thorough."

"Oh no, here we go again," Burford warned.

"What is it?" both Mabel and Charles asked.

"Another roadblock."

"We haven't gone but ten miles," Charles complained.

Burford slowed the horses and approached the military awaiting them.

"Union soldiers, Union soldiers," he kept repeating, to Charles and Mabel's "Good, good."

"Morning," the soldier said to them. "Heading into Higgins Ridge?"

"Just passing through. We're working our way to Pittsburgh," Charles told him, leaning over Mabel and the children to converse with the soldier who stood at the carriage window.

"Well, we've an incident in Higgins Ridge. During the night, Hooligans sympathetic to the Rebel cause let all the farmers', pigs, cattle, horses, hens and roosters out. The hens are on top of barns, the cattle have stampeded through and ruined the corn crops, the pigs and horses are cavorting in the fields and eating all the produce from the gardens. Looks like a tornado struck Higgins Ridge."

Charles pushed on his glasses. They'd begun to slide down his nose constantly; he was forever pushing them back onto his face. He wrinkled his nose, looked at Mabel and shook his head.

"Any reason we can't keep going?" Mabel asked.

The soldier laughed. "Plenty. Some of the ruffians are still there, been a little shooting." He looked at Danny and Beth and to Charles and Mabel who could see he had questions. But the soldier did not inquire of their business and motioned them through. "Have a safe journey," he said waving them on and signaling to the soldiers to let them pass.

Burford drove the horses briskly through chickens, pigs and horses that cluttered the roadway. At times startling their horses, bouncing hens scurried out of the way. Pigs oinked and rolled in the dirt, horses chewed at the fresh thick grass that lined the road. Danny and Beth climbed on Charles' and Mabel's lap to get a look, grinning and reaching their arms out wanting to touch the real life farming dysfunction. Burford was smiling too. There was something nice about seeing the animals free, even if it had been accomplished by the Rebels.

Mingus O'Brien had been unable to contact Editor Whitethorn, having made himself elusive in recent weeks. Mingus wandered into the hotel across the street from the *News Herald*. He had a bite to eat, stretching his time at the window seat where he sat staring at the boarded up newspaper office where there was no sign of life.

"Ever see anyone come and go from the *News Herald?*" he asked the waitress.

"Nah, not for a while. Too many folks were traipsing through wantin' to know 'bout the war," she frowned. "I miss them... Victor, Mabel, Whitethorn and Victor's sister..."

Mingus laughed. "Sister? That ain't his sister. You talkin' 'bout Annie?"

She nodded, still pouting, her bottom lip down turned, her eyes sad.

"If that's his sister than somebody better speak to their parents. They do some squealin' over there..." Mingus looked at her to gauge her readiness for gossip. She looked genuinely interested but not maliciously so.

"Ya see, I live next door to those two," he whistled, "they aint no brother and sister, I'll tell ya that."

She shrugged and nodded then glanced nostalgically at the boarded building.

"I know something..." Mingus let slip, trying to impress her.

She nodded and again shrugged. If there's one thing a waitress learns, it's to feign indifference about many things, particularly gossip which you hear a lot of, much of it false. Act like you don't care and you're less likely to be blamed when it spreads and more likely to be on the receiving end of some juicy tidbits.

"I know who Black Pansy is," Mingus said, looking across the street to the newspaper office. "And it's not some man down in Baton Rouge. Nope. It's a woman and I know who. I think Editor Whitethorn will pay a pretty penny to someone to keep the world from knowin' it's Mab... not a man." He looked at the waitress, reading her expression. *Had she recognized the slip of tongue?* She continued feigning indifference.

"Would you like anything else?" she asked him in a bored tone.

"No thanks," he said, rising to leave, looking again toward the *News Herald.*

The waitress went to the kitchen. "Don't repeat this, please don't..."

"What, what?" the cook asked.

The waitress looked into the restaurant to see if there were patrons who might hear, she whispered. "I think... not sure... but pretty sure..."

"What, what?"

"I think Mabel McCrutchon is Black Pansy."

The cook gasped. "The pretty Negro girl who used to work over there?"

"You think she's Negro? I never noticed. Noticed she was pretty though, wish I looked like that. Anyway, don't tell anybody 'cause I'm not sure."

"K, won't tell no one, lips are sealed he said and returned to the chicken he was cutting up."

An hour later, the cook told the butcher when he came with a delivery. The waitress told the next shift waitress who told several close acquaintances who came to dine. The butcher told the knife sharpener who told the shoeshine man. The shoeshine man told every man who came for a shoeshine, including Pittsburgh's mayor who told his wife who told all her church friends who went on to tell their neighbors. Within two days there were none in Pittsburgh who did not know Mabel McCrutchon was Black Pansy, and with competing newspapers finding out, it would soon be known across the nation and into Canada.

Everyone except Whitethorn had heard the news. Having become so reclusive, all that mattered to him was the simplicity of receiving Mabel's chapters and taking them to the newspaper that printed and delivered them. There was not much more for Whitethorn to do except go to the bank, deposit wealth and retrieve telegrams from newspapers across the country and Canada who also wanted to run the *American Heroes* chapters. When Whitethorn received Mabel's tawdry chapters, he knew his fate was sealed. *She's finally done it,* he thought.

He closed his eyes and envisioned his new home. He'd have a long drive put in and a fancy carriage house with flowers all around. He stayed up late at night with pen and paper, calculating his growing volume of sales. The hints of vulgarity and impropriety that Mabel wove into the story created a scandal that was discussed on Pittsburgh's front stoops, the taverns and at church socials. Most thought it improper, sinful and immoral yet everyone seemed to know the storyline. Tsk, tsk, Mabel McCrutchon was on everyone's lips. Auntie Louisa and Mabel's mother Vivian were highly embarrassed and chose not to go out for when they did they were bombarded with people shaming their daughter one moment and asking if there were any new chapters the next. Mabel's father had to run the errands and dodge the multitudes.

They were reading it in Wethersfield, Connecticut too. Charles mother kept a copy hidden in her knitting basket and his sisters had them secreted under their mattresses keeping it from their husbands who had copies hidden themselves. Needless to say, the nightlife in those bedrooms intensified immensely, neither husband nor wife admitting to reading such smut though clearly by their eagerness they had.

"I see the author of that wretched story, *American Heroes*, is not a man but a woman," Charles mother Clarrisa said to his Auntie Lena who had not read the book nor had any intention of reading the book, being much too engrossed in reading Thoreau.

"She's from Pittsburgh, isn't that where Charles is?" Clarrisa said, her dry crepey skin hanging in fine lines about her slender bony face. Clarrisa loved to linger in her nightclothes until long after lunch. She would drag out breakfast of coffee and pastries then linger over brunch of eggs and soft cheeses, then more coffee, then after the noon church bells rang she'd slowly take herself up the long sweeping marble stairway to her private bedroom where she'd retire until she heard the church bells ring twice, then with help from her favorite female servant, a Scottish girl from the highlands, she'd get dressed in her afternoon attire, then slowly make her way down the sweeping circular marble stairway again to have lunch or on nice days in the sunroom where two servants attended to the needs of three-hundred different exotic potted plants and flowers.

Charles father, Frederick Churchill was not home much, he and his wife spoke about three times a week. They conversed about their adult children, their grandchildren, their enormous shipyard enterprises, the servants and their needs. When finished, Samuel would reach into his vest pocket, pull out his pocket watch, wind it, then kiss her on the cheek delicately and with sincere admiration. After all, she had bore him ten children.

Clarrisa had no thoughts on where Samuel was on the nights he did not come home. No one inquired, especially not she for fear the honest man may tell her. She had, after the birth of their tenth child, decided that sexual relations brought more children and that she had enough of those. It had been many years since she'd had any type of sexual exchange, although she could not help but notice that reading *American Heroes* aroused her. Clarrisa wasn't sure how to incorporate that into her conventional life style. Clarrisa had begun having fantasies about giving the day off to all the servants except the elder Italian hothouse gardener, who in his fifties, looked capable of reintroducing her body to the touch of a man. Whether he'd be interested probably depended on whether she smiled, which she rarely did, mostly due to boredom, but

American Heroes was livening households. It wasn't out of the question that the Churchill estate would be one of them.

"I've finally heard about *American Heroes*," Lena told her sister-in-law Clarrisa, a few mornings later, who raised her eyebrows, bringing Lena to chuckle. The women were quite different from one another. Clarrisa was tall and slender, Lena was tall and heavy. Clarrisa had been blessed with a beautiful face, Lena a beautiful heart. Lena resided several doors down, in a guest cottage of one of the estates on Bluebird Pond, a community within Wethersfield, also known as "the cove." Her deceased husband had been an ironworker. He had not left her wealthy but had not left her wanting either. She had one handyman whom she could call on and an Irish girl in her employ for seven years. None of the Bluebird Pond Churchill's would have any Negro servants; paid employees yes but as strict Abolitionists they believed strongly that the black man was equal to any white man.

Lena learned of *American Heroes* through her Irish servant. Lena was open-minded, though not a crude woman, quite the contrary. Lena was a practical, fun-loving woman who was well read and understood the minds of the younger generation.

"Charles and Burford? Are you as excited as I about returning home?"

"I am anxious as a hawk overlooking a wren's nest," Burford said, "These horses are made of steel. Mr. Charles, what are you going to do with these fine horses once we get home?"

"I'm going to give them to you Burford."

"Oh don't joke like that Mr. Charles, why I love these horses, I mean it. What's going to happen to them? They need rest and tender loving care."

"That's why I'm giving them to you Burford. They deserve a good home."

"Mr. Charles, you're not that rich are you?"

"No Burford, I'm not... but my father is," he said then looked to Mabel's face for her reaction. She was seriously considering what he'd just said and she was not smiling. She knew all too well that having a lot of money meant nothing toward having a happy marriage. The happiest married couples she'd known were the ones who put heart and soul before everything else. It seemed to Mabel that prosperity complicated life. Yes, she loved pretty dresses and nice hotels but she knew that Charles Churchill had something that his father's money could not buy. If his father disowned him, Charles would still make a fine husband and with his great sense of humor and passion for fun, he would be a fine father. But did she want to have children? She looked at Danny and Beth, one asleep on her lap and the other on Charles lap. They were peaceful bringing something into her life that was absent before. She was not convinced she wanted any children... ever. But she and Charles had not discussed that, every man wants children. *Will he still desire me if I tell him I'm not interested in children?*

It was late on a Sunday night when Victor and Annie were awoken by a loud knock at their door.

"What time is it?" Victor asked, startled that at that hour someone would intrude on them. He fumbled for his timepiece, "Two o'clock?!" He crawled from bed, "Keep yourself covered up Annie, stay in here."

"Whose there?"

"It's me, Mr. Whitethorn."

Victor threw open the door. "It couldn't wait?"

Whitethorn shook his head. Victor brought him in and had him sit at the table. Annie came in, covering her delicate slender frame in a long white cotton nightdress. She looked alluring in the dim light, her thin, fine, blonde hair pinned up casually. Without asking, she put out a plate of her cookies and a pitcher of fresh milk. Whitethorn smiled and went right for the cookies. She poured him milk.

"I need you to come back to work," he said sheepishly.

"I can do that," Victor said, pleased with the offer.

"I want to return to normal, I'm going to re-open the office and return to putting out a weekly newspaper."

Victor burrowed his brow and fiddled with a dishcloth. He looked to Annie, gauging her reaction. She nodded faintly and had a faint matching smirk.

"What about *American Heroes?*" Victor asked suspiciously.

Whitethorn put his head down.

"I suppose you've heard everyone in town knows it's Mabel," Victor said coarsely.

Whitethorn nodded. "I didn't find out until today. Mr. Burns at the bank, he finally told me. I feel ashamed Victor. I was making all this money, and poor Mabel..." he looked meekly at Victor, "and what I did to you. I let all this wealth go to my head. It's right what the preachers say about money, it does evil things to a man."

"Wealth? You bringing in that much?"

Whitethorn nodded. You and Mabel are the only friends I've got and I treated you both badly."

Victor patted him on the shoulder.

Whitethorn smiled. "What do ya say tomorrow we pull the boards of the office windows, unlock the door and start writin' stories about the war and how folks can help the slaves that are coming north."

"Sounds good to me," Victor told him.

"Me too," Annie said then went to Victor's side and from his position on the chair he hugged her small waist.

"What about *American Heroes?*" Victor asked Whitethorn, "and what about Mabel?" Victor chuckled, "Did you read that tawdry chapter?"

Whitethorn nodded, his eyes grew wide at the thought of it.

"Geesh," Victor said with an enormous grin, "what got into her?"

Charles snuggled into Mabel as they drove late into the night. They had only a few miles before they would reach Pittsburgh. The last several days had been filled with the sights of Union soldiers heading south. Worried that they may find themselves in the midst of a battlefield they pushed the horses like never before. When they got to within three miles of Pittsburgh, Burford apologized to the horses, promised them he'd make it up to them, then spurred them into a trot, then a canter, then into a full run. It was as if the horses knew the good life awaited them. They ran through the darkened night. They ran so fiercely Danny and Beth awoke. The carriage shook so severely the adults feared it would dismantle. Even Burford was frightened. For the first time during the whole journey, he had lost control of the horses. But he'd spurred them on and they sensed the urgency. They did not slow their pace until they reached the outskirts of Pittsburgh.

Burford pulled up to Mabel's home and Charles escorted her quietly up the flower-strewn red brick walkway to the large white door. A lantern hung near the door. Mabel clutched the shiny brass door latch. It was shortly after midnight and the two lovers lingered on the porch. Charles nibbled at her ear and kissed her neck. She giggled and with his promise to see her in three days, she kissed his lips succulently and said good-bye. He scurried back to the carriage and she entered her beloved home.

It was dark inside but immediately Mabel knew, she was not alone.

"I thought I heard hoof beats," her father said from his chair in the dark.

"Father!" Mabel rushed to him and wrapped her arms around his neck.

"Wonderful to have you home Mabel."

"Oh father it's wonderful to be home." She let out the deepest sigh and her father recognized it had not been an easy trip. "Father I saw the Crocker Plantation! I saw where your great-grandmother lived as a slave. I discovered the story. I felt her too father, it was frightful, the winds blew fiercely... I think I saw her... Oh father!" Mabel fell into his arms and let loose the floodgates of her grief. He patted her and warmly comforted her as he always had.

"Mabel... I hate to bring this up now... I know you're tired but..."

"What is it Father, is mother alright? Is Aunt Louisa?"

"Yes, they're fine... as can be expected."

"Oh no... what's happened?"

"Someone found out that you are the author of *American Heroes*."

"Oh dear," she stumbled to the couch and fell into it. "And some people know I'm Black Pansy?"

"Not some people Mabel. All people."

"Oh dear me," Mabel's voice trembled.

"Not just you. Your mother and Auntie Louisa have confined themselves to home. It seems the whole city has read your latest writing."

"Oh my..." Mabel's heart rose and fell to the depths of her gut. "The latest?" she questioned.

"Yes... the very latest, the story about the soldier and..."

"That's enough Father, I know the story you speak of," she sighed heavily.

"What do you suggest I do?"

"I don't have the faintest idea child. I have not read the story but have heard *all* about it."

"Is Mother angry?"

"Not as angry at you, as all of Pittsburgh appears to be at her, for raising a sinful girl."

"Oh dear..."

He laughed. "What I don't understand is how the righteous know so many of the finer points of your story."

Mabel laughed and her father laughed again with her and the two laughed heartily and arm in arm walked to their rooms.

"Good night Father."

"Good night Sweetheart."

Victor and Whitethorn pulled off the boards from the windows at the *News Herald*. People were coming in droves to complain about *American Heroes* and in the same breath asking when the next chapter would be out. Whitethorn would only shake his head and wave them off with his hand.

"I've got a newspaper to run," he told them.

Victor handled the incoming war stories and Whitethorn delivered the copy to the printer. Once a week they planned to deliver what Whitethorn promised would be "the best damn paper in Pittsburgh."

The bell on the door jingled constantly but both Victor and Whitethorn were stunned when it jiggled then presented Charles Churchill.

"Good morning!" he said as if he'd never been gone. He had no idea that the office had been boarded up nor had he heard about Black Pansy. Victor and Whitethorn both looked at him but said nothing.

"No good morning from you two? Have you not missed me?"

"Mr. Whitethorn, I think you should be the one to tell him."

"Tell me what?"

Whitethorn clammed up.

"Come back here," Victor told Charles, then led him past Mabel's desk, which Charles patted when he walked by.

"Remember how we sent Mabel home because of that incident out front? Remember that young man called Mabel a..." Victor said and Charles stopped him.

"Yes, of course," Charles rolled his eyes, "how could I forget that? And you punched him," Charles did a little boxing with his fists. "I appreciated that."

Victor was stone faced. "I'm not sure but I think you better get Mabel outa' Pittsburgh."

"Whatever for?"

"Because everyone, and I mean *everyone* knows Mabel is Black Pansy."

Charles face turned pale and the smile left his face.

Victor nodded and was grave about the situation. "She's penning into dangerous territory Charles. No woman should talk like that where people can hear, let alone spell it out to the whole world."

"Uh huh, uh huh," Charles mumbled. "I haven't read it."

Victor shook his head disgustedly, "Well you're the only one who hasn't."

Whitethorn walked back to join them. "You see Charles, I'm in a bind here. Tempers are high on account 'a the war. I don't think it wise for Mabel to come around here. Not wise for Mabel to come around... anywhere round here. It's probably not safe. They'd probably mob her."

Charles was sympathetic but stunned; he hadn't prepared himself for this.

"And Charles, I'd like for you to accompany me to the bank. I have a very large sum of money and most of it belongs to Mabel."

"Really?" Charles laughed uncomfortably as if he could not believe what he'd heard.

Victor nodded. "Whitethorn syndicated the story across the country and into Canada. Hundreds of papers pay him for the rights."

Charles laughed uncontrollably; he had to hold on to a counter he was laughing so hard.

Whitethorn smiled, relieved that at least Charles was not angry with him. "Mabel's a very wealthy woman," he said proudly.

Victor nodded, "Very... very wealthy."

"Well that's wonderful. Mabel will be thrilled... I think..." Charles said as they all three contemplated, "or... maybe not so much." Charles pushed his glasses back up his nose repeatedly. "I need some new glasses," he mumbled. "Thanks fellas for the talk... thanks," he said then hurried out the door.

Mabel spent her first days home in her garden. It was not easy to unwind after the ordeals they'd experienced. Some she forgot and some ordeals that seemed trivial at the time, now rose to her thoughts and troubled her. She tossed and turned in the hammock, unable to get comfortable but appreciating it better than being confined to the carriage. She pined over Danny and Beth. She'd been anxious to return but hadn't understood that she would never see the children again. The bond between them had grown and now she felt a great loss.

"You're suffering from exhaustion," Auntie Louisa told her, "you'll feel better soon," then went to confide in Mabel's parents.

"She's deeply melancholic," Auntie told them. "What's to become of her when she ventures into town and is scorned or worse?"

"There will be no venturing into town," her father said, "my understanding is that she and Charles are to be leaving soon to Connecticut. There's been a messenger boy every day this week, carrying notes from Charles."

Auntie Louisa twisted a handkerchief she held in her hands. She'd never seen Mabel so distraught. "Traveling again with a man to whom she is not married?" She shook her head. "I said nothing before but look what it's brought." She walked to the window and peered out at Mabel's body lying limply in the hammock, in a beautiful full white dress, tied at the waist with a large bow. Her hair hung wild and free, one arm dangled loosely over the side of the hammock, her leg on the opposite side dangled down to the ground, firmly touching.

Mabel's mother stood behind Auntie Louisa and gazed at her daughter. Thin, white, silk, draping curtains hid the two women. "I fear I've been too protective of her," Vivian said.

Mabel's father twisted sharply in his chair, incredulous of her words. He and Louisa shared glances. Neither responded but chose to let Vivian speak her remorse, whether true or not.

"I wanted everything for my daughter," Vivian said, drawing closer to the window and pulling back the curtains to see her more clearly.

Mabel's father could not hold his tongue, "Vivian, you wanted everything for yourself. You were never pleased with the color of her skin."

Trancelike, Vivian turned her head toward him; her eyes were glazed and yellowed with age. She shook her head no then turned back to gaze at her lovely daughter. "I know how cruel the world can be. The minute I set eyes on that baby girl, I knew she was to be treated differently. I believe I've done a fine job," she let go of the curtain and turned to her husband. "She tells me she's quite wealthy now from the proceeds of her story. She's in love and about to marry one of Connecticut's more respectable gentlemen. He's quite handsome." They both remained silent. Vivian smiled and again pulled back the curtain. "I believe I've done a fine job as a mother... a fine job."

Charles' mother, Clarrisa, followed her usual morning routine then made her way up the wide, sweeping, marbled staircase, pausing every few steps to take a breath. Once settled in her room, surrounded in silken fabrics, perfume bottles and colorful, untouched bowls of fresh fruit, she lay down on her bed and propped herself with several large pillows. The window by her side was open two-thirds and a soft breeze blew at the curtains. The songbirds chorused and the smell of lilacs was carried in the breeze. Clarrisa was pleased. All the children were grown and it had been three weeks since any uncomfortable family crisis had arisen. No grand children in trouble at school, no squabbles between sister-in-laws and no business rivals in the world of shipping magnates attempting to destroy them. No, everything was peaceful and beautiful on Bluebird Pond. She folded her hands on her chest and closed her eyes. Her breathing slowed and her heart beat rhythmically. For twenty minutes, she lay in this position, a faint smile on her face, until she was disturbed by a light tap on the door.

"Yes? What is it?" she said annoyed at the disturbance.

"Mrs. Churchill, I thought you might want the newspaper. It arrived rather late this morning."

This was an untruth. Every morning the newspaper boy was prompt. The servant who was first to retrieve it would carefully read it, scan it for the latest news, fold it back up again, concealing that anyone had dared read it first, then delivered it to Clarrisa, the head of the house. But this morning the servant had stumbled across a story on page two about the identity of the author, Black Pansy of *American Heroes*, and revealed her to be a Miss Mabel

McCrutchon from Pittsburgh. On the society page, a reporter had gotten wind of the relationship between Charles and Miss McCrutchon and posted it. The paper had spent all morning going through the hands of each servant in the household, including the gardeners, who had all been reading, *American Heroes.* By the time the servant handed the newspaper to Clarrisa, it was terribly dog-eared, so he rushed quickly from the room. Clarrisa smiled when she saw the story about *American Heroes. I knew that story had a woman's touch,* she thought, proud of her sex. *And that a woman can be so bold,* she mused pleasantly. *Good for her.* She laid the paper on her chest, closed her eyes, and inhaled the fresh spring breeze. She opened her eyes and they began following through the latest news about home and abroad. When she reached the society page, she snuggled in better, making herself comfortable, as this was her favorite section. Who was marrying whom, who attended what university, who traveled to Europe or the Orient and the obituaries. Her eyes darted back and forth, back and forth then stopped dead on the name of her dear son Charles Churchill. Clarrisa sat up, pulled the paper up close to her face and read about Charles "presumed" engagement with a Miss Mabel McCrutchon of Pittsburgh, Pennsylvania. Nothing was mentioned about Miss McCrutchon being one and the same young lady who had penned the scandalous *American Heroes* series, they didn't have to! Everyone would make the connection. Why even she had a copy under her mattress! (A piece of trivia with which all the servants were aware). Clarrisa missed her scheduled return downstairs for brunch and stayed in her room, in bed, all day.

Charles rented a small carriage for the duration of his stay in Pittsburgh and did the driving himself. Mabel sat next to him as they trotted through the streets to meet and say a final good bye to those she was close to. Charles pulled to the curb, hopped out, quickly wrapped the reins round the hitching post and assisted Mabel down. Her hat was securely tied and her face hidden. Nonetheless, he hurried her into the hotel across from the newly reopened *News Herald* office. Burford was there to greet them, along with his wife, an attractive woman who made him an excellent companion. They brought all four children who shared the beauty of their mother and the firm bone structure of their father. Life was better for Burford after returning home, the compensation from Charles left him and his family secure, and ready to build upon the financial boost he'd received from driving Charles to New Orleans and back.

Annie and Victor were there and in love as much as ever. Whitethorn was there to wish Mabel and Charles well on their journey and new life together in Connecticut.

In between the laughing and talking, they ate fried chicken, potatoes and coleslaw. They'd barely finished eating when Charles, wisely, *told* Mabel they must go. Nervously he looked around. If word got around that Mabel was at the hotel, crowds would gather, crowds still unsure of their feelings for the girl who penned the great stories that they desperately needed to keep their minds off the "God awful war."

Tears were shed and promises were made to reunite but all knew in their hearts... they may never meet again.

Bluebird Pond

"The journey is not near as far," Charles told Mabel, "but just as dangerous. The war has divided the country, no one is of calm mind."

She said nothing as the small carriage rambled through the streets of Pittsburgh. Mabel knew they'd reached their first destination when she saw other travelers standing around various wagons. Charles bought passage for them through an outfit called, 'Appalachian Wagon Travel'. They had no illegal stolen slaves, just he and Mabel. As long as Mabel, "kept her head down," he told her, all would be fine. He did not feel she need worry about their noticing that she was "Colored."

"The war is not solely fought because of the Negro," she reminded him. "The politics of agriculture where the farmer who uses Negro slaves has an advantage over the farmer who does not..."

"Wise to keep your thoughts to yourself Mabel," he said to her while waiting for his turn to square away his paperwork and get them situated in a wagon that would be shared with another couple. "Good practice for meeting my mother." His words surprised her. She had not thought much about meeting his mother.

Once the wagons were assigned, Mabel and Charles found they'd been paired with a French-Canadian and his British wife, Pierre and Jane. They were headed all the way to Nova Scotia, Pierre having brought Jane to Indiana to start a new life. Jane had detested pioneering so they were returning to Nova Scotia where Jane's family awaited.

Pierre was loath to return. Jane's British family were not fond of him simply because he was of French "stock" as they put it. Pierre found it difficult to live in Nova Scotia, as it had been the homeland of the French until the British drove them out. "Nova Scotia was first Acadia... New France," he enjoyed reminding them.

Jane and Mabel enjoyed one another's company. Mabel was well-read, Jane, though not as well-read, had read a few of the same books, and they passed the hours away discussing various stories. Charles kept one ear on their conversation, fearing Mabel may be tempted to reveal her writing success and the other on Pierre who droned on too much about the British, the ethnicity to which Charles belonged.

At night, the wagons circled and the travelers retrieved their musical instruments. One of the more popular songs was, *Oh Susanna*, which Charles reminded everyone was more popular for travelers heading to California than Connecticut. That statement made everyone laugh and Mabel playfully lead them in one more round of the chorus. *Camptown Races* was another popular tune as were tunes referring to Negro slaves to which Mabel didn't seem to notice but knew every word and sang from her heart.

Charles rarely joined in the singing but appreciated seeing Mabel enjoy herself. He was content to sit by the fire with Pierre who knew much about the latest news from both armies. When they were alone, Mabel would question Charles thoroughly and use the information in her story that she worked on profusely, telling Jane and Pierre, "It's my journal."

The days were long and many nights were cold. They passed through forests of white pine, maple and hemlock. Two scouts on horseback rode ahead, returning with any news of danger. Their days had been blessed with peace during a time when the lives of thousands were lost. Brother against brother, family against family, the nation torn apart. The outfit downplayed any negative episodes but in the distance, the travelers saw clouds of smoke and the too familiar sound of cannons reached their ears. They were told nothing, the outfit relying on safe travels to be their vanguard. There were days when the outfit would announce a day of fishing. All knew it was to wait for safe passage but none protested, trusting the wisdom of the outfit and appreciating the soothing elements of nature, rushing water and tall endless trees.

Along the journey, Charles would point out Quakers. "How do you know they're Quakers?" Mabel would ask.

"The men wear collarless coats and wide brimmed black hats. The women and children wear very simple clothes. No adornment. And I know a Quaker wagon when I see one."

He knew they were drawing closer to Connecticut when along the way he began running into Quakers that he knew or recognized. Though Mabel could see and tell by their conversations that Charles was apprehensive about seeing his parents and she meeting them, he looked forward to it.

Though they are "a strange family," as he put it, they were quite fun to be around and usually kind and loving to one another. Charles warned Mabel to not ask too many questions regarding his mother and father's relationship, as he was not sure his father did not have another "wife" somewhere. His mother and father both seemed content with the relationship; they were loving partners but had not shared a bed as long as he could remember. "My father is very discrete about it," Charles told her thoughtfully, "and there's a lot of great gossip in the family regarding this topic although it is usually carried on by my brothers' wives," he put his head down. "We don't particularly care to discuss it." He looked at her seeking mercy. She was seeing his vulnerable side.

"Please tell me more about your family's home in Wethersfield," Mabel asked Charles as the wagons lumbered along and they reclined on top of colorful quilts.

"My family has been in Wethersfield since 1649."

"Really..."

"It's one of the oldest settlements in the United States."

"What took them to Connecticut?"

"Great river flows to the sea. My father and his brothers build ships on the harbor for merchants who export timber and grain to the Caribbean. The merchants return with rum and molasses, sugar, salt..." he looked to see if she thought of the slaves who worked on those humid islands to produce the precious commodities. Her expression told him she did.

"Our home is on Bluebird Pond," he said changing the subject. "Big beautiful home, surrounded by an acre of lawn, flowers and gardens. Although the garden isn't as cozy and personable as yours," he drew comfort thinking of Mabel's garden and she looked a bit homesick at the thought but quickly put it aside.

"Who lives in the Great House?"

Charles laughed heartily. "Very good question. My mother and father, their five servants and two gardeners are the official residents but my sisters still hold bedrooms and their children and my brother's children visit often. They all live nearby."

Arriving in New Haven, Connecticut, Mabel and Charles said their good-byes to Pierre and Jane. They'd developed a cordial friendship but believed they would not see one another again.

While Charles procured a carriage and driver to take them to Wethersfield, he had Mabel sit outside in front of the carriage company on an ornate iron bench. She sat and admired the beauty of Connecticut in the spring. A light sea breeze blew as vendors paraded by in carts and wagons. The pace was slow, people were friendly and because slavery was abolished many years back, Charles encouraged Mabel to be free as she was.

"Let your hair down," he told her and grabbed at her hat she held in her hand. "Get rid of this old thing," he said pulling it from her and walking to a trash barrel where he tossed it in.

Mabel looked as if he'd wrenched a puppy from her hands. She smiled timidly then went to the barrel to retrieve it. The barrel was tall and empty. Mabel had to bend at the waist almost throwing herself into the barrel. She struggled to reach it, while Charles stood idly by, embarrassed.

"Charles!" he heard a man's voice say.

It was Malcolm Ivers with his young wife Natalie, neighbors of the Churchill's on Bluebird Pond. The sound of Mabel rattling the barrel distracted them. Malcolm and Natalie both turned to look.

"Charles," Mabel's voice echoed in the barrel, "will you come help me retrieve this hat?"

In disarray from the long journey, not having freshened up since the day before, Mabel pulled her head out. She'd not heard Malcolm greeting Charles so was quite surprised and even more embarrassed.

"Oh hello," she said softly. Her thoughts went first to her unruly hair. Her hands felt for the degree of disarray. Understanding it was unpresentable, Mabel quickly put her hat on bringing a giggled outburst from Natalie and a big grin from Malcolm.

Mabel looked at the trash barrel then back to Natalie and Malcolm. "Oh no... it isn't... I didn't..." she put her hand on top of her hat pushing it firmly on her head. "It's my hat. You see, it's very important to me this hat..."

Charles stood smiling. He loved Mabel and everything about her. He loved seeing her talk her way out of her first Connecticut social faux pas.

"This hat has been everywhere with me," she said in a high-pitched trembling voice. "It has protected me."

Malcolm and Natalie looked bewilderedly at one another, shrugged, smiled at Charles and nodded politely at Mabel. Malcolm tipped his hat, took one last wayward glance at Mabel and arm in arm he and Natalie strode off.

Mabel pouted and returned to her spot on the bench.

"You're very tired love," Charles tried comforting her.

"Yes. I'm plumb exhausted. But that does not excuse me from humiliating you and making a fool of myself in front of your friends."

"They're my parent's neighbors."

"Well, my first impression should sit well with them. Your mother will get an earful, I know how people talk."

"At Bluebird Pond?" he said teasing her. "Talk about others?" he laughed and Mabel heard something in his laugh. *Was it a bit devilish?*

Mabel stewed on the bench while Charles arranged with the carriage company to deliver them to the Cove. He left the storefront office with paperwork in hand. Folding it securely he placed it in the inside pocket of his silk vest.

"Mabel, we are forty miles from the Cove. We'll stay here this evening. There's an inn on the outskirts of town. It will offer us more privacy. Are you up for a walk? I'll have our bags delivered but what say you and I walk in this brisk Atlantic air?"

She nodded pitifully. He put his arm tenderly around her waist. She tied the hat ribbons under her chin and they walked slowly up the road to the inn.

It was an uphill climb to the inn. Mabel enjoyed Charles hand on her waist and she sensed he enjoyed having it there. They'd refrained from any intimacy. Not since their trip to New Orleans had they been alone together. Due to their not being married, they behaved platonically on the wagon trip and when they arrived at the inn Charles booked them in separate rooms for which Mabel was grateful. She needed the luxury of brushing out her hair, bathing and grooming in private. And she needed rest. She'd been looking forward to meeting Charles' family but now she felt doubt and the confidence she naturally possessed seemed to dissipate into the misty sea air. Before bathing, she had a good cry but it only seemed to weaken her. *Where was the strong confident nature of her former self?* She stewed and lay about the bed in her filthy dress, too tired to rise. She fell asleep and did not awaken until the wee hours of the morning when all was quiet except the simple banging of shutters from the sea breezes. She lamented that she'd

190

lost her opportunity to eat and bathe. The inn offered a warm bath only until eight o'clock. With all the strength she could muster, she washed up with a large pitcher of water. She did her best to comb the tangles from her hair. She put fresh clothes on but they did not energize her. She could sleep for days. She began to question if she cared much whether the Churchill's found her pleasant or not. She sank back onto the bed and fell asleep until the next morning when she heard a loud knocking at her door.

"Mabel... Mabel?" she heard Charles voice.

With difficulty, she pulled herself from the bed and pulled open the door.

"Oh dear," Charles said when he saw the dark circles under her eyes and her puffy face. "I see you're not feeling well. You look terrible. It's all my fault. I've been dragging you all over the countryside..." he paused then couldn't resist a jab, "although it was your very bold writing under the pen name of Black Pansy that contributed to our leaving Pittsburgh."

Mabel glared at him, then looked away and nodded.

"How's the ol' story coming along?" he jested.

She resented his enthusiasm first thing in the morning. *What is he so happy about?* She waved her hand in the air dismissively. "I've not been writing much lately... but I will," she said with a hint of threat. "Do they know?"

"About Black Pansy?" Charles said lacking concern, "of course not. How could they? We are far, far, away from all that." He closed the door behind him and put his hands on her waist. "You're plain and simply Mabel McCrutchon from a lovely little garden, from a delightful home in Pittsburgh."

Mabel nodded and grabbed her hat.

The carriage horses cantered briskly through the marshland meadows where farmers toiled cutting hay. Beyond the low meadows and vernal pools lay thick forests of oak, maple and elm. Across the river cattle grazed on tall spring grasses in the sleepy, warm sun.

"Can you smell the onions?" Charles asked the unusually quiet Mabel who stuck her nose up and sniffed.

"Yes, I do smell onions."

"Would you like to hear the story of the Onion Maidens?"

She smiled and grabbed at his forearm with both hands and rested her head against his shoulder.

"The Onion Maidens did the work of weeding and hoeing the onions. With the money they received, they bought beautiful silk dresses. They were so beautiful in their finest silk, they remain a legend to this day. And today, my father's shipyard works with the farmers who export hemp, Indian corn and seeds... lots of seeds are grown here."

"And onions. Don't forget the onions."

"No, of course not, nor ever the Onion Maidens."

"Do you think I'll wind up an Onion Maiden?"

He pulled back and looked at her, surprised she'd forgotten. He sat back and patted her thigh with the arm he'd wrapped around the lower part of her waist. He looked out upon the hay fields thoughtfully. "Have you forgotten? You've quite a nest egg from the syndication of *American Heroes*."

"Actually, I had forgotten. Funny isn't it... how things change?"

"Change?" he said, his voice insecure.

Charles' mother kept silent about Mabel and Black Pansy. She had no idea her servants knew every detail. Clarrisa would do nothing to tarnish Charles' name, nor hers. She would do all in her power to prevent Wethersfield from knowing the truth about Miss McCrutchon. She would pull Charles aside and ask him nicely to discontinue his relationship with her. If that proved unsuccessful, she would insist he not use her last name.

When Clarrisa received Charles letter saying he was coming, she had informed the servants and asked them to prepare a hearty welcome. The servants got together for tea and compared their knowledge. Some of the stories about Black Pansy had grown ridiculous. "She'd come from the Wild West where she'd been a saloon girl." She "had been the wife of a pirate " or "the wife of a Confederate general." In all instances, she'd been a woman of the world with a mind of her own.

As the carriage drew near Wethersfield and the Cove where the Churchill estate butted up to Bluebird Pond and a large expanse of green, Mabel's spirits picked up. The long driveway lined with flowering cherry trees welcomed them. The afternoon sun shined brightly on the white home and struck the enormous brass door handle of the oversized door. Charles' father and his brothers built ships and he'd learned to think it wise to have wide entries. But *that* wide a doorway was unnecessary and was a frequent family joke.

Clarrisa's servant Liza, hurried to open the door but Clarrisa rudely brushed her aside. Offended, Liza retreated to the servants' parlor where they had agreed to meet and exchange gossip. Clarrisa swung open the door. The sun shone so brightly on her, it was difficult to read her expression but Mabel could tell by Charles' and her warm affection that they were very close, in spite of what Charles may have implied and in regard to his closer relationship with his Auntie Lena.

Other than Clarrisa giving Mabel the once over and she feeling it derogatory, Charles' mother was overtly friendly albeit a little pushy about sending Mabel off with the servants to clean up after the "long ordeal." Liza, the servant in charge of the main floor, was enlisted with the task of showing Mabel to her room and drawing her a bath while Mabel studied the architecture of the home, the tallest ceilings she'd ever seen and rooms so wide she couldn't help but wonder if Frederick Churchill's shipbuilding influence wasn't at play throughout the house. Mabel still had her hat on when she and Liza entered the guest quarters. When Mabel removed her hat and Liza, a very white skinned English girl saw Mabel's face she was stunned. Mabel, immediately offended by not only Liza's bad manners but her shallowness of mind, held the young woman's gaze. Liza became flustered, showed Mabel where everything was, then quickly ran out and to the servant's parlor.

"She's Negro!" Liza squealed. "She's Negro!" she squealed again, kicking her feet excitedly under the chair where she sat with two other servants.

"Really!" the other two said, eyes wide.

"It didn't say that in the paper," one said to her while the other agreed.

Liza kept squealing over and over in a high pitch. "She's a Negro!"

"Shh..." the others told her. "Shh..."

Mabel sat angrily in the tub using the bubble bath provided. Her exquisite brown skin contrasted beautifully against the white bubbles. Her dark brown eyes were glassy from recent tears shed. One well-formed arm and slender shapely leg hung gracefully from the side of the white porcelain tub, its brass, claw feet ornamentally holding the tub in place. Mabel wished she could stay in there forever, perhaps slide into the water, and drown, accidentally on purpose. But she knew the manners her mother and her Aunt Louisa had taught her must come into play now, in spite of her deeply bruised feelings. Numbly she rose from the tub. Standing nude, her light-brown hour-glass figure faced the doorway, white suds stuck here and there, including in her chocolate brown hair she'd pinned up gracefully with several wet wisps of long hair sticking sensuously to her dripping wet body. The door opened without a knock. It was Charles. Too late for manners, he stared at her beauty. From deep within, beyond the realms of sexuality, above the heights of intellectualism, somewhere where people's souls collide, clash and fall in love he felt for her a fire, a love, a need, a want and a satisfaction of knowing she was his.

"Oh my God," he said, deeply moved by all of her loveliness. He shook his head in disbelief. "I've made love to you in the moonlight and in a hay barn but... you are... more lovely..."

She smiled only lightly. Her modesty had her hurriedly reaching for a towel but unbeknownst to either of them, before her hand touched the towel, a gardener walked by and Charles had foolishly left the door ajar. The gardener hurried to the parlor where Liza was still squealing, "She's a Negro, she's a Negro."

"She is a beautiful woman," the gardener said with a cat-like grin. He let out a deep sigh. "She is the most beautiful woman I have ever seen."

The servant girls laughed at him until they saw how deeply moved he was.

They weren't sure whether to feel guilty or ashamed.

By the time Mabel made her way downstairs Charles' father had arrived, having left the shipyards early in order to greet Charles and his "lady friend." Frederick was all business all the time. Not that he wasn't jovial, he was a lot of fun, when he was around, which was infrequent. Like Charles, Frederick wore a gold pocket watch and chain clipped to his vest. But where Charles would look occasionally, Samuel would look continually at the pocket watch, as if someone or something had ownership of his time. Mabel noticed right away that Frederick Churchill lived in two worlds and that pocket watch helped him navigate between them.

It was obvious that Frederick was smitten with Mabel from the beginning. He fired questions at her. Impressed with her intellect, he kept raising his eyebrows and nodding at Charles, pointing at Mabel each time he agreed with her. Finally, he said to Charles, "You should marry this girl."

"I plan on it Father. Mabel has agreed to marry me."

Clarrisa blew a deep disgusting breath from her belly.

Frederick slapped Charles on the back, looked at his pocket watch, promised to return as soon as work was finished and made his exit.

Clarrisa was unfazed by her husband's departure even though she would not see him again until the following afternoon. Frederick Churchill's family life on Bluebird Pond was sporadic. Where he took his meals or slept when away was a mystery. Though it would be easy to figure out, none endeavored.

Mabel was left alone with Clarrisa, who was silent and in bad sorts making Mabel long for her Auntie Louisa and even her mother, whom she realized now, truly loved her. But the silence was broken by a chain of Charles' siblings with their spouses and their children flowing through the wide door, filling up and warming the house with their presence and friendly exuberance.

"Thomas," Charles said with his hand on the shoulder of his brother, the eldest in the family, "this is my fiancé' Mabel McCrutchon."

Clarrisa winced then blurted out from her luxury chair near the foyer, "No need of last names Charles, let's not be formal."

Charles glanced his mother's way but she was not foremost on his mind.

"Sophia," he said motioning to his sister, a handsome tall brunette looking much like himself, "come, come, you're next in line. Sophia, meet Mabel McCrutchon."

"Last names only, Charles," his mother shouted again, to which he responded, "Yes Mother," then rolled his eyes.

"John, you're next." John was the shortest of the boys, a stocky fellow with sandy brown hair, a round chubby face and crystal blue eyes like his mother. "John... Mabel... Mabel... John," Charles said, while children got underfoot but reached up and smiled at Mabel. "Hello Mabel," began a chorus of young voices.

Charles' introductions went on with Joseph, Nathan, Prudence, Emily, August and Flora. By the time all the Churchill introductions were through, siblings' spouses were introduced. The spouses were friendly but the exuberance and confidence rested in the personalities of the Churchill's and Mabel felt quite at home.

A long table was filled. The evening was spent being waited on by servants, eating Wethersfield's agricultural bounty and discussing the war. Thomas, John and Joseph had finished their schooling, all three had gone to Harvard. Nathan and August were working in their father's shipyards. The young men emotionally expressed an obligation to serve the Union, but none spoke of enlistment.

"I'm all for liberating the Negro from his servitude but not sure I want to risk my life over it," Joseph confessed.

"Nor I," said Thomas, "I've a family and a farm. We own no slaves, never have. Why should we..."

August cut him off, "It's an ugly institution that must be stopped. I've been debating enlisting. I can handle myself with a gun."

The table was silent for quite some time. Only the clinking of silver knives and forks on French china. The silence was broken by one of the children, Arthur, a little boy of about five.

"Are you a slave?" he asked Mabel, to a collective gasp.

"Arthur!" Charles shouted, then turned to Mabel, "I'm sorry Mabel."

She nodded and drew strength that was hers. "No, Arthur I am not a slave. Most of my ancestors were white, like you. The rest of my family are very white but for some reason I look a bit like my great-great-grandmother who was."

"Oh," Arthur said. "I think you're pretty. I'm glad you're not a slave."

"Well thank you Arthur," Mabel said, "I'm very glad I'm not either. Very, very glad."

The whole table was quiet. Clarrisa sat at the head. Mabel could see her expression. It was one of pleasure.

"I'm so sorry Mabel," Charles said to Mabel after dinner when the two took a walk along the pond.

"Charles, I always thought my mother was cruel for keeping me hidden. I thought she was ashamed of me but now I realize she was only protecting me. I always felt her love. I wish now..."

"Oh, don't be remorseful, your mother probably knows."

Mabel shook her head. "My mother and I need to talk about our feelings. When I go home..."

She looked at Charles with pleading eyes. He looked away. They'd not discussed where they would make their home but Charles had hoped it would be in Wethersfield. Mabel hadn't been out of Pittsburgh until he came into her life and now it seemed she had no interest in staying put. He put his arm around her and wrapped her shawl tightly to keep the river breeze off her back. They walked slowly back to the house.

After several quiet, uneventful days of relaxation, Charles left Mabel alone for several days while he met with the Quakers, the Society of Friends. Mabel stayed in her room, occasionally venturing outside in the nice weather. While in her room she wrote but was afraid to take her work outside for fear she would have to lie or explain herself. Clarrisa avoided conversation with her and the servants were polite. Mabel was unmoved by Clarrisa's cold shoulder, she was immune to that, which aggravated Clarrisa who turned up the iciness. Still, Mabel was unmoved. But trouble began brewing about four hours before Charles returned around seven in the evening. It was three o'clock when Mabel's door hadn't shut all the way and she heard whispering and crept quietly to the door to listen.

"I've never seen the Mistress so dour," a female voice said softly.

"Yes, she's out of sorts... it's that little Black Pansy in there, restin' up," another female's voice said sarcastically.

Mabel felt like she'd just eaten a dozen hot peppers. Heat rushed through her body. *They know.*

"Do ya think the Mistress knows she's the lil' tart whose ben' writin' them stories 'bout *American Heroes?*"

"I know it! I saw the book under her mattress when I went ta' flip it. And then I saw the newspaper had the story 'bout her son bein' engaged to Miss McCrutchon. She knows alright, it's why she's so out of sorts and taking it out on us."

"When's the lil' tart leavin'?"

"Don't know. Charles is supposed to be back tonight."

"Isn't he dreamy?"

"Yes, I'd love to pull him aside and have my way with 'em in the pot pantry."

Mabel heard laughter and more whispering but she'd heard enough. She sat upon her bed not knowing which way to proceed. As her anger welled she contemplated walking into the Servant's parlor and shocking the sass out of them. As Charles' fiancé, she had clout. But Mabel was a kind girl and would rather spend her time reading well-written literature than becoming involved with servant girls whom she would never see again. But wait. She would see them again if she stayed at Bluebird Pond, she would see them continually, day after day. *Perhaps I should befriend them*, she thought but dismissed it immediately. She had no interest in simple-minded women who spent their days talking about other people. She liked to spend her thoughts on ideas and politics, history and great literature. She looked down at her latest manuscript lying on the bed. She'd not written anything of substance in weeks. Yes, she'd been swept away with passion and yes, it was naughty but it was her best writing. Whitethorn told her that the louder the outcry over her *immoral* writing, the more the readership grew. And the deeper entrenched the country became in war, the more the public cried out for an escape. *This dreadful war... when will it end?* She looked again at her manuscript, picked it up and began writing. With a smile on her face, she thought of the two servants who were critical of her and she outlined characters as closely resembling them as possible. She went to the door to listen. It was quiet but she heard the rustle of papers in their parlor. Bravely Mabel walked to the door and poked her head into the parlor. Only one servant remained, Liza sat reading a pile of old newspapers.

"Hello," Mabel said.

Liza stiffened and straightened out the papers, used to authorities taking command of her time and attention. Mabel drew satisfaction from her fear. Mabel smiled as she leaned into the doorframe. She studied Liza's features and coloring, her expression and her emotions. Feeling uneasy about speaking up to Mabel she said nothing while Mabel made mental notes of her characteristics.

"What are you reading?" Mabel asked curiously and not without a hint of sarcasm.

"Nothing Ma'am, just the news."

She called me Ma'am. "Read any good books lately?"

Liza's face took on her own sarcastic smile. "No Ma'am, not today."

There was something in Liza's smile that captured Mabel's nature. She and Liza were more alike than she and any of the females in Charles' family. Mabel sat down.

"When you do read a story, what do you like best?"

"Oh Ma'am,"

Mabel put her hand on Liza's. "Call me Mabel. No one ever calls me Ma'am."

Liza nodded. "I like to follow two characters who are in love. And I like it when..." she stopped.

"Go on."

Liza was red, "Well... I enjoy reading..." she looked up, still red faced. "It's not proper Ma'am...sorry... Mabel. It's not proper for a lady to say. Not proper 'tall."

"Ohh..."Mabel taunted her. "You mean to tell me you like..." Mabel was delighting in catching her hypocrisy, "a story that is a wee bit... naughty?"

"Yes. That's what I'm saying." Liza understood that Mabel had heard their conversation and had gotten even with her. But Liza was to take no more of Mabel's abuse. She gathered her papers, teacup and saucer and rolled up the remaining caramel cake into a white linen napkin. "Excuse me," she said, almost pushing Mabel aside.

"You're excused," Mabel said rudely.

Liza scurried down the hall and down the gigantic stairway. Mabel scurried after her. Liza kept turning back, feeling that Mabel was stalking her but Mabel turned in the opposite direction and entered the large glassed in greenhouse. Wandering through African broad-leafed plants, agricultural seed sprouting for the summer garden, a few orchids and a collection of violets, Mabel drew strength. Surrounded by nothing but green and colorful flowers, she found a chair and sat down. She inhaled deeply the oxygen the plants gave out. Closing her eyes, she tilted her head back. Finally relaxing, she took in more deep breaths.

"Enjoying that are you Ma'am?"

Startled, Mabel stood up quickly. It was the gardener who had seen her glorious naked body when Charles foolishly left her door ajar. He'd read her risqué story and heard the terrible things the Servant girls had said about her. He had neither woman of his own nor brilliance enough to attract one. He was good with plants and that was the extent of it. In his ignorance, he'd not understood that Mabel was Charles' beloved and respected fiancée. His mind saw Mabel as a wild woman from the west who wrote tawdry novels based on her life's experiences. He believed she entered the greenhouse to seek him out. He imagined she'd seen him pass in the hallway while she stood bare and beautiful and his imagination had her wanting him as he wanted her. In his fantasies, he'd already had her, and would take her again now.

He walked to her. In his hand, he held a sharp knife he'd been using to divide rootstalks. He held it to her throat. "You like this?" he said running the blade against her soft skin but not piercing it.

Her face flushed with terror, she shook her head no. He ran the blade down the front of her dress and popped the top three buttons off with the sharp blade. He put his face into her breasts. She could feel his sharp whiskers and smell his foul breath. She glared at him, which angered him. With his free left hand, he ripped her blouse. Her full breasts spilled from her exposed corset. He ripped it again. Mabel screamed and the Gardener put his hand over her mouth. He pulled at his trousers and they dropped to the floor. He lifted the fullness of her petticoat and tried to prop himself into her.

"Mabel? Mabel?" she heard Liza calling.

Mabel's voice was muffled by the Gardener's hand on her mouth but she made enough sound that Liza heard.

"Mabel?"

Mabel stomped a foot as loudly as possible. Liza followed the noise and shrieked when she saw what the guard had come so close to doing.

"Mabel!"

The Gardener dropped his knife and let go of Mabel who trembled uncontrollably. He gathered his pants back to his waist and shot Liza a dirty look.

"Go away! Go!" Liza screamed. She carefully held Mabel and pulled the shreds of her dress to cover her bosom as she escorted her out. They left the greenhouse and walked to the massive stairway. Just when they started to climb the first stair Clarrisa came down the hallway from the kitchen. The girl's backs were to her.

"Liza?" Clarrisa asked.

"Yes Ma'am," she said timidly.

Clarrisa sensed all was not right and hurried toward them. "Liza..." she demanded, "turn around."

Liza did as she was told and Mabel's limp body swung around with her. The color had left Mabel's face and her dark eyes were frozen with the terror she'd just been victim of.

Clarrisa was disturbed when she saw the condition Mabel was in, her ripped dress, off color face and her glazed eyes.

"Good God," she mumbled angrily. "Who did this to you?"

"It was the Gardener Ma'am, I feared Mabel may be in danger so I went looking for her. He has a reputation Ma'am."

"And you never told me?"

"Yes Ma'am, I mentioned it before but you didn't believe..."

Clarrisa cut her short. "In my home? Under my roof?" she shouted.

Mabel hung there limply.

"I need to get her upstairs Ma'am. I'll put her to bed."

"Good God, I should say you will! And when you've finished come find me in the kitchen. I wish to speak with you."

"Yes Ma'am."

Liza struggled to get Mabel upstairs. Once Mabel inhaled some deep breaths, she came around more and began helping herself up the stairs.

"Thanks Liza," she said, then mustering up some dry humor, "for this I won't write about you in my story."

"Thank you Ma'am."

When Charles came home Liza and his mother, both wanting to get to him before he saw Mabel in the state she was in, descended upon him.

"It was a very close call," Liza told Charles who was enraged and wondering why the Gardener had not yet been fired.

"The man should be thrown in jail! Why haven't you summoned the Constable?"

"We'll wait for the facts," Clarrisa said not wishing to dismiss her favorite gardener. Frederick told her she was to have but one gardener and when one left there would be no replacing him.

"All the facts? Mother are you insane?"

She exposed her weak character by saying nothing.

"Thank you Liza, from the bottom of my heart," Charles said before racing up the stairs to comfort Mabel.

"Mabel!" he said running to her while she lay in bed.

He looked into her beautiful face as tears welled in her eyes then ran down her cheeks.

"I am so sorry, truly I am," he stood and looked down upon her. In a tantrum, he paced the floor not knowing what to do, think or feel. "In my own home!" he shouted loudly, his voice booming down the stairs where all could hear. The servants had gathered and Clarrisa had sent for Auntie Lena who had not yet met Mabel.

"I kept you safe through the worst of trials and in my own home you meet with this fate! I'll kill him! I'll wrap my fists around his neck and choke the life from him! I swear I will!"

Mabel shook her head and patted the bed for him to sit beside her. "It will give me ideas for my story," she joked.

He sat on the bed and buried his face in her lap.

When Charles' Auntie Lena arrived, Clarrisa whisked her away to speak privately. Charles came down the stairs just in time to hear his Auntie Lena say, "Why that's absurd! The man is still on the grounds?"

Clarrisa was tormented. She could not understand that the Gardener had shown a pattern of abuse toward women and that he was dangerous. "I wasn't there," she kept repeating. "I don't know what transpired. She may have solicited it."

"Solicited it!" Charles raged.

Auntie Lena went to Charles side, "You poor boy. Clarrisa, you know Charles wouldn't bring a woman like that here, into your home."

"She is Black Pansy."

Charles gasped. "You know about that?"

"Everybody knows about THAT!" Clarrisa bellowed. The whole house knows about THAT!"

Lena shook her head at Charles. "Black Pansy? Is that... the author... the one who wrote..."

"Yes, yes, it's my Mabel!"

"My Mabel," Clarrisa mocked him.

Lena shook a finger at her sister-in-law. "You show respect. Charles has yet to make a bad decision."

"Well he's making one now and the sooner he gets that tramp out of my house the better."

"Charles, bring Mabel to my house. I'll make her feel welcome."

Charles marched up to Mabel's room. "We're getting you out of here. That man is still on the grounds."

Mabel nodded. "Where are we going?" she asked softly.

Charles was distracted when watching her rise from the bed. She still trembled. "We're going to Auntie Lena's home. It's near, we can walk. Are you up to a nice walk?"

"Yes, that sounds nice and Auntie Lena sounds refreshing."

"Are you hungry?"

She shook her head no but he sent word for Lena to prepare a warm meal. Not a soul was in sight when Charles and Mabel descended the long flight of stairs. Clarrisa was in her bedroom and heard them leave but made no attempt to stir. She sat in front of her dressing table brushing out her thinning hair. She caught a glimpse of herself in the mirror but looked away. The door closed behind Charles and Mabel. They were off to the brighter side of Bluebird Pond.

The fresh air transformed Mabel. She would be forever cautious of men, especially gardeners, but she was strong-minded and grew stronger with each step they took toward Auntie Lena's.

"You alright?" Charles asked as he helped her walk.

"Yes. Just wondering how I can incorporate this experience into one of my episodes."

"Leave it out."

She stopped walking. She held tightly to his arm. "Where do you think I draw inspiration and ideas for my stories but from my own life."

"I guess that's true. Who are the heroes in this episode?"

"You, Auntie Lena and especially Liza. She rescued me just in time you know."

"I know, I spoke at length with her. She was very brave."

"Please see to it that she is rewarded."

"Absolutely. I will ..."

Mabel interrupted him. "No, I will."

Charles cleared his throat and loosened his shirt at the neck, "Yes, that's right. You have the ability to do that now don't you?"

Mabel said nothing but he could feel the spunk returning to her step.

For several days, Charles and Mabel lounged comfortably at Auntie Lena's. A gracious hostess, she always had bread baking, yams with fresh butter or a pie cooling in the window. Her home was but a cottage compared to her brother Frederick's. Lena loved her brother but had never been fond of Clarrisa, nor the children that took after her. Charles was a Churchill in disposition as well as name, just like his father. Clarrisa and several of the other Churchill siblings had latched on to the notoriety that being related to the Duke of Marlborough and England's Royal family brought them. One evening when the three of them were enjoying a hot cup of tea in dim candlelight and the hour was growing late, Lena let it slip that she knew more than anyone about the double life Charles' father Frederick led.

"Oh my, I've said too much," sincerely sorry she'd let it slip that she saw him on occasion when he didn't return home.

Charles was about to press her for more when there was a knock at the door. It was Charles' youngest brother August. He was nervous about arriving late but wanted to say good-bye, he was leaving in the morning to join with Union forces that were gathering at Camp Oakwood.

"You're going through with it?" Charles said, mixed emotions in his voice.

"Yes, I feel a sense of duty. President Lincoln has put out another call for volunteers. Charles, I can't sit idly by when so much is at stake." He looked at Mabel.

Why does this small portion of Negro heritage make such large impressions? Mabel thought to herself and as if August could read her thoughts he nodded to her.

"Father and some of the others send their best."

"Father is back? I hope to speak with him soon."

"Yes, he hopes to speak with you."

"*Some* of the family send their best?" Charles asked cynically. "Not *all* of the family?"

"Charles..." Lena tried to stop him.

"Yes. Mother has convinced several of the others that Mabel was ..."

"Enough" Charles said.

"My sentiments as well," Lena said, placing her oversized body back down comfortably in her chair.

"I believe Mabel," August said kindly. "I've never felt right about that gardener, he seemed to slither around. I've always hated the way he looked at my sisters. I hope you're feeling better Miss McCrutchon."

"Thank you August, and I hope you'll find luck and fulfillment in the Union Army and bring this dreadful war to a close."

"What are your plans Charles?"

"He's going to New York," Mabel butted in. "With me."

213

Charles thought it was a joke and laughed. Auntie Lena groaned. She knew Mabel was not ready to settle down, especially not at Bluebird Pond nor could she blame her. But she had hoped they would settle at least in Wethersfield. The family had been there for two hundred years.

"I'm very serious Charles. I want to find Jenny."

"Jenny?"

"Yes Jenny. New Orleans Jenny, remember? The slinky blond you seemed to know well."

August lit up. "I remember Jenny."

Charles gave August a warning glance but he missed it. "Charles used to bring Jenny for dinner. I was very little but I had butterflies for her," he laughed. "She was so pretty and had this beautiful southern accent."

"August... please."

"Oh sorry Charles," the younger brother said but Mabel could see he wasn't.

"I want to find her," Mabel turned to Charles. "You can find her can't you Charles?"

"Yes, of course the Friends will know where she is."

"We left her in a predicament, leaving with James."

"Yes, we did. And she did say she was going to New York didn't she?"

"I've not been to New York," Mabel chirped. Lena moaned again prompting a smile from Mabel.

"You'll love it," August told her.

Charles looked to August and Mabel and to his Auntie. "Sounds like we're going to New York!"

The morning Charles and Mabel prepared to leave the Cove, the water on Bluebird Pond lived up to its name. The morning sun hit the water in front of Auntie Lena's but no sun yet struck the Churchill estate where the water looked frigid and the wind created rough edges along the sandy beach in front of it. Mabel couldn't wait to leave but Charles was slow in his departure, running back and forth between his family home and Auntie Lena's. He'd spoken to his mother and she'd agreed to *try* to accept Mabel. She'd invited Mabel to come for one last dinner with the family but Mabel had refused, especially since Clarrisa was yet to remove the gardener who threatened Mabel's life and came very close to raping her.

"Charles is in a bit of a dilemma," Lena said to Mabel, her back to her while she flipped pancakes.

Mabel did not respond. She was fatigued of talking of it. Lena sensed that. "What are your plans in New York," she asked.

Mabel brightened. "Do you know Jenny?"

Lena flinched with the mention of Charles' former flame. "Yes, um hm..." she said nonchalantly. "Jenny, the one with the Southern drawl?"

215

Mabel smiled into her teacup. "Yes, that Jenny. We'll be seeking her out. Charles has sent word with his Quaker friends, she's not a Quaker..."

Lena interrupted carelessly, "No," then laughed, "no, Jenny is no Quaker," then laughed again.

Mabel took another sip of her tea but this time she was not smiling into it. "If she isn't a Quaker what's her relationship with them?"

"I've visited with Jenny only on two occasions and they were both at the large table surrounded by Charles' parents and siblings. We talked of many things, as we usually do at the supper table but I can't recall about the Quakers. I know she loves children, perhaps it has something to do with that."

"Perhaps."

"I know she wants no part in raising a family, which is why..." Lena stopped, scared she had once again revealed too much. Nervously she asked Mabel, "More tea?"

"Yes, I suspect Charles would love a family."

"And you?"

Mabel's mind wandered. Her eyes wandered out onto the pond where circling birds tilted their wings to the wind. Cattails stood tall and abundant, not yet crowding a profuse growth of purple iris and tiger lilies along the bank. The warm sun gave promise of another lovely day. "Doesn't every girl dream of having a family?" she waited for some kind of response from Lena. The silence was uncomfortable. "I'm not anxious to pop out ten children the way Clarrisa has done, why look at what it's done to her marriage. She and Frederick have not shared a bed in decades."

"Clarrisa has always been difficult. She was a sight to behold when she was young. She was very beautiful, tall, slender, porcelain skin, pretty, blue eyes. She looked a lot like..."

"Jenny? Yes, she is beautiful isn't she?"

"Yes she is," Lena submitted and with a sigh, "yes... and Clarrisa was too."

"Does Jenny have a drinking problem?" Mabel inquired still watching the birds tilt and glide.

"I'm afraid so. An emotional problem as well. Charles mentioned he saw her in New Orleans."

"Yes, and she appeared to have had too much to drink that day... although she was a great help. She was part of the plan..."

"Plan?"

Mabel assumed that Lena knew everything they'd been up to in New Orleans, she had after all, been the one to arrange Charles' connections with the Quakers, they were her old friends. "Sort of an Under Ground Railroad destination."

"Yes, yes, of course, that plan. Yes, Charles said she was fantastic living up to her end of the deal. I guess the others not so much?"

"They left her alone with the escaped children. Jenny was ill with it all."

"What's prompting you to seek her in New York? She's spends her days amongst the theatre crowd... you know... the poets, artists, novelists... she loves that crowd and New York has its share."

"Lena, I'm related to Jenny... distantly of course."

Lena was surprised at Mabel's revelation. "Related? You and Jenny Saint Francis?"

"It's a long story and a sad one but it has a happy ending..." she looked up at Lena, "that is if you believe that I'm a worthy person, worthy of living... the same as anyone who is one hundred percent white and not ninety-six percent white," she said the anger growing in her tone.

Lena sat down beside her. "Child, you are *more* valuable than the most of them. Half of 'em aren't worth a lick. And don't you ever forget that."

"I'll remember it well Lena."

"Please... call me Auntie."

Charles returned from one of his many efforts to smooth things over. "Are you sure I can't get you to stop and say good-bye to Mother?"

Lena stepped in. "Charles, for God's sake, have you forgotten what transpired? Your mother's gardener came a hair's breadth from violating your fiancé. He held a knife to her throat. Your mother accused her of soliciting! Where's your head Charles?"

"You're correct but ..."

"But what? Leave it be Charles."

"I know Mother," he looked fondly at Mabel. "I know that if she and Mabel can't work this out... well..."

"Well, you'll have to live your life without... your mother!"

Mabel shot a look at Lena. *Was she jealous of Charles' love for his mother?*

"My mother runs the Churchill clan. I know she'll eventually accept Mabel. She'll have to." He put his hand on Mabel's lap.

Mabel finished sipping her tea, rose and methodically kissed Charles on the cheek. "Has that Carriage man been waiting for two hours?"

"Yes. I'll get your bags. I had hoped..." he said to Lena who looked at him sternly.

"You had hoped to stay in Wethersfield. You would have liked to have a grand wedding right out there on the lawn." Lena waved her hand toward the direction that was the beautifully un-mowed deep green grass.

Charles nodded.

Lena leaned closely into him and whispered in his ear. "You've a few adventures yet with this girl," she said nodding her head sympathetically then shaking it. "Um mm, she is a live wire that Mabel," shaking her head again. "And be careful," she shook a finger at him, "she gets a little jealous of the other women. Better not divulge too much about your relationship with Jenny Saint Francis. And don't tell her about..."

"Lena, you are the only one who knows about that... and again I thank you so much for your assistance. I was such a boy then... it was ... difficult ... was it not?"

"Yes. It was... but we survived didn't we?"

Charles nodded and then Mabel entered the room. She'd heard everything they'd just discussed and it would not be long before she had a talk with Charles to find out just what it was Lena did not want Charles to divulge about he and Jenny Saint Francis.

Charles looked longingly at his family home as the carriage wound past the estates that backed up to Bluebird Pond. Mabel threw her nose in the air. Her hat was off but the ribbons to it she held tightly in her hands. The fresh wind blew at her hair. She closed her eyes. What a sense of freedom and relief to be on the road again. New York!

New York

There were several stops to be made where Mabel was introduced to a good many of Charles' Quaker friends. Most were literate and refined although their drab clothing frightened her. Alone in her thoughts she wondered what it would be like to belong to the Society of Friends but knew she could never give up her pretty dresses. Charles had spoiled her with the beautiful clothes he bought her. The thought of wearing plain drab, clothes for the sake of humility made no sense to her. *Isn't there beauty in nature? Aren't we to repeat it as best we can?*

"I've found where Jenny is," Charles told Mabel after making her wait in the carriage while he entered a rough area and walked into a pub.

"Charles, haven't you wondered why I want to see Jenny?"

"Of course not. I know your reason," he looked askance at her, trying his best to hide any anger.

"You do?"

"Yes. You want to know about Jenny and her great-grandfather..."

Mabel cut him short. "Yes. That's right."

"And... Benjamin Crocker."

Mabel held her hand to her heart. Her chest was pink from too much sun, her cheeks had been burnt as well but it did not hide the great flush that rushed to her face.

"Charles, if you think..."

"I know you've been thinking of him. Ever since you saw him you've had this air about you."

"Charles, you're forgetting that it was *after* I met Benjamin Crocker that we became intimate."

Thinking of intimacy made him uncomfortable. It had been a terribly long time since he had held her close and felt the loveliness of her body. He glanced down at it as he sat close to her, not hearing any of her ramblings about Benjamin Crocker. Charles knew Mabel loved him. Although he was not secure in his belief that she would stay with him or that they would make it to the altar, he would patiently wait out the days. He would indulge in her adventures, ignore her childish crushes, and occasional in poor taste passions.

Signs of war were evident everywhere they ventured. They saw soldiers walking home. Whether from illness, insanity or abandonment, they passed many a young man whose mind did not seem healthy. Each time they did Mabel wanted to stop and provide aid but Charles discouraged it. "They'll find their way," he'd say.

"Charles... what are you doing to help with the war?"

"Have you forgotten what we just went through? How you and I and Burford risked our lives to see that not five but six Colored children were freed?"

"No, I've not forgotten but what are you doing today?"

"What are you doing today?"

She kept quiet and made a mental note to prove not just to Charles but to all that she could and would have an impact on this bloody war. "I need more pens Charles. And I need to make more stops."

Charles continued gathering modest sums of money and put it with the large sum of his own money that he had wrapped in the luggage he never lost sight of. Mabel had no idea that he was acting as financier and banker for several other "missions" that were going on, not unlike the one they completed in New Orleans. Nor had Charles any idea that Mabel had once again penned an intriguing story, this time about the friendship between a Northern general, who owned slaves and a Southern Rebel leader who detested slavery. The military leader's names were changed but the story was based on truth she'd heard from Whitethorn. Since there had grown a chill between Charles and Mabel, she had plenty of time to work on her story when they stopped for lodging, each happy to be going to their own separate rooms. She'd written well into the night on many evenings and slept in the carriage during the day. She'd not yet let her readers down but kept the tawdry out of her stories, thinking that had been a mistake and hoping she could gain back their respect.

It was evening when they reached New York. The streets were alive. Horse manure was everywhere. Carriages darted in and out of alleys and streets. Horses were skittish, irritable or tired from overwork and large draft horses stood resting calmly next to wagons full of fruit and vegetables. Little boys ran around selling newspapers and delivering telegrams. Women dressed in the latest fashions walked the promenade, some with well-dressed children in tow others with handsome men, their faces pressed together, Mabel wondering what manner of bedroom talk commenced between them. Poverty stricken families in filthy clothes stood watching their sons playing marbles on the street corner and their daughters playing jacks. Music came pouring through windows and musicians stood on street corners, their violins playing sad or lively tunes, and accordion players made dreams come true for lovers willing to spare a nickel.

They were both hungry and spotted a restaurant with tables on the sidewalk out front.

"Oh let's do go there Charles, please," Mabel said lovingly, as if there had been no differences between them.

"Well..." he looked around then signaled to their carriage driver to stop. "Are you willing to carry your own weight?" he asked referring to her suitcases.

She nodded and they stepped out of the carriage and Charles paid the driver, same as he had paid every other driver they'd enlisted the services of since leaving the Cove. They grabbed their heavy luggage and set them on the sidewalk, Charles keeping a keen eye on his. Mabel paying no attention to hers. Charles spotted a newspaper rack and walked to it. "Watch my bag," he said. She nodded but continued being distracted by all the activity. "Watch my bag!" he yelled rudely. He bought a paper, returned to his luggage and she, pouting because he snapped at her, would not look at him. They took their seats at a table outside the restaurant but the noise of the streets, the smell of horse manure, burnt meat and every other imaginable human smell, including rotting produce had them think otherwise about the outdoor dining and grabbed their luggage and went inside. They had to step down when they walked in and Mabel hadn't noticed so took a tumble but corrected her fall. She laughed and was happy again at the thought of a nice meal. They both agreed on a private table in the corner and sat down. The waiter was quick with a menu and glasses of water.

"So how do you like New York?" Charles asked her.

"I do... I think I do... but the noise takes getting used to."

"And the smell," he laughed. "All the neighborhoods are not like this. We're on the end where poor immigrants live, those who come into the country with little assets. There are other neighborhoods... my father has friends..." he let it drop, not sure he wanted to visit his father's elite friends with *Black Pansy* in tow. He'd had enough of that.

"Lovely homes, no doubt?"

He nodded.

"Where's Jenny's place?"

"She's in the SoHo district, that's where the Bohemians live," he said sarcastically.

"Charles, I thought you appreciated artists."

"I do but the ones Jenny tends to associate with..." he got a terse look on his face and Mabel wondered if it had anything to do with he and Lena's secret.

"Does Jenny have history with one of these *artists?*"

Charles nodded.

"Care to elaborate?"

"No," he said and his expression let her know he didn't appreciate her prying.

"Why not?"

He ignored her and looked around the restaurant, looking for a distraction. The waiter came and took their order of fish and fried potatoes. While usually they took pains to use good manners at the dinner table, they were a lot more relaxed about the delicious food and ate heartily. After dinner, Charles implored her to not let his bag out of her sight. He needed to ask people the directions to SoHo. He was gone fifteen minutes then returned with a smile. "Seven blocks over."

"Seven blocks? That's an awfully long walk."

"You said you would carry your own weight."

She looked down at her heavy bag. Charles laughed and bent down and kissed her on the cheek. She looked into his deep-set eyes and the ring of fire encircling his iris. She admired the way he stood tall, his muscles naturally strong. His hair had grown long and thick, covering his ears. He usually kept it behind his ears but now locks covered his left ear. She reached up and with her finger tucked his hair behind his ear prompting a serious look from him.

"Shall we go?"

They didn't have to wait long before they found a carriage waiting to carry them to SoHo.

"Big cities are made up of neighborhoods. London, Paris, San Francisco, they're all like this. You never know what to expect. You can turn a corner and the whole street is a different culture," Charles said of the vibrant nature of cities.

"What type of culture does Jenny live in?" Mabel asked as she noticed the mood of the neighborhood changing.

Charles did not like that question and chose not to answer it. "Let's be happy," he said, putting his arm around her waist. She looked into his eyes. He bent down and kissed her lips. She nestled her head into his neck, felt his hair against her cheek. She brushed her nose against his skin. He could feel and hear her breath in his ear. Their pleasure was interrupted by the sudden stop of the carriage. "SoHo" the driver shouted.

"I have Jenny's address but we're more likely to find her in a bar near her address," he said sarcastically.

"Charles, that's not nice."

"No it isn't but it's true."

Charles found the building, a tall brownstone in a tree-lined neighborhood. Luckily, she lived at the bottom. It was an attractive building where two women sat out front on the stoop chatting.

"Either of you know Jenny?" Charles said then went on to describe her, "tall, blond, very pretty..."

"Charles..." Mabel interrupted, "give them her last name, not how beautiful she is."

"Jenny lives right through there," the women told him.

"Wait Mabel. Let me make sure she's here."

Charles knocked on the door the women had given him. It was the right number, it matched with his note. There was no answer. He knocked again louder. Still no answer. One more time he knocked, finally the door opened, slowly and cautiously. He could see her bulging, hazel-blue eyes peeking around the door. *He'd know those eyes anywhere and that smile... his heart felt a little pang.*

"Charles!" he heard Mabel's voice.

Jenny smiled. "You braught' her, I see," she said, with the same thick southern accent he'd grown to love. She stood beautifully erect, a bit on the thin side but that was her usual *unwilling to eat* physique.

Without Mabel peering over his shoulder and watching his every move and dart of eye, he was able to glance at Jenny, see what she wore, feel her presence, sense her presence and detect any abnormalities either in her or in himself that might create friction.

There were none. Just the electricity that had once been there, still working its magic but when before it capitulated into something beautiful when their bodies met, now it arched, with nowhere to go. He was hungry though, denied way too long of the touch a woman can offer a young man so Jenny could feel his longing for her, knowing it wasn't exclusively for her but for any beautiful woman who should come within a foot of him. She smiled and turned in such a way that exposed and let fall over her shoulder the silkiness of the evening dress she wore. Jenny loved attention from men. She could make a man feel like a king but Charles felt she would never love just one man and her sexual appetite combined with her love of spirits brought only grief to herself and the men who loved her. The night Charles had come upon her ... it pained him to think of it... with two men in her bed... *And to think my mother loves Jenny and hates Mabel, she is so wrong about them both!*

"Charles!" he heard Mabel calling.

Sheepishly he looked at Jenny. "I believe that's your cousin," he said then smiled, believing Jenny would take pressure off he and Mabel's relationship for a few days.

Jenny did not respond.

The *News Herald* was a lively meeting place. Reliable sources came in to help Victor and Whitethorn report the status of the war.

Their latest story, alongside Mabel's *American Heroes*, was that of Kentucky. As Pennsylvania's neighbor, Kentucky's role was of great interest to Pittsburgh. There were no planned invasions of Kentucky, unless Rebel Armies came to occupy it. Kentucky's governor was implored to preserve the state's neutrality. If he was unable to, Union soldiers would be sent there to do it for him.

The hotel restaurant across the street was the place to go for those who wanted to argue war issues. An argument about the name of the war, *War of Rebellion*, used frequently by the Union Army, *Freedom War*, the term favored by Negroes, *War for Southern Independence* and *War of Northern Aggression*, favored by the Rebels, became so heated they had to take it outside. Some witnesses reported that guns were drawn. The next day another argument broke out regarding the boundary line two surveyors, Mr. Mason and Mr. Dixon drew before the war. Whether or not that was an accurate spot, between Pennsylvania and Maryland to separate the free Northern States from the Southern Slave Sates, was a contentious issue for weeks.

And there were always folks coming in and asking about Mabel. The community loved the story and had grown proud of its popularity. Miners in Alaska read it. Spaniards and Germans read it and it was rumored that one of the members of the Royal Family in London was overheard talking about it. Word was they were quite proud that their distant American cousin, Charles Churchill, was engaged to the author, Black Pansy, but would never go on record as such. Every day folks came in asking Whitethorn when the next installment would be out. "I'll tell you what I tell everyone else. It comes when it comes and I never know when it's coming," he told them.

Whitethorn was proud of Mabel and made sure that the profits went mostly to her, with a fifteen percent cut for himself, out of which he paid Victor regular bonuses and compensated well, the printers and newspaper that distributed it for him.

Jenny greeted Mabel kindly. She'd thought a lot about their meeting in New Orleans. Mabel had seen her at her worst. She'd been there by herself, abandoned by the others and in such a state of boredom and fear, she'd drunk too much, and for that she apologized to Mabel.

"I am truly sa'rry," Jenny said. Mabel smiled when she spoke, she'd grown to like the sound of her accent.

"No apologies necessary. I've come for a reason."

Jenny shared glances with Charles making Mabel feel they were poking fun at her. She ignored them and continued. "I want to... need to know more about my past. I want to know everything you know. I suppose..." she hesitated, it was difficult to speak of, especially with the gardener's attempted assault on her, "we're cousins?"

Mabel would have never thought Jenny's bulging eyes could get any larger but they did. And Mabel was tired of the glances she and Charles kept exchanging but waited patiently for Jenny's answer.

"Cuz'ins? Well, I 'spose... but down sa'th if a masta' takes lib'aties with a Negro slave and a child rez'ultz from that... union..." she paused and again glanced at Charles before continuing, "they hawd'ly call that child a cuz'in."

Mabel put her head down. She felt an instant swelling of her cheeks that spread across her face and to her ears. She looked to Charles but his face was not turned toward hers but toward Jenny and the look he had was of mortification. Jenny saw that look and being a compassionate woman and developing a fondness for Mabel spoke softly.

"But yes, I ass'ume we are... Cuz'ins, as you put it," then she smiled genuinely and Mabel felt a welcoming in her eyes and warmth flowing from her heart.

The three spent the evening talking of old Crocker family history, telling Charles what she knew about the Quakers in the New York area, the ideas they had and about those who'd collected contributions for the cause of aiding Negro children and seeking their freedom. Nothing was mentioned about Jenny and Charles former relationship nor did Jenny taunt Charles the way she had in New Orleans but nor had she had any liquor that evening.

Charles father, Frederick Churchill was pleased when he received a letter from the English Churchill's congratulating him on his son Charles' engagement to such a woman of such fine literary accomplishment.

"You're a reminder that America has its share of Puritans," Frederick said snidely to Clarrisa during one of his rare evenings at the dinner table with the whole family, including Auntie Lena.

Clarrisa had not fared well since Mabel's visit. She slouched and never smiled and her face had taken a downward slide. She spent every waking moment trying to convince everyone attached to the Churchill estate, including the servants, that Mabel McCrutchon was a very bad woman and that Charles was making a huge error. Charles' siblings would nod in agreement, just to appease her. Most of his siblings were indifferent to Mabel. Charles had brought other women to the dinner table and they were not sure they should be distressed over his latest. Some felt he may never marry.

"But the English Churchill's..." Clarrisa said, then paused making sure *everyone* at the table was listening, "can't truly mean that Black Pansy is a literary accomplishment." She shook her head dismally.

"I think she's jealous," Prudence whispered to her sister Flora.

"They do!" Frederick said, "you've seen the letter. They're proud of our association with her. They've invited Charles and her to England!"

233

Clarrisa lifted the large silver gravy ladle and slowly spilled the thick warm liquid into her bowl while she planned her next words. "I have never received an invitation to their home. Why on earth would they invite a woman who writes smut? It doesn't make sense and I refuse to believe it."

"Well, I have just fired your gardener. Do you believe that?" he said curtly.

"You did not! Not against my wishes!"

"I did and he's been removed to the Wethersfield jail. I'll have no more word of it. If you insist, I'll grant you a replacement gardener. Please pass the pickles."

The following evening, Jenny took Charles and Mabel to meet the artists, writers, musicians and poets she called friends. They were to meet in a studio off the main thoroughfare. Jenny pulled them down an alleyway and down a flight of stairs that descended into a basement. She led them down a long, dark hallway. As they drew closer, the sound of music and laughter bellowed into the hallway. Mabel could hear singing but not the sort she'd heard gathered around her piano on holidays. More the sultry sound of a woman's voice and the baritone of a man's. Mabel was enticed. Charles was put out. He knew Jenny had a variety of social groups but there was one social stratum she gravitated toward. Like Jenny, they loved weeks where all they did was drink spirits for days at a time and Charles was quite sure they were taking advantage of opium. Mabel's experience with opium was non-existent, having only read about it in the newspaper. But when the door swung open and Jenny's friends were glassy eyed and reclining over lounge chairs set up haphazardly she knew immediately what she was experiencing. Mabel looked at Charles. He nodded then looked away. Jenny went to her friends and was soon in a back room returning later more glassy-eyed than before. The energy had left her body and she, like the others enjoyed reclining in the chairs listening to the mellow sounds of an African drumbeat, a ukulele and a xylophone. The trio was to the musicians, a bit of a joke, but even Charles and Mabel had to admit they held extraordinary talent. "They could make our shoelaces sound beautiful," he said, rolled his eyes and shrugged. It didn't take long before men were drawing close to Jenny who, adoring attention, allowed touching of her skin and person the way Mabel would never consider. Yet Mabel watched in amazement how Jenny could, in front of them all, let go of social inhibitions and let men touch her in places no woman should publicly. Mabel looked away. She had had enough. She looked to Charles to remove her and he, ready to retreat himself, having seen enough years ago, went to Jenny and said they would be leaving and would see her later at her flat. Jenny protested, with what little energy she had then resigned him away to Mabel for the duration of the evening. Charles and Mabel were happy to be back out on the street again, even if it was loud and bustling. They walked arm in arm to a small restaurant where they enjoyed a hot beverage.

"That's revolting!" Mabel said, removing her shawl and settling into her chair.

"I know, I know. I'm just as disgusted as you are. She's been doing this for years, seems to enjoy it. I grew tired of it long ago. Jenny and her men..."

Mabel saw an opening and grabbed it. "Her men?"

Charles knew he'd stumbled. "She loves men, most men, the attention from men, sex with men, sex with more than one man..."

"Oh my."

Charles nodded.

"Did you... I mean have you ever... uh... did you and she and ..."

"No. So I seem the sort of fellow who would engage in THAT? Albeit it may appear pleasant in theory..."

"Charles!"

"In theory... just in theory Mabel."

"Well how do you know then?"

Charles looked around for a waitress to refill his cup. He tried to drop the subject but Mabel was not about to let up.

"Charles... how do you know Jenny enjoys sex with more than one man? I mean that's a pretty strong statement to make..."

"Because I saw her!" he blurted.

His outburst frightened Mabel. Charles was usually quite the gentleman.

"I'm sorry Mabel, forgive me but your prying is bringing back uncomfortable memories. I try to forget..."

"What happened?"

"We were courting. She was young, fresh, intelligent and ..." he wasn't sure he should go on but Mabel waited, "beautiful," he finished. "Very, very, *very* beautiful. I had no idea that she was as promiscuous as she was. My God that woman... she has one hearty appetite for the male species. Good God. It was so humiliating."

"What happened!" she implored him to go on.

"We'd made a date, set a time for me to pick her up."

"Yes."

"She didn't answer her door and I was worried about her so I went in. It wasn't locked." He looked at her as if he were ashamed, as if he'd been the one at fault. "She must have forgotten our date. The door to the bedroom was open..." he looked away, it was painful to think of, even after several years.

"Yes," Mabel said, her eyes growing larger.

Charles grew bold. "There she was, stark naked, two men, also stark naked... all three..." he winced, "performing the sex act. They were all over her body Mabel. Quite active the three of them, it was dreadfully embarrassing and humiliating."

"I guess that was the end of that?"

He shook his head no.

"No?"

He shook it again.

"No?"

"Pray tell..."

"We'd been courting, as I mentioned before. I cared for her but I wanted nothing to do with a woman like that. Good God, no gentleman wants a woman like that."

"So? You did what after seeing that?"

"I did nothing! I gave up on Jenny Saint Francis. Until..."

"What?"

"Until she came to me and told me she was pregnant and that I was the father."

A hummingbird could have flown into the restaurant and dove into Mabel's mouth it was open so wide. "Charles! You've a child?"

"No, no, no... I don't think... no... well... no, pretty sure it's not mine."

"Pretty sure! That's not something that's addressed lightly! You either do or you don't."

He leaned forward and spoke in a low but angry tone. "Listen, how am I supposed to believe the boy is mine when she had all these other men in her bedroom? What am I supposed to think?"

"Have you seen him?"

He shook his head no.

"You and Jenny may have a child together and you've never *ever* seen him?"

Charles was feeling ashamed and hung his head like a little boy.

"Don't you think it's time you saw the child? Do you give her money?"

Charles shook his head no.

"Charles! You don't help support the boy?"

He shook his head no again. "If I did, that would be admitting he's my child and I'm certain he's not."

"How can you be sure?"

"Jenny's Quaker friends help Jenny's sister take care of him. They've all told me he doesn't look at all like me."

"Where is he?"

"Here in New York."

"Well don't you think it's time we saw him?"

"No."

"Charles Churchill you're going to go see that child. I'll take a look at him. If he looks *anything* like you, we'll take him and raise him ourselves."

"Mabel, I've thought long and hard about this. I calculated the timing of our intimate acts and researched thoroughly the men she was intimate with, there are five men beside myself. Five Mabel. Five! In the period of one month!"

"Oh my, she does have a voracious appetite doesn't she? Who were the men and what did they look like?" she said, taking her pen out of her purse and beginning to take notes.

"What? Are you putting this in your story?"

She laughed, "No, but some of the bits and pieces may fit together nicely in a chapter someday. Tell me what did they look like?"

"One was tall and thin, very narrow face, long pointed nose. Another was short and stubby, big round face, freckles, I've heard the child looks like him."

"Yes but you have a brother who fits that description."

"This is true."

"And you're tall and thin, your face is rather narrow."

"You're making me feel terrible Mabel. Can we stop?"

"We must see him."

"Come on Mabel. Let's go. Jenny's probably through with her rendezvous by now. Once the drugs wear off she's done."

"Mabel... why did we come to New York? So you could punish and torment me for loving someone else?"

She smiled sympathetically. "I need her."

Charles glasses fell to the end of his nose.

"When are you going to replace those?"

"As soon as you get a new hat."

They had a nice tension-relieving laugh but now it was Charles who would not let up.

"Please Mabel, tell me. Why did we come to New York. I would have taken you back to New Orleans someday."

"Someday? I want to go now Charles. That place has a pull on me. I can't bear it. I have to go back I must!"

"What does Jenny have to do with it?"

"I don't know, I can't explain it.

"You'd not been away from Pittsburgh before meeting me. Now you've no desire to settle down."

She was thoughtful. "I'd like to go to London some day."

"As would I."

"Do you know where Jennie's sister lives?"

"I have her address. I've not been there but I suspect I can find it. It's near here."

"Think it's too late to go now?"

He laughed heartily, "It's never too late in this city."

Before long they stood in front of a small house surrounded by a black wrought iron fence. There was light glowing inside.

"There's Jenny's sister, I recognize her," he whispered.

"Look there's the child," she whispered back.

"I see that but the light is too faint. Oh Mabel how did I let you talk me into this?"

"Same way you talked me into going to New Orleans."

"What shall we do now?"

"Charles, I'll go to the door. I'll pretend I'm lost. I'll be friendly enough, she'll let me in."

"What if he looks like me?"

"We'll take him with us and I'll settle down."

Mabel opened the gate and rapped on the door. In no time, Jenny's sister had let her in. Charles waited and waited. Finally, he sat down on the stone foundation supporting the fence. Eventually Mabel left the house. "He's not your son," she said.

"How do you know?"

"He's Benjamin Crocker's."

Victor arrived earlier than Whitethorn. He opened the office and began work on his unfinished journalism. When Whitethorn arrived, he was jovial and carried a competitor's paper under his arm. "Look here," he told Victor, pulling the paper out and pointing to an article about *American Heroes*. "Rebel soldiers are reading it in their tents! They're trading whiskey for it!"

"Have you heard from Mabel?"

"She's in New York. I'm worried about her Victor. Something's amiss."

"She didn't stay long in Connecticut. Maybe she didn't like the scenery."

Whitethorn shook his head of white unruly hair. "No, there was a difference in her tone in this chapter."

Victor chuckled, "Every chapter has a different tone. She's wild with that pen."

"True," he said but Victor detected fear on his face. "She's mentioned opium."

"Opium? You think Mabel's smoking opium."

"I sure hope not."

"Crocker! From New Orleans? The plantation with the racehorses, that Crocker? The boy is Crocker's? That makes six different lovers in a month! And those are the ones we know about. Shame on her for not admitting that. How do you know Crocker is the father?"

"I asked. And he looks just like him."

"But you're a complete stranger."

"I told her right away who I was, that's why I was in there so long. She's a cousin you know."

"I suppose... if you want to claim the Saint Francis sisters as relations."

"Charles, how very unkind of you."

"Well... now I know the truth."

"I have to return tomorrow."

"Why?"

"There was an artist there. He wants to sketch me. I said I'd return tomorrow."

Charles waited for Mabel all day while an artist meticulously drew her features. He was a gifted artist who captured her beauty and playful qualities while not neglecting the depth in her eyes. Within three days, the sketch had found its way to the front cover of *Harper's Weekly*.

Everywhere they went people recognized her as Black Pansy, she was deluged with requests for autographs. Charles couldn't wait to get her out of New York before the city turned her into another Jenny. Mabel thrived in the attention. Charles began to sulk.

"Did ya see?" Liza asked the other servants. "Did ya see the picture of Mabel on the front of *Harper's Weekly*? Lookie there," she said slapping it down on the tea table in the Servant's parlor. "I'm going to leave it on Clarrisa's dressing table. She'll get a kick outa that one, she will."

Charles' father left one on the kitchen table, Lena left a copy on the divan, Charles' sister left one on the bookcase and two of Charles' brothers each left a copy on chairs. All thought sure they were the only one to share the good news to the lady of the house that Mabel McCrutchon had made a splash in New York City. Clarrisa was angry and made it a point to let everyone know that seven copies of *Harpers Weekly* made their way into the house and if she found out who the culprits were she'd remove them permanently from her welcome list. Charles' father was amused but the servants were frightened yet they delighted in it and late into the night sat together laughing over it.

It was on a Sunday evening when Charles told Mabel that he had to return to his family in Connecticut and by Tuesday evening, he was gone.

"But you can't leave me here by myself," she pleaded.

"You're welcome to come," he told her, wishing she would have a change heart. They made plans to meet in New Orleans at the end of summer. Charles was trusted to manage her royalties from *American Heroes*, he'd discussed it with Whitethorn before leaving Pittsburgh.

"I'll be happy to meet you in New Orleans so that you may pursue your interest in Benjamin Crocker."

The look in her eyes at the mention of Crocker brought a great shiver to Charles' spine. Her dark eyes opened widely but no smile companied them. Her eyebrows raised and he could see her mind had drifted far away. Her expression became curious.

"Yes," she said and began fiddling with a ribbon that adorned the waist of her long dress. "I have much to pursue at the Crocker mansion. Charles," she raised the pitch of her voice, "there's something going on there." She stared at him waiting for his response. She respected Charles brilliance and adored his compassion.

He looked bewildered and shrugged lightly, wishing to avoid the esoteric realm she'd fallen into over the Crocker Mansion and Jenny's Saint Francis ancestral home, whose grand but violent days had passed.

"That's what it is Charles, I'm sure of it. My ancestors are beckoning me. There is something not right there."

"But is it your business?"

She shot him a look half way between disdain and wisdom. He could see she debated his remark. He also knew she was very stubborn and that they would both be in New Orleans in the fall investigating Benjamin Crocker, even though the country was in the midst of a nasty war.

Charles spoke privately with Jenny before he left. "I trust you'll take good care of Mabel."

The smile she wore told Charles he'd misspoken. He looked into her bulging, hazel-blue eyes, tinged with thin red blood vessels.

"I'll watch her I 'spose, we'll make quilts, just like all us Suth'n girls do."

"Jenny..."

She knew what he was going to ask and she weakened. She was standing behind a ladder back chair, her hands gripped the top tightly. She pursed her lips and held back her emotions.

"Don't force me Cha'ls, I don't wish ta speak of it."

"Is it true Jenny," he begged, "is your child Benjamin Crocker's son?"

Her eyes welled, her eyebrows furrowed and she continued pursing her lips. She nodded.

"Why didn't you tell me! Why did you let me go on thinking..."

She stopped him abruptly. "Oh come now Cha'ls, yew' knew the boy wasn't yaws'."

He could see she was uncomfortable. She hated being vulnerable.

"You let it hang over me. Yes, I was quite sure he wasn't mine... but not positive."

She nodded and the tears began to flow. She found a hankie on the china cupboard and dabbed her eyes. She swung around and sat down in the chair.

He pulled up the second wooden chair and the two sat facing one another. Her fingers twisted the moist hankie, nervously wrapping them around her fingers. Her eyes so red and swollen Charles felt remorse he'd brought it up.

"I had to know for sure. The boy's getting older now, he needs his father and financial support."

She nodded then broke into a shrill sob biting her lip in a desperate attempt to control it.

"He doesn' know Cha'ls, please..." she rested her hand on his.

He put his hand on hers and spoke softly. "He must be told."

She returned to her usual prideful demeanor, "Wey'll see 'bout thay't." Then shot him that haughty look he'd grown to know as *her mask*.

"You know Mabel is drawn to Benjamin?"

"All the gals 'r drawn ta' Crocker," she laughed cynically. Then looked at him as if he were a fool.

He let it drop. Charles Churchill knew better than to give fuel to her fire. Besides, Mabel had been convincing that she was following her instincts. He had a busy agenda of his own. Within three weeks, he was to meet with the Quakers and advise his father regarding the family's shipbuilding enterprise. There would be a large formal family dinner where the whole clan would be pulling on him to break ties with Mabel. All this while worrying about Mabel traveling in trains and carriages down to New Orleans in the midst of a war, with unstable, promiscuous, sultry Jenny Saint Francis who drank too much and cavorted in opium bars.

Jenny sat staring into space. He stood up and patted her twice on the shoulder, then left the room before Mabel finished bathing.

Charles stood in the doorway and watched Mabel as she reclined on her bed with pen in hand. "You look beautiful when you're thinking," he said softly. She barely smiled as she was deep into a paragraph and did not wish to lose her thoughts.

"Of course, you always look beautiful..."

Mabel brought her finger to her lips, "Shh," she said, loving the attention but frowning that he was interrupting her thoughts.

"Remember the first day we met?"

She let the pen drop then sighed dramatically, "You're not going to let me write are you?"

"No..." he smiled eyeing the feminine way her body lay upon the bed. Her dress was crisp, its black and white stripes ran vertically with a starchy white collar, its lace accentuating her neck. She tilted her head up, thinking it gave a more flattering view. He came and sat next to her.

"We need to wed. Shall we set a date?" he asked pressing his face into her hair, inhaling deeply the essence of her Devon violet perfume.

She was silent.

His hand patted her hips, "That's fine," he said feeling rejected but good-natured about it. He started to rise.

"Please... I look forward to being your wife. I miss our intimacy, but..."

He nodded. He hated the thought of being away from her. "I'm more than concerned for your safety. In New Orleans, you portrayed yourself as being my servant. What will you do this time?"

"I know, I know Charles. Jenny and I have talked it over. Believe me, she'll make a good Slaver. I hope she doesn't take it to extremes."

"Yes, she's one for the drama isn't she? Wear your hat. If they can't see your face, they can't begin to question. If you stay at her family mansion, you should be safe, unless the Rebel Army is camped out on the lawn," he laughed.

"That's not funny."

"No it isn't and you'll run into soldiers a plenty on the train. Keep your head down. That *Harpers Weekly* story and picture of you could cause problems, some may recognize you."

"I'll be careful. We're getting a sleeping compartment, I'll stay inside most of the time."

He shot her a doubtful look, knowing how much she loved attention.

"No, this time I understand. I need to uncover more of my family history through Benjamin Crocker and through Jenny if I can get her to talk more about her family. This trip is business, all business."

"I'll take your word on that." He then smiled mischievously, "Want to get married this fall in New Orleans?"

She admired his humor, raised an eyebrow and stared thoughtfully off into space.

"Mabel you are lost in a sea of thoughts. Go to New Orleans, discover yourself, uncover what you feel needs exposure, you'll make a better wife if you get this behind you."

"A better wife," she said snidely then rested her head on his knee. He brushed his hand across her hair.

"Are you looking forward to seeing your family?"

"Sometimes but then other moments have me cringing. I'm disappointed in their self-centeredness. I didn't see that in them when we were children."

She didn't respond. She was again lost in her own thoughts.

The weather was warming as quickly as the war. Every day the headlines grew more gruesome. The war was on everyone's mind, especially his family when Charles reached Wethersfield. One by one, his siblings began trailing into the lavish estate on Bluebird Pond, their children and spouses in tow. They were not void of kindness but Charles grew fatigued at listening to their selfish jabber.

At dinner Charles' father, Frederick, sat at the head of the table. Charles' mother, Clarrisa sat at the other end. Because of the large turnout in welcoming Charles home, a smaller table for the children had been set up. For quite some time the conversation consisted mainly of politics and the war. Then it shifted to the Churchill shipyards, then he had to listen to the mundane stories from each sibling regarding their home lives. Not one person at the table inquired about Mabel. It was as if she didn't exist. He felt certain they had forgotten her.

His brother Joseph managed the welders of the shipyards. He expected way too much from the employees, Charles father had come to their defense more than once while Joseph spoke. He then droned on about his dandy game of golf and how he'd beaten the other chaps. Prudence and Emily got into a loud conversation about their love of fashion, their high-pitched voices at the table was distracting. Charles' little sister Flora, the baby of the family, played her role well, monopolizing everyone's time and patience regarding her allergies until as usual they became fatigued and ignored her entirely, except Charles who kept offering healthy suggestions. After receiving her fill from him, Flora smiled broadly and asked loudly, "How's Mabel?" Not because she cared to know but because she wished to stir up controversy at the table. When all eyes were on her, Charles could see she was pleased. He felt alone and abandoned and compelled to answer. "She's quite well Flora, thank you for asking."

There was an uncomfortable silence at the table. Their somber faces stared at him.

"I'm glad you've gotten over her," the eldest sibling Thomas said to a chorus of "um hmm, yes, me too and amen to that."

"No! There will be no amens to *that* because Mabel and I will be marrying this fall in New Orleans."

As the gasps went around in waves, he felt sure it created white caps on the pond he could see from his spot at the table.

"But Charles," his oldest sister Sophia protested. "Surely you understand the damage that would do to our family name?"

"I'm not sure I understand what you're implying."

Sophia looked around for help.

"You're on your own darling," Clarrisa said, loving every moment of the contention, waiting for it to escalate.

"She's not in the same social strata... Charles, we're Churchill's for God's sake!" Joseph sniped.

Charles' voice trembled. This situation frightened him as much or more as any he'd encountered throughout his ordeals of late. But he held firm. He was, after all, the most courageous of all the siblings. "Churchill's?" He laughed. "None of you live up to the Churchill name our grandparents and their grandparents worked hard to protect. Have you forgotten father's mother was an Erskine? An indentured servant from Scotland?"

"He's right!" Charles father sided with him. "The Churchill's were kind and compassionate. Those of you who lack that characteristic take after your mother. She bears the Churchill name through marriage only."

"Father! That was uncalled for," Sophia said protecting her mother and defending herself.

"I found Mabel refreshing," Charles' youngest brother, August, said supportively. "And real pretty."

"If you like saloon girls," Emily said to snickers.

"How dare you! Especially you Emily. Talk about tainting the Churchill name!" Charles shouted to more snickers.

Clarrisa could hold her tongue no more, "Charles, the girl wrote a vulgar story. The whole world is reading her promiscuous pen." She looked around the table, overly proud of hearing herself talk.

Charles narrowed his eyes and pointed at all of them except August and his father. "And I'll bet every single one of you has read her *vulgar* stories." Many of his siblings averted his eyes but his mother raged on.

She'd read those vulgar stories and enjoyed every word of them until she found out the author was engaged to her son. She believed it was one thing to read them, quite another to have the author in your home. "We'll not have that girl in this family!"

"Come now Mother," Charles began slower, calmer. "Could it be that her Anglo blood has just a touch of Negro blood?"

"That too," Sophia said snidely.

"Sophia!" Charles' father shouted. "We are Abolitionists! This family sees the Colored race as equals."

"I do," August spoke up.

Charles watched his mother as her shaking hands finished off another glass of champagne. While Sophia's back was turned Clarrisa grabbed her daughter's glass and finished off her champagne, then held the glass in the air, "More champagne!" she shouted as the servant scurried over to fill it.

"Mabel is a sweet Presbyterian girl from Pittsburgh! Enough!" Charles shouted.

Day after day Mabel lay on the bed, pen in her ink-stained hand. She brooded over Charles and feeling she'd taken him for granted brought remorse. She looked up to see Jenny's slender, sultry body leaning into the doorframe.

"What ah' you writin' bout' now Miss Black Pan-say?"

"I'm writing a story about a minister, this one's a bit sad but ministers are heroes, don't you think?"

"Ah' haven't spent time with any mini'stas lately, Miss Black Pan-say, sounds lyke you need a change. You need some graft and corruption in thos' stories. Change yo' clothes, I'm taken' you uptawn."

"Uptown? What's uptown?"

"Fifth ava-nu, that's what's uptawn. Don' you wan na see New Yawk's underwarld?"

"Underworld? I suppose it would do a girl good to get out a little, especially if it would make my stories more exciting. I have run out of ideas. The minister story was a little dull."

"I'll bet," Jenny said with a wry smile.

Jenny waited patiently for one of the finer carriages to come along. One with big white horses whose hooves were painted black from the same can of paint that blackened the carriage. They'd both taken care to primp. Mabel, more than she'd like to admit. Jenny as much as she could. Mabel found a pink rose and twisted it into her hair, saving a few curls for around her face. Jenny dug out a gold broach and matching necklace. Mabel wore a dress that covered her up to her neck. Jenny hung the heavy broach in the middle of her bosom, enabling the weight to pull the silky fabric of her dress down, revealing cleavage supported by a tight corset that she hoped by nights end some handsome man would remove. Mabel added blush to her cheeks. Jenny added black to her eyes. She'd almost convinced Mabel to let her dab some of the black onto her eyes but Mabel remembered that she was engaged and with the *Harpers Weekly* photo, feared people may recognize her.

The driver knew exactly what club Jenny sought and it wasn't long before Jenny grabbed Mabel's hand and like two schoolgirls, they clamored down from the carriage. Mabel stood outside the club looking into the window.

Well-dressed patrons, couples mostly, with a few dapper men who looked twice at them, walked the small flight of steps into the high classed club.

"I approve," Mabel said, the pink rose in her hair flashing out at Jenny whose broach had fallen dangerously low.

"Not thay't one, this one," Jenny said yanking Mabel into a dark stairwell that led down a long flight of steps and down a narrow, dark, dank hallway, smelling of alcohol and urine. Before Mabel could protest, Jenny had knocked a tune onto a solid door where a heavyset black man answered. He immediately recognized Jenny and escorted the two across the empty dirty room to another door. He took out a huge ring of long silver keys and unlocked the second door.

"You alright Miss?" he asked Mabel but before she could answer, Jenny had pulled her inside.

Mabel stood close to the door, hoping she could pound on it if she needed out. Jenny tried pulling Mabel further into the club but

256

Mabel would not budge. Jenny waved her off and headed toward the bar where most recognized and welcomed her.

From her spot by the door Mabel gazed out at a large window that looked onto a ten by fifteen foot walled garden where small pink climbing roses bloomed and several chairs were placed next to a few small bushes. There was a spittoon for men to spit their chewed tobacco and an old violin was on a stand.

Inside there were three round poker tables. Under the table were four compartments, cubbies where the players could hide their money and cards.

All three tables were full, an ongoing game at each. The room was thick with smoke, much of it cigars. There was a trio playing a style of music unfamiliar to Mabel. A swanky saxophone, a guitar and a piano that she recognized had been tuned every other key slightly off to give it a tinny sound. She turned to her right and saw three women whom she was sure were prostitutes. They sat near a door that Mabel was convinced opened into their *house of ill repute*.

"Hi there," a slim, dirty-blonde man, about twenty-eight with a sallow complexion said to her. His eyes were horizontally slender giving the impression he couldn't open them all the way.

"Hello," Mabel said giving him only brief eye contact before returning to the variety of sights before her.

"Kinda' strange," he said with a slight southern accent. "At least for me it is," he said with a smile Mabel found dopey but cute.

"I'm glad to hear you say that," she scowled at the room then turned and gave him her full attention.

"Where you from?" he asked, then smiled, squinting his narrow, hazel-brown eyes even further.

"Pittsburgh," she shouted over the noise.

"Oh," he shook his head knowingly. "You look familiar, have we met?"

She tilted her head shyly, smiled faintly and shook her head no. His silent staring made her uncomfortable so when another young man came to introduce himself she was overtly friendly with him. He took it as a sign she was interested and he pushed himself in front of the Southerner, who was more intelligent and self-confident than Mabel gave him credit for.

With this new fellow standing too close to her and aggressively asking questions, she returned her attention to the Southerner. "Excuse me Sir," she said to the man bearing down on her, "this gentleman and I were talking."

The Southerner was amused at his turn of luck. The other fellow took the hint and left.

"Come on, let's go outside the Southerner said to Mabel and with impeccable manners, he escorted her outside to the walled garden.

"A little bit quieter out here," she said and sat down in a wrought iron chair with sun- faded cushions.

"A little bit. I'm Monroe. I'm a lawyer from Lafayette, Louisiana."

Those words played nicely in Mabel's mind and Monroe could see she was pleased.

"My friend... I mean my cousin," she corrected, "Jenny and I are leaving for Louisiana soon."

"Oh? With the country at war? Is that wise?"

"Yes, we'll be fine."

Monroe recognized that Mabel was of trace African ancestry. He was thoughtful but silent. Mabel knew what he was thinking. *I'm just like everyone else,* she thought. *Why must the color of my skin be such an issue?*

"I know I've seen you somewhere before," he squinted his eyes and pulled his head back as if to get a larger view of her, making her terribly uncomfortable.

" Harpers Weekly?" she asked.

"No, I don't read that. Are you a model?"

She smiled and rolled her eyes, leaving it vague.

"I know where it was," he said pointing his finger at her. "New Orleans. I saw you at the hotel."

She was surprised at the co-incidence.

"You were with another gentleman and a colored carriage driver."

Mabel wished she could remove herself from the situation. She liked being more autonomous.

"I'm sorry. You're very striking. Men notice beautiful women."

She nodded.

"What's a beautiful girl like you going to New Orleans for, under the worst of situations?"

"My family is from there, I've some business to attend to."

"What's the family name?"

She glared at him. "You ask a dreadful lot of questions."

He laughed. "Sorry, I'm a lawyer. Investigating comes natural. I've been in Louisiana all my life, I know a lot of people, I thought I might know or have heard of your family."

"Crocker," she said fiercely.

He smiled and she could tell he thought she was lying.

"Saint Francis."

He nodded. "I could believe that."

"What? Believe what?" she asked anxiously.

"I've known a few of the St Francis's and I can see it in you. But Crocker, no way."

"Really? Why?"

"Because the Crocker's are lily white, every last one of them. While the St Francis have color in their skin."

"Really?" Mabel was perplexed. She looked through the glass for a glance at Jenny who was still at the bar but keenly aware of Mabel visiting with the gentleman. She was already watching them. Mabel looked away. "See the slender blond at the bar?"

He was discrete in his looking but Jenny was staring at them both.

"Yes, I see her."

"Care to take a wild guess? Saint Francis or Crocker?"

"Definitely Crocker. She looks just like the Crocker's. They're all lily white like that and most of them have those big bulging blue eyes."

Mabel was aghast.

"Miss?" the lawyer asked her.

Mabel tried to appear unmoved. "'McCrutchon. Mabel McCrutchon."

"Well Miss McCrutchon, I have a train to catch. Here's my card. If you need the services of a lawyer while you're in New Orleans, don't hesitate to call. Keep your head down."

She frowned. "I have a hat."

He shot her one last slanted smile, one last slanted glance, bowed his head gentlemanly, then took his leave.

Monroe's seat had not grown cold when a different fellow came and sat down. She welcomed someone to talk to. The chat between she and Monroe had left her bewildered and fatigued.

"Are you OK?" the fellow asked.

She nodded.

"Would you like to go for a walk"?

Mabel laughed and the release energized her. "I don't even know your name. Why would I walk with a stranger and where would we go?"

"I'm no stranger. I'm one of Jenny's friends. I'm Christopher. And if you look closely, you'll see there's a hidden gate on that fence, behind the vines. It's only a narrow space between buildings but it's quiet and not as strange as all this. Besides, Jenny asked me to keep an eye on you."

Mabel looked toward Jenny, still sitting at the bar. "She's a good heart, isn't she?"

"Yeah, Jenny's great."

Mabel gathered her full, crispy dress and she and the tall black-haired stranger ducked through the gate.

"This is nice!" she said, surprised at the deep green vines that clung to the sides of both buildings as they walked through the narrow corridor.

They walked around the buildings and found themselves out on busy Fifth Avenue.

"Are you hungry? Let me buy you a bite to eat."

She liked the way the streetlamps lit up Christopher's green eyes. "Sure!"

They found a small restaurant. They laughed about the menu that offered Italian chicken, Chinese fried rice or Irish stew. "This is New York!" he said.

"Yes, it certainly is."

They spent over an hour nibbling at their food, each sharing bites of the others choice. Mabel laughed and let loose. After dinner they strolled slowly back to the corridor between the two buildings but before they reached the gate, in a movement practiced and perfected, Christopher gently swung Mabel around and planted her back up against the wall. Before she could say no he planted a delicious kiss on her reddened lips. He held her there, she did not struggle. Her lips were full, sweet and to his liking. She looked into his sparkling green eyes, begging for another. He kissed her again. Her breathing grew heavy.

He looked down at her full breasts rising and falling with each heavy inhale. Thinking her experienced in necking behind nightclubs, his rough hand grabbed at her backside, then he reached around and started to unbuckle his trousers.

"No! You will not!" she shouted. Slapped his face, hard, turned and ran through the gate. She quickly shut the gate and saw a lock, slid it across, locking Christopher out. Before she had a chance to straighten herself up, she saw Jenny's concerned face. Jenny motioned her to come in.

"Time to go?" Jenny asked. Mabel appreciated her compassion and nodded sheepishly.

Neither spoke much during the ride home. Mabel tried to sort out her thoughts over what Monroe had said about the Crocker's being lily white with bulging eyes and the Saint Francis's being more colored skin. Jenny spent her time wondering what Monroe had said to Mabel that had them looking at her that way. She'd seen Monroe before at social events... in New Orleans.

"Mabel darlin', Ah can see somethin' is troublin' you. You wanna talk about it?" Jenny asked sympathetically after several days of Mabel staying to herself in her room.

Mabel was spread out on her bed, her faded red-checkered cotton dress fanned out around her. "I wonder sometimes Jenny, if I'll make Charles a good wife."

"Do ya love heym?"

"I think so."

"Think so's not good en'uf," Jenny said kicking at one of the legs of Mabel's brass bed.

Mabel's dark eyes looked up at Jenny with a childish expression. "Charles was the first man to kiss me."

"Is that so," Jenny's smile was more a smirk but Mabel ignored it knowing that she and Charles were lovers in the past and she was probably jealous.

"I get a little carried away sometimes," Mabel said looking into Jenny's big, bulging hazel-blue eyes that were once again bloodshot.

"Carried ah'way'?"

Mabel couldn't look Jenny in the eyes, as she spoke she fiddled with the pages of her journal. "Like your friend Christopher... the other night.

Jenny was loving this, "Christa'fha? You and Christa'fha?"

"No, not that."

Jenny was disappointed. "Oh, Ah thought Ah was in for a good stor'ay."

"I let him kiss me twice."

Jenny laughed. "Ya' worr'aid 'bout two lil' kisses? Oh my, I got way more'n 'at to be worried 'bout. I shore wish all Ah had to wor'ay 'bout were two lil' kisses!"

"There was another fellow too, I let him kiss me. I never told Charles."

Jenny looked incredulous. "Oh dea' God, you're bein' ridiculous and childish and yo' makin' me feel lik' a tray'ump."

"I'm sorry, it's just that..."

"It's jus' thay't you wanna' be a good lil girl and now you feel tainted. Is that it?"

"Yes, I suppose it is."

"Well Ah' think you owed those three lil' kisses to yo'self. You and Charles are goin' ta' be mayr'ad fo' a lifetime, that was yo' chance ta' taste the fruit of anutha' man's lips. And Ah can tell ya right now Christa'fha has more 'n kisses ta' give a wo'man and that ya missed out if ya didn't have a lil' taste a' him," Jenny shrugged, "but thay's yo' choice. Ya don' hav' ta tell Charles either, just be a good lil' girl from now on. Ya hear?"

Mabel nodded, "Thanks Jenny, I feel better, it was eating away at me."

"Ah know tha' feelin," Jenny said curtly then turned and walked out of the bedroom.

Mabel was determined to figure out the mysteries of the Saint Francis and Crocker mansions. The information Monroe told her about Jenny looking like a Crocker therefore making Benjamin look like a Saint Francis was troubling. She'd thought Benjamin Crocker looked a lot like her, the same skin tone, same hair, and similar eyes. Why would Jenny look like a Crocker? It was all so confusing she grew anxious for the day they left for New Orleans so she could try to sort it all out. Until then, it would eat away at her. Dead ancestors or not, made no difference to her. Someday she would have her own children and they would know the truth, whatever that might be.

The day arrived when Jenny and Mabel said goodbye to New York. Jenny teased Mabel for days ahead of their departure. It was for Mabel's safety that she pose as Jenny's Negro servant and Mabel knew that, but she was a moody girl and prone to episodes of haughtiness. There would be none of that. Jenny also warned Mabel she could wind up at New Orleans auction block if she didn't stick by her side. Mabel knew all that, she'd been through it all before. Jenny tried to buy Mabel a new hat but Mabel refused. Her old hat had seen many adventures and she'd grown fond of it. Besides, Charles bought it for her and it brought her great comfort as she sat hiding within it when the train rolled out of the station.

Stops were frequent in the heavily populated areas of the east. There were occasions when the two rode by carriage, then were on the train again. As the train headed south, the train picked up and transported wounded Rebel soldiers. Because Mabel and Jenny had a sleeping compartment, they were obliged to give up their seats to military when asked. Both were disturbed by the experience, Jenny had the harder time coping with the sight of young men missing limbs, on crutches and loud screams of terror that came day and night from soldiers awakened from their nightmares. Moans were heard throughout the train, there was no escape from them, much as Jenny tried.

"You look dreadful," Mabel said to her.

"Ah feel drayd'ful. Ah can't slee'up. Ah feel lyke I rey'cognyze some 'o these boys." She shook her head then stared off into the scene in front of her.

Mabel kept penning away. *American Heroes* had come alive again. There had been no better opportunity for her to see firsthand the true American hero. To pose the question to the world, what was a hero, who were our heroes and why?

It was early morning in the Churchill estate on Bluebird Pond, in Wethersfield, Connecticut. Clarrisa had invited two of her daughters for lunch, the oldest and the youngest, Sophia and Flora. Sophia to provide the fire, Flora the kerosene. Sophia had a beautiful young woman staying at their home, the daughter of a close friend. Sasha was twenty, culturally accomplished and as the daughter of a diplomat, quite politically astute. Clarrisa knew Charles would find her attractive. It was a delicate situation and Clarrisa planned carefully to have her daughters unknowingly do the dirty work.

A table was set in the greenhouse, the very spot where Mabel had been held with a knife to her throat and almost raped. Clarrisa felt confident her daughters would not notice and they did not as they removed their napkin rings and placed their large white, linen napkins on their laps.

"This is delightful Mother, I'm so glad you thought of this," Sofia said as their servant, Bruce, ladled steamy clam chowder into her bowl. That Clarrisa had chosen that spot was not lost on Bruce who scowled.

"Is something wrong with Bruce?" Sophia whispered.

"Oh, there's always a petty argument afoot with the servants, nothing for us to worry about. How are things at home Sophia?"

"Fine Mother, the children are away for the week and their father and I are going sailing tomorrow. I'm looking forward to it."

"Well, cover your face with a hat, you know what the summer sun can do to our white skin... but don't you have a houseguest?"

"Sasha," Flora chimed in then laughed.

"Why do you laugh Flora? What do you find so hilarious about Sasha?"

"That silly little French accent and those tight fitting corsets that push her breasts up into everyone's face. Her teeny, tiny nose and the perfumed hanky she waves about."

Clarrisa loved what she was hearing, she'd not met Sasha. She sounded *perfect*.

"I do believe you're jealous Flora and I can see why. She's gorgeous and all the men adore her."

"Will she be sailing with you tomorrow?" Clarrisa asked.

"No, Sasha is looking forward to having a quiet day by herself. We're giving all the servants a day off. She said she's using the day to pamper herself."

"She uses every day to pamper herself," Flora sniped.

Clarrisa's mind spun wildly out of control picturing Charles comfortably walking into his sister's 'empty' home in Wethersfield to retrieve papers for his mother and finding Sasha alone and freshly pampered.

"Mother... Mother! Your mind is miles away, do come back to us here at the table."

"Oh yes, I'm here. I was just thinking of the papers I asked you to sign. Have you signed them yet dear?"

"I did and I meant to bring them. They're sitting on my dressing table."

Clarrisa smiled but stopped when Bruce glared at her, "More chowder Ma'am," he asked.

Clarrisa shook her head no, the flesh on her face hanging in an unhappy smile. *Bruce knows too much of my business, perhaps it's time I let him go,* she thought.

Flora looked at her mother and the interaction between she and Bruce. Flora looked around the room and remembered the incident with the gardener. Bruce read her thoughts, nodded and retreated to the kitchen. "Anyone seen Charles?" Flora asked.

"No, and I'm angry with that brother of mine. We had a dinner, invited him and he didn't show," Sophia complained as she took a bite of crusty bread, then a heaping spoonful of chowder.

"He's staying at Auntie Lena's, they're very busy. They're working with the Underground Railroad you know. Charles has helped to free a lot of slaves."

"Yes, Flora, we're all keenly aware of Charles' work. I brag about him every day. But he musn't be so busy that he neglects family," Sophia lectured.

Flora disassociated her thoughts from her sister's chatter and looked around the room thinking of the gardener and how he accosted Mabel. She quivered and saw Bruce looking straight at her.

As the afternoon came to a close Clarrisa sent a note to Charles:

Would you be a dear and go by your sister Sophia's tomorrow? No one will be home. She has left papers for me on her dressing table. I trust you're going into Wethersfield?
Love, Mother

Charles was indeed going into Wethersfield and was happy to do a favor for his mother. He'd felt horribly guilty after the argument at the dining table. He'd been hard on her. Any chance to make it up to her was welcomed. He was having new glasses made, he would pick them up. He stopped at Sophia's before going for his glasses that had gotten so bad about sliding down his nose, he'd quit wearing them. He could see well up close but distance was blurry.

Charles found Sophia's hidden key and let himself in. He went into her dressing room and as planned, the papers were on her dressing table. He started whistling and scurried down the steep flight of stairs in the tall, boxy house.

"Helloooo..." came a sweet voice.

Charles stopped in the middle of the stairs. "Sophia? Mother said you'd be away."

"No, not Sophia," came the soft voice with a French accent.

Charles walked back up the stairs and came face to face with Sasha. He'd not been that close to a woman since he left Mabel in New York.

"Hellooo," Sasha waved her perfumed hanky at Charles who stared at her heavily corseted body. With light brown curly hair, properly pinned up and dressed in a pink velvet dress that matched her pink cheeks, Charles couldn't help but be taken in by her charms. After all, he and Mabel had not been intimate since returning from their trip to the south and whether it was appropriate or not his masculine desires were on edge.

"I'm Sasha, I'm Sophia's friend."

She was so close to him, the word friend came out a breathy wind that hit on the side of his neck, sending a chilly spiral down his entire body.

Sasha stood and smiled, exposing a full, protruding, attractive set of slightly offset teeth.

Very pretty, he thought.

Not to be rude he introduced himself. When he started to leave to go into Wethersfield, Sasha asked if she could accompany him. She said she'd been needing to go to town.

"Of course," Charles said politely. And thus began the *friendship* of Charles and Sasha who were soon seen walking and talking along Bluebird Pond, on carriage rides to view Connecticut's orchards and occasionally dining together in town. Such was the relationship so fruitful for Sasha and the prospect of marrying a Churchill so encouraging, she had suspended leaving indefinitely.

The daily onslaught of wounded soldiers brought great despair to Mabel. If able, the soldiers smiled at her. Not one soldier was unkind to her. She didn't understand. They were fighting for the right of the agricultural south to continue holding Colored people in bondage. Didn't they see she was Jenny's colored servant? She had to hide that she could read or write. Where were the heroes in the midst of all this human confusion of sacrifice? *Charles!* her empty heart cried out. *Charles!*

It was another lovely day when Charles and Sasha went again, to what had become their favorite picnic spot. He took out a thick wool blanket and shook it, the wind catching it, dancing it before it touched the soft blades of grass. The sunlight caught words stamped into the wool. *Property of the United States Army, Union forces.*

"What is that Charles?"

He'd grown so accustomed to seeing it, he'd grown not to notice. He lifted up the corner and read it. Yes, it's a military blanket."

She laughed. " Why do you have it?"

His face grew serious but she continued flippantly.

"Stop!" he said. "The war is not to laugh of. Not today, not now, not ever!"

She looked perplexed and hurt. He reached and grabbed her into his arms and kissed her roughly. She backed off but then smiled.

"Although it was a bit rough for a first kiss, I'm pleased to see your intentions are more than friendship."

He leaned into her again pressing her back down onto the blanket. He kissed her again, not much softer. He could feel himself growing erect and kissed her again and again and she kissed him back again and again. He pulled himself up and sat upright.

"I can't!" he said angrily. "I'm engaged, I told you that from the beginning."

Sasha came up from behind him and hung her head over his shoulder, "Sometimes plans change," she said then kissed him on the neck.

"Not these plans. I'm going to marry Mabel. I'm ashamed that I've carried on this way. It's not like me."

"You're a man. Men have needs," she said tempting him to kiss her again.

"I'm sorry that I've misled you. I don't know what got into me," he said turning around into her fully corseted bodice, her breasts overflowing like water over a fountain.

She laughed. "I should have never mentioned the war."

"No, you shouldn't have."

Several days later Charles found himself at the long Churchill traditional dining table with most of the family present. It was Sunday evening and Charles father, Frederick had pulled himself away from his *obligations* to attend. Clarrisa sat next to him, she did not look well.

Charles' sister and her husband arrived late and brought along Monica. Charles avoided eye contact with the beauty. Since he'd openly courted her, his silence appeared odd and worried Clarrisa.

The meal and conversation ran smoothly, no arguments. There came a point in the evening where everyone was silent and all that could be heard were the children playing in the other room.

"I saw you the other day Charles," his sister Flora said.

Everyone turned and looked at him. The whole family knew that Flora was a trouble starter and all waited for the ensuing fireworks.

Charles did not know how to respond and so remained silent but due to Flora's husband not taking his eyes off Sasha all evening, Flora needed some way and someone to punish. "Yes," she said, "on the grassy knoll, just before the woodlands. You were with someone. Was that you Sasha?" Flora said looking to her husband as if warning him. "You looked both to be..." she paused and laughed for full effect, "enjoying yourselves."

Charles was a favorite of the family and they all had at one time or another fallen victim to Flora's venomous mouth so all were sympathetic and embarrassed for him, all except Clarrisa whose smile ran ear to ear.

"Have you heard from Mabel?" Flora asked, to gasps.

"No, no I haven't."

"Oh yes you have," Flora said then leaned across the table and handed an envelope to him, giving Sasha a snide look as she did. "One of the servants gave it to me. They were afraid Mother would get a hold of it and you'd never read it. Better give Black Pansy another address," she said sarcastically as she looked around at the variety of emotions each family member bore. The evening's entertainment was over.

One evening as the train rumbled over the tracks, one of the wounded soldiers started playing a flute. Shortly, another soldier joined him with a banjo. It was an unusual folk tune, one Mabel's grandmother had sung to her.

In the flight of the birds
In the roar of the streams
Comes the sound of our earth
And the makings of our dreams

Mabel recognized the tune and couldn't help but sing out. The soldiers played it again but this time livelier and Mabel's voice rang out pitch perfect and pure. Soon other soldiers gathered around and their spirits were lifted. No one cared that Mabel was Colored nor did Mabel care that these boys were fighting a war to keep her from freedom. Not at this moment. They transcended the place where human differences mattered, that universal place that can be reached through the sound of the flute and the high soprano of a young woman separated from the man she loves.

When they arrived safely in New Orleans, Jenny let out a sigh of relief. "Trains, carr'ages, Ahm so damned ti' ed of it. If Ah see anutha' carpet bag I'm goin'a die on the spot."

Mabel chuckled as she looked at the crowd of people all carrying carpetbags. "What an ingenious way of using old carpets. That company is doing well, I read about it in the newspapers."

Jenny gave her a miserable look, "An' did you eva' see so many newspa'pa's? What's gonna happen ta all thos' trees now that mankind has discov'ed newsprey'nt? Good Lord."

"I'm surprised at all the cameras," Mabel said looking around, worrying about being recognized.

"Imaj'gen all the wa'r photos they'll come out wey'th. We'll neva' see tha' end a this bloody wa'r. We'll be lookin' at severed limbs fo' eva."

They both looked sadly at one another. Mabel nodded and wondered if Charles' brother August had joined the Union forces as planned.

"Wey'll, it's off ta Saint Francis Plantay'tion, or what's ley'ft of it. My Dadee's mun-ey has been used fa otha' thangs, God rey'st his soul but I weysh I'd had the foresi'ght ta spend some of it on that crumblin' mansion. I just don't hay've the hart."

"Are you sure we'll be alone?"

"Unley'ess the Rebel soldiers hav' may'd a hospital or a morgue out of it, yes, wey'll be alone."

Mabel got to thinking again about Jenny looking like a Crocker. She wasn't sure how she would unravel the mystery. Maybe she could plan questions and ask them to her when she drank too much, which was often.

"Tuck yo' hat on yo' pretta' little head Miss Black Pansy. We're in slay've country now. Time ta be serious."

Mabel felt a surge of love coming from Jenny's big oversized eyes. She tied the strings of her hat securely under her chin and patted the top of it. She thought of Charles and Burford and felt a pang of loneliness.

It was eerie pulling up the road to Saint Francis. Mabel remembered clearly the apparitions of spirits and the blow to her heart when Jenny had popped off about her great-grandfather raping the Crocker servant, who Mabel deciphered by the story, was her great-grandmother. The last time they were there, it had been windy. Now it was warm and calm. She'd read the papers and understood that southern men were enlisting in the army leaving the wives, slaves and children to carry on the work. Many of the slaves were running off, either joining up with the Underground Railroad or making their way north to free states. But there were thousands of slaves still dutifully tending to the crops, not sure what the future had in store for them.

Corners on the white stucco mansion had crumbled while they were gone, reminding them of life's temporary nature. It was a tall stately place, even after all these years. Jenny had a large ring of rusty keys and in no time was pushing open the massive doors. Looking inside Mabel was reminded of the children Jenny had taken in. Another heart pang, Mabel missed Beth and Danny.

"You Okay? Jenny asked her.

"You should be a mother, you're good at it," Mabel said forgetting that Jenny was a mother and she was not good at it.

Jenny said nothing, just looked away and continued her ritual of opening up the estate. Mabel had not seen the whole mansion and looked forward to exploring. For now, she was grateful to Jenny who showed her to her room and apologized for the humble arrangement. Mabel made herself at home and was relieved to finally remove her hat.

Sasha knew Charles routine and arranged to see him almost daily. She was beautiful and the temptation was great. She appeared intelligent and could hold her own but Charles felt she wasn't genuine. It became apparent to him how desperate she was to marry a rich man when he heard from Sophia that Sasha's father had lost a lot of his wealth by investing in southern agriculture, especially cotton. The war was devastating the crop because farmers left the farms to fight and slaves were running off. He grew angry at the thought that Sasha was preying on him for his wealthy inheritance. He contemplated preying on her. He knew that she would succumb to him if he began kissing her and the thought was quite pleasurable. It had been such a long time since he'd enjoyed the soft warm curves of a female, and she had those. He was certain though, that Mabel would find out. Every day he

279

waited for the local newspaper to print a lie about his relationship with Sasha and every night he fanaticized about making it true. *'Tis a curse to be a man without a woman.* He ripped open the letter from Mabel, read it, then angrily crumpled it and threw it on the floor.

Mabel made a chart of her ancestry:
Mabel's father Lionel
His father Lawrence
Lawrence's father Albert who married a mulatto slave (Lionel's grandmother, Mary, she was a Crocker)
Mary's mother, Sarah? (a Crocker slave)

Mabel did not know Mary's mother's name. Was it Sarah? She could not remember. Phinius Crocker has been blamed for the abuse of Sarah that led to the birth of Mary. But Jenny had made it clear it was her great-grandfather, Saint Francis who abused Sarah, not Phinius. But Sarah was a Crocker, who were her parents? Would she ever know the truth? Did she want to know?

This would make me both a Crocker and a Saint Francis. She needed to speak with Jenny. She could contain it no more.

Sasha waited until Charles' Auntie Lena left for the day then entered the house without knocking. She found Charles eating a late breakfast at the table. She could see the sun shining on Bluebird Pond through the window. Charles was stunned that she was so brazen to enter uninvited.

"I had to see you Charles," she said, soft light brown curls brushing her rosy pink cheeks, her perfume filling the air. Charles heart raced. *No one is here but us.*

"I've grown so fond of you and I can feel you desire me, a woman knows these things. It's quite flattering, really it is Charles, why do you run from it?"

She walked closer. His heart raced faster. She took a lock of his hair and twisted it round her finger. She wet her lips then bent down to kiss him.

"Something is bothering me," Mabel said to Jenny in the large living room that had few furnishings and all were covered with blankets and had been for almost two decades.

"Dear God, Ah knew this was coming. Aren't you goin' ta wait till this bourbon hits me?"

"No, but I did consider that. People often speak freely when they're..."

"Drunk? It's alr'rhyt, I know what Ah am... I just wish Ah wasn't but go ahay'd... ask me. Whay't is it you wanna know Miss Black Pansy?"

"Why do you look like a Crocker when you're a Saint Francis?"

Jenny saddened. Mabel had not yet seen her reach that deep into despair. She was sorry now she'd said anything.

"Now what may'kes you say thay't? You meet one Crocker and one Saint Francis and you be'come the ex'pert?"

"It was Monroe who planted the thought."

"Who the he'yll is Monroe?"

"He's a lawyer from Lafayette?"

"Good Lord. Was thay't who you were talking to at the club? That blonde fellow?"

"Yes. He said you look exactly like a Crocker and he described Benjamin Crocker when he described a Saint Francis."

Jenny was silent and Mabel could see that she was not only hurt but she was angrier than she'd ever seen her.

"Get away from me! I've told you time and again that I'm engaged. What happened between us, that one time in the meadow..."

Sasha was not deterred, "It was wonderful Charles, I know it's meant to be..."

"No, how many times and how many ways do I have to say it? I'm leaving tomorrow."

"You are?"

"Yes," he lied but now knew he must. He'd finish his meeting with the Quakers and be off to New Orleans. *I'm not safe here.*

"Ah was my fatha's favorite chil'yd," Jenny said somberly. "All my life everyone told me Ah didn't look ly'ke the other Saint Charles children. Ah got so tie'erd a' hear'in it, afta' awhi'l Ah jus quit hearin' it. Honestly Mabel, to this day Ah don't know why Ah look ly'ke a Crocker. Ah loved my Daddee and he sho' loved me."

"What about your Mother?"

"My motha' was busy with chu'ch. She taught Sun'da sc'hool. She kinda igno'rd me. She wa'nt mean tho', she was a kind wo'man."

"Did your father love her?"

Jenny laughed. "Tha'y had twelve chil'drun ta'getha, musta' loved her fo thay't. But I think he loved me mo're."

Mabel felt bad that she was putting Jenny through all this. She had unintendedly reduced her to a pathetic picture of the past. "Does Benjamin Crocker know anything?"

"No."

"Are you sure?"

"No."

"Tomorrow will you take me over there so I can get acquainted with him?"

"No," Jenny said, the mischievousness returning to her big, hazel-blue, eyes. "Tha's a war goin' on. He's prob'ly out fight'in, less his bum knee got him out'a goin. He fell off a' one a' his race hor'ses a few yea's bay'ak. What bus'ness is all this to you?"

"I'm not sure."

"You writin' a stor'ee 'bout me?"

Mabel shook her head no.

Very early the next day Mabel walked to the Crocker mansion. It was quiet, the birds were peaceful and the sounds of slaves and old, white farmers working in the fields and orchards were all around her. When she approached, she walked past the front entrance and went behind where three Colored women with their hair wrapped in colorful cotton turbans, and wore long, printed cotton dresses while hanging wet clothes on a line behind the kitchen. They said nothing to her, but turned their backs continuing with their work.

"Is Benjamin Crocker here?"

"Yes Maam, he's in the parlor."

"May I be announced?"

One of the young women shrugged, finished hanging a tablecloth and motioned Mabel to follow her. The sun was yet to reach inside the home, the large oak trees saw to that. Benjamin Crocker sat at a table going over papers and receipts.

"Sir? This lay'dee is here to see you."

"Thank you Claudette. Hello!" he said to Mabel genuinely pleased to see her, putting her at ease.

"Hello. We've met before, I can see you remember."

"A man does not forget a beautiful woman. What brings you to Crocker Plantation?"

"Family history."

"Oh?"

My great-grandmother lived here," she paused, "as a slave."

"Yes. I remember you mentioned you were... a Crocker."

"I'm rather confused about it all, I was hoping you could help me sort it out."

Benjamin smiled and went to the cabinet, strained to reach a top bookshelf and retrieved a large ledger. "We keep all the records of our slaves. How long ago was it?"

"It was when Phinius Crocker was master here."

Benjamin smiled broadly. "Phinius was my great-great-grandfather. He was a good, kind man."

Mabel smiled. A year ago, she wouldn't have believed it but now that she knew it was Jenny's ancestor who raped her great-great-grandmother, she was willing to consider, maybe.

Benjamin felt her apprehension. "Are you from the north?"

"Yes." Mabel stood up and looked over his shoulder as his soft hands turned the tall lined pages of the book.

"Here's Phinius, his wife, their children and the seventeen slaves they had living with them. What was your ancestor's name?"

"Her daughter's name was Mary."

"I see no Mary."

"Is there a Sarah?"

Benjamin's finger scrolled through, "No, no Sarah... oh wait, something's been crossed out. It looks like it says Sarah. Does it look like that to you?"

Mabel beamed. "Yes, and that would fit the story."

"Please, tell me the story."

Mabel sat back down again and snuggled comfortably into the cushioned chair.

"Would you care for a hot cup of Sassafras?" he asked her.

"Sure."

The story I was always told was that Sarah was abused by her master, Phinius Crocker."

Benjamin frowned.

"The child who came of the abuse was my father's grandmother Mary. Phinius' wife was so jealous she gave the child to a woman in her church."

"I'm sorry to hear that story. I've heard nothing but good things about Phinius."

"Well, as it turns out it wasn't Phinius but it was the master of the Saint Francis plantation. He raped her," Mabel said angrily.

"So... it wasn't Phinius?"

"No. But he was blamed for it. After they took the baby away from Sarah, she was so distraught she couldn't work, they sold her. She was never heard from again."

"And Mary?

"Mary was a beautiful mulatto slave who my great-grandfather, Albert McCrutchon fell in love with."

"And here you are..." he smiled. "The rooms of these old plantations have their stories to tell. Since we're being candid..." he looked for her approval to delve deeper.

"Sure, go ahead."

"Negro women are very beautiful. As your great-grandfather did, many men fall in love with them... father children."

"Make more slaves... Sarah pulled a plow!"

"Without getting into the politics of slavery Mabel, what I'm trying to state is that there are many love stories between the whites and their colored slaves."

Mabel looked at the three young women still hanging clothes on the line outside the kitchen. "They don't seem happy to me."

"As I stated, I'm not interested in the politics of slavery, we'll let the war for southern independence decide that. But I will say... you'd be wise to marry a white man, that would dilute that little bit of colored blood you carry in your veins and your children won't have to fear getting abducted and sold on an auction block."

"I'm proud of my African bloodline."

"Just a bit of advice. These are dangerous times," he said with a threatening look that sent a blood-curdling chill down her spine.

"Masta Crocker?" Claudette interrupted.

"Yes, Claudette."

"Mrs. Long is here to see you."

"Benjamin, good morning," a friendly, middle-aged, dowdy woman said as she pushed her way in. "I've redone all the records, I wanted you to see them before Reginald."

"Mrs. Long," Benjamin stopped her and Mabel could see he'd grown terribly uncomfortable. "Are we finished here Miss McCrutchon?"

"Yes, I'll see myself out."

"Claudette will see you out," he said rudely, changing Mabel's impression of him from advocate to adversary.

Mabel let Claudette lead her into the kitchen but then she stopped and listened. Claudette let Mabel stand behind the wall and listen to Benjamin and Mrs. Long.

"Benjamin, all the records have been changed. The words 'Colored' have been removed. Once we pay Reginald the three-hundred-dollars, he said he would substitute the census records for the originals and we can relax. No more fearing the world will discover our Negro ancestry."

"Yes, Mrs. Long, that will be a relief."

Mabel and Claudette stared at one another. Claudette's jaw dropped in disbelief and she and Mabel tiptoed out of the room.

"Jenny, will you escort me to Lafayette?"

"Lafayette? Way up there?"

"Yes, I need to see the lawyer I met in New York, Monroe."

"Thay'ts a long drive, all tha' way up there."

"Please?"

"Wey'll hav' ta continue our masta'-servant relay'shon'ship."

"I know, I know and I'll have to keep my hat on so no one sees me."

"Lil Miss Black Pansy... are we goin' to Lafayette lookin' fo' trouble?"

"I've found the trouble, looking now to solve it."

"Lafayette, that's Cajun country. Is that where the handsome lawya' lives?"

Fortunately for Mabel and Jenny, Monroe had not yet left for the courthouse. If they had been an hour later, they'd have missed him for several days as he was planning time away with a female and was to leave straight from the courthouse.

Pleased to see Mabel again, Monroe agreed to return when finished at the courthouse. He hurried off but did a double take of Jenny on his way out the door.

"You must have an adventure for me," Monroe said when he returned from the courthouse.

Jenny had gone to browse the shops but Mabel had waited outside the locked office of *Monroe Smith Attorney at Law*. Once inside she could see he was accomplished and respected in his field and that he'd been an athlete in college playing both rugby and baseball. He kept his appearance professional, down to the smallest detail, including white spats on black boots and he kept his office orderly.

"When we spoke in New York you said you knew Benjamin Crocker."

"Not well but we've met, through friends. What's up?" He asked and leaned against his oak desk then glanced at a Waterbury school clock hanging on the wall.

"Benjamin is bribing an official at the courthouse."

"Bribing him to do what?"

"Switch out census records that show he and others have Negro ancestry."

"Can you prove it?"

"His servant Claudette heard him say it, so did I."

"Hmm, the testimony of two Colored women..."

"Monroe, perhaps you didn't notice but Benjamin looks as Colored as I do. I came all the way to New Orleans during time of war. It may sound strange to you but a woman has her intuition and her hunches. They may not always be right but this time they were. And I'm being led."

"Led?" he said looking up at the clock again.

"Yes. Led by my ancestor."

"Would this be a dead ancestor?" he said and Mabel saw again his squinted eyes and squinted smile, mannerisms that had struck her when meeting him at the club on Fifth Avenue.

"We needn't include that, I shouldn't have mentioned it," she said, fearing she may be losing his respect.

He looked up again at the school clock, its brass pendulum steadily swinging back and forth.

"Why do you keep looking at that clock?"

He squinted out another one of his smiles, "I'd arranged to meet someone at the courthouse, I left early. I expect she'll come here. We were going to a quaint country resort... nothing for you to worry about."

The door opened and Jenny walked in looking striking in a new dress and hat. Mabel could see that Monroe found Jenny appealing and she appeared to be teasing him unforgivably.

"What courthouse?" he asked Mabel.

"Jenny, what courthouse serves your estate?"

"Saint Francis Parish courthouse, of cou'se." She smiled and flirted some more with Monroe who seemed to welcome the attention.

"Am I correct in assuming that you are a Saint Francis?"

"Ah am," she said, flashing her enormous hazel-blue eyes at him.

"Does St. Francis Parish have a genealogical society?"

"It does, mah neigh'bor, Benjamin Crocker, he's the presi'dant."

"Mabel, do you have the funds to hire me and take this to court?"

"She does," Jenny said, then drew close to him and whispered, "she's Black Pansy."

"Black Pansy?" he shook his head. "Is that supposed to mean something?"

Jenny continued parading around the room in her new clothes while Mabel sat feeling a bit helpless and frustrated.

"Why evra' one in the whole country is readin' her *American Heroes* stor'as," she flashed her eyes again at him, well aware the effect they had on men.

Monroe looked sharply at Mabel. He pointed at her, "You? That's you?"

Mabel smiled.

"You see Mon'row, the girl's got all the mun'ee in tha world ta buy a law'ya."

The door opened and in walked a woman looking every bit as stylish as Jenny.

"Gloria," Monroe greeted her.

Jenny's disappointment was obvious, Mabel felt sorry for her as she watched Jenny's hope fade.

"Jenny, Mabel, meet my sister Gloria."

Traveling to New Orleans, Charles took many of the same trains and carriages as Mabel. He went anxiously to Saint Francis Plantation and was terrified to find Mabel and Jenny were not there. He thought of going to the Crocker Plantation to inquire but feared discovering that Mabel had struck up a romance with Benjamin. Charles returned to the hotel where he and Mabel stayed previously, hoping she'd think to look for him there. After several days of worry, he was eating breakfast and a man at a table across from him was reading a newspaper. Charles could clearly read the headlines.

AMERICAN HEROES AUTHOR, BLACK PANSY GOES TO TRIAL FRIDAY

Charles heart went straight to his gut. *Oh good Lord, what trouble is Mabel in now?*

Monroe and Jenny were suited for one another. Mabel was left to spend long hours alone with her writing. She sometimes would accompany the two lovebirds on various outings, as was the case on the Wednesday evening before the trial. Monroe had insisted they all go to a quiet restaurant where they could dine outside on a patio and eat fabulous Acadian food.

After their dishes of shrimp and spicy rice arrived at the table, Monroe told them parentally, "I've several things to discuss with you ladies."

Mabel and Jenny stared wide-eyed, Mabel with her big browns, Jenny with her hazel-blues.

"First you Jenny. You haven't been honest with me. You should have told me you have a child. When you marry me, I'll adopt him."

Both girls gasped. Monroe was proposing marriage. It was a strange way to go about it but Jenny was beyond pleased.

"You should know I would find these things out. I'm a lawyer for God's sake."

"The next is also about you Jenny. I hate to disappoint you but all the digging into old census records has brought new light into your identity."

Jenny leaned back in her chair, resigned to finally hear the truth.

"Your father was in love with another woman, Mrs. Crocker. She died, leaving a child, a little girl born in 1840. Mrs. Crocker's husband accused Saint Francis of being the father. That was never proven and genealogical interviews with relatives make it clear he was not. It appears your father, Saint Francis, loved Mrs. Crocker but did not break his marriage vows to his wife. Old family interviews reveal that Crocker abandoned you after your mother died and Saint Francis felt so bad about it he and his wife adopted you. You say your father adored you and your mother ignored you, this is why. I've seen pictures of Mrs. Crocker and you're a spittin' image of her, probably brought great joy to Saint Francis to see your face every day, a reminder of Mrs. Crocker."

"Wey'll, wey'll, we'yll..." is all Jenny could say but both Mabel and Monroe saw and felt her relief.

"And Benjamin Crocker? He's a Saint Francis, sort of. Saint Francis' wife, the woman you thought was your mother, had a liaison with old man Crocker, before most of your siblings, the Saint Francis children, were born. That's probably why Crocker accused Saint Francis of fathering Jenny, because Crocker fathered a child with Saint Francis' wife. That child was Benjamin Crocker. He was raised as a Crocker by a Crocker auntie.

Again, "Wey'll, wey'll, we'yll..." was all Jenny could say.

The courtroom overflowed with newspaper reporters, legal representatives, relatives of the defendants and curious and concerned citizens. Sitting in the courtroom on polished oak benches, Mabel sat proudly next to Monroe, Jenny and Claudette. Benjamin Crocker sat on the other side of the courtroom, not far from the Confederate flag. Unbeknownst to Mabel, Charles Churchill sat in the very back.

The judge, a stern, middle-aged, man called Monroe and Benjamin's attorney to "Approach the bench." The judge quietly whispered, "What are you doing?"

"Your honor," Monroe began, "the plaintiff has good reason to pursue damages against Mr. Crocker for reasons of lying to government census officials and changing government records."

"It's nonsense," the judge said then looked at the crowd of reporters. "You've made a fiasco of my courtroom."

"Your Honor," Benjamin Crocker's attorney said, "my client was acting in good faith."

The judge scowled at Crocker's attorney, "I've questioned Reginald and he admitted to taking a bribe of three-hundred dollars to switch census records. Are you prepared for that?"

"No Your Honor, we had believed otherwise."

"Monroe? Is your client willing to accept a guilty plea from Mr. Crocker and a fine of twelve-hundred dollars?"

"I'll discuss this with her."

"This court is dismissed until three-o'clock this afternoon."

Reporters swarmed Mabel. Clipboards hit her in the head and men with rolled up sleeves were ready to go to work on the fraud story regarding the famous author Black Pansy. Monroe tried standing between Mabel and the reporters but was pushed and shoved out of the way. From the crowd emerged Charles, he reached through and grabbed Mabel's hand tightly.

"Charles!"

He pulled her toward him and gallantly hollered at the crowd. "Stand back, stand back, let the lady through."

"Miss McCrutchon," a reporter shouted, "when did you find out the ethnicities were being changed in the census records?"

"Miss McCrutchon," another reporter said standing in front of her, blocking her exit, "were any of these changes your relatives?"

"Miss McCrutchon..."

"Let the lady through!" Charles demanded.

"Meet me at my office!" Monroe shouted over the top of the crowd of men's heads."

"Yes!" she shouted back and Charles and she ran from the courthouse.

"I'm so proud of Mabel," Victor said to Whitethorn when he read the telegram of her success in the courtroom.

"She'll be home soon," Whitethorn told him. "It will be nice to have her back again.

Confessions

After court, Monroe and Jenny left for a few days, leaving Mabel and Charles alone in Monroe's Lafayette home.

"I've missed you terribly," Charles told her. Her face was browner than the last time he saw her, "The southern sun has tanned your skin."

She flushed, "I got careless about my hat."

She wore a white dress with long, tight-fitting sleeves with crocheted lace at the bottom, and a high collar that extended to beneath her chin. Small white, pearl buttons ran down the front. Several white silky bows garnished the blouse and more bows pulled and draped the fashion of the skirt.

Charles admired her style and ran his finger down the sleeve, needing to initiate intimacy but it having been so long he wondered if he dare.

Mabel sensed his precaution, grabbed his hand, and walked to the bedroom. Her long, dark hair hung down in well-arranged curls. With her right hand, she pulled her hair back revealing the back of her dress. "I must get out of this dress. Charles, all these buttons that run down the back a' this dress, could you do me a big favor and unbutton me?"

Charles melted. One by one, his big clumsy fingers unbuttoned her dress, revealing the gentle slope of her back as it ran down to her backside. He pulled the fabric of the dress from her shoulders, first the left, then the right. He kissed the back of her neck. The dress lay situated upon her breasts, he reached his hands into the cups of the dress and felt her warm soft, full breasts. She shivered. He continued kissing her neck and she continued shivering.

"Charles," she said.

"Yes," he whispered, still behind her, his hands still actively, gently caressing that which he'd missed and desperately desired.

"I kissed another man."

"I kissed another woman," he said, lost in the pleasure of the moment and the warmth of her body.

"I suppose we're even then," she said, glad to have it off her conscious but a bit disheartened that he'd strayed.

"I suppose."

The breath from his deep voice tickled down her back.

"Did you venture deeper than a kiss?" she asked, then turned to face him, her long dark eyelashes and big sparkling brown eyes questioned.

"No, I fought her off," he said in a teasing tone.

"You have far too many buttons on your shirt, Charles."

"Yes, I know."

He felt like he would explode while waiting for her to delicately unbutton each one. When she finished, he could feel her fingernails against his skin as she removed his shirt. Her eyes took in his well-defined chest. He backed her up to the bed, she lay down and he placed his bare chest upon hers. He snuggled into her neck and the bed of curls that smelled familiarly sweet. He struggled to remove her weighty dress and mumbled something about "all the buttons and bows" but finally the two lay entirely unclothed. He entered her and she winced then succumbed to the great pleasure that had been hers in other hotels, meadows and barns, that which she had yearned more of. The pain of being away from her, the betrayal of his family and the sad affairs of the war flooded his mind but the rhythmic sliding together of their bodies eased his pain and the crescendo they reached... together... and the soft panting she did and the release her voice sang out let him know their love was again ignited. Mabel could see a tear in his eye. That tear she would always remember as one that told her his love was genuine. She believed that he would be forever faithful.

"Mabel, I've something else to tell you."
Her look was one of fear.
"I've enlisted in the Union Army."
She gasped. "Oh Charles... when... how much time do we have?"
"None."
"None?"
"This is our last night together. I must leave tomorrow. I'm to meet up with my brother's regiment in Kentucky."
"Oh dear."
"I'm sorry. Duty called. I couldn't bear seeing what was unfolding. I must be a part of it."

"I understand but I'll worry every day. I'll wait for you to return and I won't kiss anyone else. I promise."

"Nor will I. I promise."

"Good bye Mabel, my sweet little Black Pansy. Until we meet again."

Mabel returned to Pittsburgh and continued writing. She went often to the *News Herald* and spent time in the hotel across the street waiting for the day when Charles would return. But he did not return. One day, in late September when she lay in her garden hammock her Auntie Louisa was the one who volunteered to present her with the fateful news that her fiancé, Charles Churchill had been killed in South Carolina fighting for the Union. Her world lay frozen in time. Day after day, she basked in the memories of the beauty of their love. Their trips together, their playful arguments, their serious talks, their delicate unforgettable lovemaking. Each time she thought of him she could smell his scent, feel his warm caresses and picture his glasses as they slid down his nose. How he'd cared for her, protected her and kept her safe. She cried when she envisioned his face, his deep-set eyes, the twinkle in them and his brown curly hair and smile. She would give anything to hold him again, hear his laughter. She would even forgive his mother. If only.

The leaves in Mabel's garden began to fall. The trees became baron and the air was cold but Mabel continued lying in her garden hammock. Her summer birds had flown south for the winter and the flowers had all died. She continued writing *American Heroes* and had the country in tears. Her bank account continued growing and men came from far and wide to pursue her, but she was not interested. She had lost weight and all the color from the southern sun had faded. She wore the same white dress day in and day out for it had been the one she wore the last time she saw Charles. Neither her mother nor her auntie could convince her to wear something else, nor to wash it. "He touched it," she would say, dreamily, her eyes staring off in space.

The war raged on and tens of thousands of young men died, mostly from disease. Mabel saw men returning with afflictions she would not wish on anyone. Battles were won and they were lost. One Northern lieutenant fell in love with a Rebel girl so surrendered his regiment to the south, creating shame and an uproar across the prairie state he represented. The whole country was saddened, North and South. Because of Mabel's ability to emphasize with all walks of life, the whole country read her stories. She longed to bring them together again, as one nation. Her fame grew in Europe and again British Royalty had extended an invitation for her to visit but Mabel was unmoved.

It was early December when the snow lay several inches on the ground. Mabel's hammock was stiff with ice but she bundled in a wool blanket and lay upon it in the barren garden. She used to find her garden cheerful in winter but no more. She'd been swinging in her hammock for almost an hour and had grown very cold. She was about to return to the warm house when she heard the sound of branches breaking. She knew those to be the branches the gardener had tossed over the tall northern wooden fence during the summer. The cracking grew louder. "Who's there?"

There was no response. Fearfully she rose to exit the garden but stopped when she saw the top of a soldier's Union cap above the top of the fence. Bravely but hesitantly, she walked to the fence. She stepped on a rock and peered over.

"Hello Black Pansy," he said, his glasses sliding down his bony nose, a warm smile on his face.

"Charles! Charles! Oh my God! You're alive!"

"I am and I've come to claim my bride."

"Stay there I'll come around... no, you come around," she said franticly.

"Mother! Father! "Auntie Louisa! Everyone! It's Charles! He's alive! He's alive! Dear God... thank you!"

Mabel McCrutchon and Charles Churchill were married on Christmas Day. They made their home in Wethersfield, Connecticut on Bluebird Pond, some distance from the Churchill family estate, in a small cottage, where Black Pansy continued to write about *American Heroes*.

The End

Book Two of Civil War Era Romances: *__Blue Violet__*

As the Civil War threatens the serenity of the small Louisiana town of Spanish Springs, Sasha Holmes overhears the gossip of jealous girls, suggesting that her heritage is not pure white. Her search for answers leads her to the advice not to dig too deep. When she meets Adam, the charismatic black son of a white Planter, she's determined to have him, no matter what. When suitor Jack Caruthers, discovers that her affections have gone elsewhere, he intensifies his charm. As the Confederacy builds, Sasha struggles to grasp the meaning behind her family secrets and choose between two men... before the war brings it all tumbling down...

http://www.amazon.com/dp/B018ZWX0R4

Book Three of Civil War Era Romances: *__"Black Lilac"__*

As he stepped toward the house where Sabina lay resting, the words grew louder... *black lilac... black lilac...*

Sabina... the sheltered black daughter of a white man, has fair skin... enough to pass for white, but she struggles with the morality of such deception, especially during the Civil War. When Samuel, a gorgeous black man she's grown up with, is not ready for her advances, she moves on to Randall Asbury, a white Carpetbagger from the North, whom she scoots out of town before her identity is revealed. But is it wise to leave Samuel behind? With that gorgeous smile? After leaving... Sabina knows she must return before she commits to living a lie with Randall. But will returning home reveal her lie *and* her chance at love?

http://www.amazon.com/dp/B01EKJMTKA

Book Four of Civil War Era Romances: *__"Ellie"__*

Just hours after her lover's death, Ellie meets Evan, a handsome mulatto. She's struggling to regain her integrity... he's anxious to take it. He *loves* women. Black, white, mulatto... he enjoys them all. He's the privileged son of a wealthy South Carolina planter, who welcomed him into his home while the boy's mother, a slave, was left to plant rice in knee-deep mud. After his white family grew bitter toward his father's favoritism, Evan was sent away with a small fortune. And then he met Ellie. She was good at smelling money... but the thumping in her heart began right away.

Should she fall for a wealthy, eligible bachelor... a heart breaker... serious about only one thing... the beautiful women who taunted him? After meeting Ellie, Evan wasn't sure what was more dangerous, white carpetbaggers or her temperament. Could he enjoy Ellie's beauty and then walk away? Not if she had anything to say about it.

https://www.amazon.com/dp/B01LWVNCTS

Link to other books by Suellen Ocean:

http://www.amazon.com/s/ref=nb_sb_noss?url=search-alias%3Ddigital-text&field-keywords=Suellen+Ocean&x=3&y=12